SECRET OF THE GLEN

SECRET OF THE GLEN

Mary Mackie

CHIVERS
THORNDIKE

This Large Print book is published by BBC Audiobooks Ltd, Bath, England and by Thorndike Press®, Waterville, Maine, USA.

Published in 2006 in the U.K. by arrangement with the Author.

Published in 2006 in the U.S. by arrangement with Juliet Burton Literary Agency

U.K. Hardcover ISBN 10: 1–4056–3850–8 (Chivers Large Print)
                ISBN 13: 978 1 405 63850 0
U.K. Softcover ISBN 10: 1–4056–3851–6 (Camden Large Print)
                ISBN 13: 978 1 405 63851 7
U.S. Softcover ISBN 0–7862–8991–0 (British Favorites)

The text of this Large Print edition is unabridged.
Other aspects of the book may vary from the original edition.

Set in 16 pt. New Times Roman.

Printed in Great Britain on acid-free paper.

British Library Cataloguing in Publication Data available

Library of Congress Cataloging-in-Publication Data

Mackie, Mary.
        Secret of the Glen / by Mary Mackie—Large print ed.
            p.   cm.
        "Thorndike Press large print British Favorites."
        ISBN 0–7862–8991–0 (lg. print : sc : alk. paper)
            1. Americans—Scotland—Fiction. 2. Large type books. I. Title.
PR6063.A2454S44 2006
823'.914—dc22   2006028926

ONE

At London's Heathrow airport, the young woman who now called herself Alix Grant boarded yet another plane. She huddled into her corner seat, ignoring the other passengers —even the overweight woman who plumped down next to her and might have started a conversation had not Alix resolutely stared out of the window, sun-glasses in place and body-language screaming, 'Leave me alone!' She knew she was over-reacting, getting paranoid, but she would not feel safe until she had reached her final destination. If then.

The flight from London to Edinburgh was a brief hop compared to flights she had made across the vast distances of the States and the Atlantic Ocean. Soon they were descending through clouds that clung like fog to the windows, down into rain that drifted in sheets over the grey buildings of the Scottish capital. Trees showed as green swathes, blotched with dull yellows and reds. As the plane circled for its landing, the Firth of Forth glinted leaden below, and Alix spotted the gaunt castle perched on its rock—familiar from travelogues and movies. Claudia had made a film here once, a quarter of a century ago, when—

1

No! Alix sat up, glancing guiltily around her. Such was her state of mind that she half believed that thoughts alone might betray her secret. Idiot! If this went on, she'd have to find herself a shrink, or go completely crazy.

Headachy and deadly tired after weeks of sleepless nights, she followed the stream of passengers and retrieved her suitcases. Glimpsed in a mirrored surface, she was just one of the crowd around the carousel, a tall, slender girl with a close-cropped cap of dark hair streaked with crimson, and shadows under anxious grey eyes. Ever since she had had her long mane of sun-streaked fair hair chopped off and dyed near-black, and especially since she had added those crimson streaks, her reflection came as a shock. She hardly knew herself. No one else could possibly recognize her. And even supposing someone did trace her as far as Edinburgh, here the signs would melt into Scottish mists. She hoped.

On the main concourse she scanned the crowd for a sign of the man who had promised to meet her. She had never met Sir Anthony McKenzie but recently his soft Scots voice had become familiar over the telephone as they finalized arrangements for her journey to the place he had selected as a bolt-hole. No, that sounded too dramatic. What she hoped to find was a haven, a temporary refuge where she might sort herself out before facing the

2

world again.

She noticed someone waving—someone who was making a bee-line towards her—a young woman whose coppery hair bounced round the shoulders of a shiny scarlet raincoat. Smiling brightly, she paused in front of Alix, saying triumphantly, 'Alix Grant, I presume.'

'How . . .' Alix felt bemused and befuddled.

'You look as if you're trying to melt into the scenery. Relax, for heaven's sake, you're only drawing attention! Besides . . . Daddy did warn me about the hair.' She surveyed Alix's black scarecrow crop with its crimson streaks, amusement sparkling in her green eyes. 'Cool! Hi. I'm Cat. Cat McKenzie—Catriona, that is. I'm Sir Anthony's daughter. He sends his apologies. Had to see an important patient at short notice, so I came in his place.'

Her voice was much too loud, making Alix fear eavesdroppers, but the concourse was noisy, people bustling about their own business. No one showed the least interest in two young women meeting each other. Offering her hand, she murmured, 'Glad to know you.'

'Yes, me too,' came the smiling reply. 'Welcome to Scotland. Look, unless you're desperately in need of a drink or anything I want to get started a.s.a.p. It's a long drive to Lachanbrae and they're forecasting mist on the hills.'

3

After a quick trip to the bathroom facilities, and with a take-out cup of coffee clutched in one hand, Alix followed her new acquaintance out to the car park. Catriona pushed the luggage trolley, her raincoat hood pulled up against the drizzle that seeped from drifting layers of steel-grey cloud.

Sir Anthony's daughter drove a compact Fiat, the same shining red as her raincoat. With its wipers swishing and its driver chatting gaily, the little car headed away, passing through the outskirts of the city and on towards hills obscured by rain and mist.

Alix sat quietly, letting Catriona's bright voice flow over her as the warmth in the car dried the rain from her alien red-streaked hair. Behind closed eyelids her thoughts swam in circles. She hadn't slept in thirty-six hours. Her body-clock was still on Central Standard Time, setting-off-to-work time, but here in Scotland it was early afternoon. She felt as though only part of her was here. The rest was in scattered fragments torn off during the past few nightmare weeks.

Trying to keep awake, she tuned in to what Catriona was saying: '. . . exciting, isn't it? Just like one of your mother's films. You've flown in under a false name, and I'm spiriting you away to hiding.'

Alarm jerked Alix wider awake. 'You know about that?'

'Of course! Daddy told me all about it.'

4

'He shouldn't have done that. It was between him and me. He promised—'

The red-head flung her an amused glance. 'Don't be silly. That didn't include me. I'm his daughter. He knows he can trust me to keep your little secret. Don't worry, your real identity is totally safe with me. But I have to admit I adore a hint of intrigue.'

Alix couldn't share her companion's delight. She didn't find her situation exciting and intriguing: she found it exhausting and troubling and thoroughly unwelcome. Nor did she entirely trust Catriona McKenzie to keep such a secret. Oh, what was she doing here, in a country she had never visited before, where she knew no one?

But that, of course, was the whole point of this journey.

Through drifts of rain, higher hills rose ahead, slate blue behind grey weather, with their heights lost in a ceiling of mist-like cloud. Maybe this unknown, shrouded land offered shelter and anonymity, she thought, and as she allowed herself to relax sleep dropped round her like a black curtain.

She woke abruptly, her neck cricked and aching, to find the car travelling along a high road, curving round a shoulder of mountain trailed with veils of mist. Far below, she made out the grey expanse of a lake surrounded by autumnal trees.

'With us again?' Catriona asked with a

laugh, still revelling in the adventure. 'Feeling better?'

'A little'

'You're jetlagged. It's always worse coming west to east, don't you find? Anyway, we're almost there, look.'

Alix peered through the side window. Wet sheep huddled beneath outcrops of rock, finding little shelter on the bare hillside. Then as the car rounded a bend and began to run down toward the lake, she saw a village nestling at the near end of the valley, roofs peeping among trees.

'There's Lachanbrae,' said Catriona. 'The lake's called Loch Lachan, and we've just come around the flank of Ben Lachan. It's familiar territory to me, of course. I often drive over to see Drummond.'

'Drummond?' Alix queried.

Catriona flung her a laughing glance. 'Did you not hear me say earlier? Drummond is the factor at Glenwhinnie estate.'

'The factor? What's that?'

'That's what we call an estate manager. In other words, he's Dame Janet's right hand man. He's the boss around here. And I warn you . . .' she was still smiling, but her eyes held a warning glint, 'he's mine, and if I catch you flirting with him . . .'

What a silly, superficial girl Catriona was. Alix had no intention of getting involved or interfering with the status quo around here.

Far from it, she wanted only to hide away like a gopher down a hole. 'No problem,' she murmured indifferently, and turned her head to watch the view as the car followed the narrow road along the side of the wind-tossed lake—wind-tossed *loch*, she corrected the thought with a little jerk of mingled excitement and apprehension. She was in Scotland. Scotland!

The village was little more than a collection of small grey houses strung along narrow lanes around a central square of grass where oak trees spread wet, yellowing leaves. Another row of cottages faced the ruffled loch, and beyond them the road ran on through a tunnel of trees that met overhead, dripping with rain. Twilight reigned there as the daylight began to fail.

Catriona slowed the car to turn in between open gates that flanked the entry to a long driveway. 'That's the lodge, look.' She nodded to where a compact grey house stood to their right, half hidden by a huge copper beech. Alix caught no more than a glimpse of her future hideaway as the car accelerated up the drive. 'We have to get the key from the big house,' Catriona explained.

On either side, pale aspens shivered in wind and rain, lining the snaking drive like sentinels. Beyond them, through gathering twilight, Alix began to discern the dark bulk of a large house standing behind high walls. Mist wreathed round its stacked chimneys and angled roofline, and no lights showed at leaded windows. An archway in the wall allowed the car to drive on through into a courtyard where yew trees, clipped into upturned cones, grew around a broad lawn.

The house occupied three sides of the courtyard, two wings extending out to meet the wall, with a central block boasting a flight of stairs up to a shadowed porch. However, Catriona pulled off to one side, where a less imposing door gave access to the west wing.

'Looks as if nobody's about,' Catriona said, scanning blank, unlighted windows that reflected sombre grey gleams from the sky. 'We should have used the mobile to warn them we were on our way. Never mind, we'll find someone.'

Alix forced her aching legs out of the car. Her weary body followed. Drizzling rain dewed on her face and hair as she followed Catriona towards a small side porch. How much longer before she could sleep? All she wanted to do was lie down and sleep. Then she heard a door slam. A man was coming from the main part of the house, tall and thin, shoulders hunched beneath a waxed jacket whose hood was pulled up.

'Hello, Mr Gordon!' Catriona called.

'Who's that?' he demanded, his voice sharp and suspicious, strongly accented.

'It's me—Catriona McKenzie. You were

expecting us, weren't you? This is Alix Grant. She's renting the lodge. My father arranged it with Dame Janet. Could we possibly have the key, please?'

The man made no reply until he was close enough to see Alix clearly. Peering at her across a flattened nose, he said doubtfully, 'Aye, well, mebbe ye can, at that. Come in oot o' the weather.'

Brushing between them, he opened the door and led the way into a gloomy hallway where stairs climbed up against one wall and further areas were lost in shadow. A door by the foot of the stairs led into a small office, revealed in all its clutter when Mr Gordon snapped on a light and ushered them inside.

Blinking in the brightness, Alix saw a desk with a computer on it, several framed photos of beaming children, scattered papers, piled filing trays, mugs stuffed with pens and pencils, much-marked calendars and charts on the walls, and a board bearing hooks from which hung several sets of keys.

Mr Gordon took down one set, weighing the keys in his hand as he gave Alix a suspicious look. 'Ye'll have some identification on ye, I don't doot.'

After a moment puzzling over his accent, Alix muttered, 'Oh, er . . .' She had nothing with her in the name of Grant—she had not expected to be called to explain herself, not quite so soon.

9

Catriona came to the rescue, still enjoying the subterfuge. 'Goodness me!' she exclaimed with a laugh. 'Don't you believe us, Mr Gordon? You know who I am. And you were expecting Alix to arrive today, weren't you? Why should we lie about it?'

The man afforded her one of his dark, dour looks. 'It's as well tae be sure. Wi' Dame Janet away tae Inverness and the factor no' here, I'm responsible if things go awry.' But he held out the keys and dropped them into Alix's hand, his pale eyes unnervingly intent on her face. 'The lodge is ready for ye. I lit the fire mysel', this afternoon.'

'That's kind of you,' Alix said, wishing she were out of that claustrophobic office. With three of them crowded into the space in front of the desk it felt like a closet.

'Ye're welcome,' he replied with another beady look, and held open the door, inviting her to leave at once. She did so gladly.

But as she stepped into the vestibule, the outer door opened with a rush of wind and a spatter of raindrops. Alix almost collided with the tall and solid form of the man who came in. Rain glittered in the unruly tumble of his dark hair and spotted the shoulders of an old camouflage jacket as he adjusted his upturned collar, glancing from Alix to Mr Gordon and back to Alix in mild enquiry.

'Hello? Who—'

From the doorway behind Alix, Catriona

10

cried archly, 'Oh, there you are, Drummond. Just in time. This is Alix Grant, your new tenant for the lodge. Flown all the way from America.'

The Glenwhinnie estate manager seemed transfixed by the sight of Alix. Had he recognized her? Oh, God . . .

A rivulet of rain ran down his hard cheek in the moment before he collected himself and held out his hand. 'Miss Grant. Welcome to Glenwhinnie. How do you do.'

'Hi,' Alix replied, reassured by the firmness of his handshake. He had a direct, enquiring gaze, too. Maybe too direct—she found it disconcerting. But his deep baritone voice was as soothing as hot chocolate, made even more attractive by the Scots burr of his accent.

Realizing he was still holding her hand, she relaxed her grip and he let go, saying, 'Excuse my surprise, but we were expecting a man. I'm sure Dame Janet said *Mr* Grant.'

'Aye, she did,' the other man confirmed darkly. 'I thought mysel' that was so. Alex Grant—Alexander, so I thought.'

Catriona chattered, 'It's Alix. She spells it with an "i". Short for Alexis.'

Alix forced her mouth to curve, wishing her brain would wake up. The red-head was far too free with information. 'I guess there was a misunderstanding. Natural enough. Does it matter?'

Mr Gordon started to say something about

her staying alone at the lodge, but the estate manager, evidently the boss here, cut him short: 'No, it doesn't make the slightest difference. You're very welcome, Miss Grant. It will be good to have someone in the lodge through the winter. Keep it aired.'

'In which case . . .' Alix muttered, 'can I get right to it? I'm deathly tired.'

'Yes, of course. Sorry.' The factor stepped aside to let her by. 'Catriona knows the way. I hope you'll be comfortable. If there's anything you need, don't hesitate to ask. You'll find the office number, and some other useful contacts, on a note-pad by the phone.'

'Oh, I'm sure she can cope,' Catriona answered, a hand on Alix's arm urging her outside. 'Come on, Alix, let's get you settled in.'

As the red Fiat sped back down the drive between shaking aspens all but lost in gathering darkness, Catriona said, 'I wonder what made them think you were a man? I'm sure Daddy wouldn't have misled them. Why should he?"

'I've no idea. Like they said—my name, probably.' Alix couldn't be bothered to think about it. 'For one mad moment there, I thought he'd recognized me. Especially when you told him my name was Alexis.'

'Oh, don't be silly. Nobody here bothers with Hollywood gossip. Besides, most of the papers refer to you as "Lexie". That's what

12

your family called you, isn't it?'

'That's what my father . . .' Oh, it was all too complicated. 'Sorry, Catriona, my brain's not working right.'

'Oh, please! Call me Cat. Just Cat.'

Alix stretched her heavy eyelids. 'You have claws?'

'You'll find that out if I catch you being too friendly with Drummond.'

A weary laugh escaped Alix. 'I guarantee you, that's one bone we'll never have to pick. Just let me hibernate here, get my head together, and I'll be off and away again, like I was never here. Last thing I need is any extra baggage.'

*   *   *

The lodge, huddled behind trees and overgrown shrubs, was built of stone, and bigger than Alix had realized. A high-sloped roof and tall chimneys towered over bay windows that would give a good view of anyone coming to or from the big house. By its small gate, the copper beech dripped water from dark red leaves as Alix brushed past with Catriona at her heels.

Unlocking the front door, she found herself in a small hallway boasting a coat-rack made of antlers and an old bench carved of oak, worn shiny black by time. Stairs covered in well-worn carpet climbed up into shadows.

Catriona shivered, 'Feels like a fridge. I wonder how long it's been empty?'

Alix tried the remaining door, which to her immense relief gave onto a comfortable, if old-fashioned, sitting room where a peat fire glowed bright, shedding warmth across furniture of old oak, with a settee and armchairs covered in rust-coloured velour. It smelled of lavender polish, old wood, and a slight mustiness that told of long months without a resident. But the firelight gleamed on old brass and on the glass of pictures of mountains and lochs and deer, and a flip of a light switch bathed the room in a warm golden glow that seemed to welcome her. As if the lodge had been lonely, waiting to be loved again. Waiting just for her, maybe?

Idiot! Alix derided herself—jetlag was making her fanciful. Any comfy warm room would have seemed like heaven the state she was in.

Catriona had gone to open a door in the far corner of the room. 'Thought so. Here's the kitchen. All provisioned, by the look of it. You'll have Ailie Gordon to thank for that. She's Murdo's wife, keeps house for Dame Janet. Look, I don't know about you, but I'm dying for a coffee. I'll put the kettle on. Then we can get your stuff out of the car and you can take it upstairs while I make us both a drink. OK?'

'Sounds good to me.'

14

The bay window of the main front bedroom had a wide view, down the drive to the right, with a dark sweep of mountainside rising against a still-pale sky. Turning to look to her left, Alix could see past the copper beech to the gateway, with glimpses of the darkening, misted loch in the distance behind trees. The room had a window seat, and a sturdy table which might serve as a desk. It was just perfect for a study, Alix decided. Towards the rear of the house lay a bathroom with quaint brass fittings, and along a narrow landing a second bedroom overlooked a tangled garden. This room was secluded, private, and small enough to be easily warmed to cosiness. Here Alix left her suitcases. She would unpack them later. A hot drink was her first priority, followed by food, and then sleep. Lots of sleep.

Catriona stayed only long enough to drink a cup of coffee, then said she had to be going. No, not all the way to Edinburgh. 'I'll be staying overnight with . . .' She smiled a feline smile. 'Let's just say I won't be far from here. Anyway, I'm sure Daddy will be in touch soon. It's just that he's so busy . . .'

'No matter. I'm fine. Tell him thank you from me, will you?' The last words came through a yawn. 'Oh, excuse me. I'm bushed.'

Pursing her lips and narrowing her gleaming eyes, Catriona stroked an end of coppery hair down her nose. 'I wonder what the people around here would say if they knew they had a runaway celebrity staying in their midst. I hope the paparazzi don't find out.'

'Don't mention that word!' said Alix with feeling. 'I came here to get away from all that hassle. And I'm not a celebrity. No way!'

'If you say so.'

'Cat . . . you will be discreet, won't you? I mean it. This is not a game.'

'Oh, don't worry, I know how to keep my mouth shut when I want to. Even with Drummond. There'll be no secrets given away during pillow-talk, don't you fret.'

'You mean . . .' Alix said slowly, frowning, 'you and he . . . ?'

'Where do you think I'll be sleeping tonight?'

'Oh. Sorry, I hadn't . . .' She shook her thick head. 'No, nothing.' Funny, she did not recall sensing the least hint of a sexual buzz between Catriona and the Glenwhinnie factor. Not that she'd been exactly on the ball, intuition-wise.

Catriona smirked. 'Don't be misled by the way he acted so cool tonight. That was for Murdo Gordon's benefit. They're all a bit tight-laced up here. It's a small community, given to gossip. The Glenwhinnie factor has to preserve his image.' Her smile turned lascivious as she added, 'In public, anyway. In private, he's . . . well, as I said, I can be discreet when I need to. Oh—mustn't forget that laptop you asked for. It's on the back seat of the car. Come out with me and fetch it.

16

And then I really must be going.'

* * *

Alix slept badly that first night. The wind soughing through wet trees sounded nothing like the roar of the city that, at home in Greenwich Village, had lulled her to sleep. Nor was it like the wind on the Kansas prairie, where she had grown up. Around her the lodge creaked and groaned while she bundled herself in thick blankets and shivered.

For a few days she remained indoors, unsettled by the upheaval in her life and afraid of making contact with people who watched TV and read newspapers. Happily, the Glenwhinnie housekeeper had thought of everything in the way of grocery provisions, even to dried milk and half-baked bread that would keep for weeks. Sooner or later Alix would need to venture out, but for now she was content to remain in isolation, incognito, sleeping off the jet-lag and the stress. The lodge provided a fair supply of eclectic reading matter, a few magazines, old hardbacks and dog-eared paperbacks, and the television, though antiquated, worked well enough despite a tendency to snow over for no apparent reason. There were enough US shows to make her feel slightly less of a stranger in a strange land.

The weather aided her hibernating instinct:

17

it remained cold, grey, wet and misty, though it was still only September. How long would she be able to stand being alone? Could she make it all through the winter? How long a time would elapse before she had the nerve to go back, to face the questions, the peeking and prying . . .

No. Stop. Don't even think about it yet.

As an antidote to loneliness—and to bleak thoughts—she set her mind to work, setting a big table by the bay window in the front bedroom, with her notebooks around and the laptop computer connecting her, when necessary, to the information highway of the internet. Ever since moving to New York, five or six years ago, as a student, she had supported herself with part-time work, both as a waitress and helping out in a second-hand book-shop. Extra pin money had come from writing bits and pieces for newspapers and magazines, including articles telling of the many interesting places to be visited around New York State, and in the city itself. Slowly she had built on that success and had hoped some day to earn her living from writing. Recently a publisher had commissioned her to do the text for a new travel book for visitors to New York State. Back in the spring she had wished for more free time to work on the project.

Well, now she had her wish.

From the bay window where she sat, she

had a clear view of the rain-swept Glenwhinnie driveway. Occasionally a vehicle passed, travelling the lochside road or coming to or from the big house. In particular Alix became used to seeing a battered red pick-up and a yellow Range Rover, both with 'Glenwhinnie Estate' blazoned on the side. Other than this infrequent road traffic there was little sign of life. Except for the birds, and an occasional squirrel. After New York, it was intensely quiet and dreary, like a ghost valley, shrouded in mists that sometimes lifted to become low cloud hanging halfway up the mountainsides, dripping rain.

From feeling safe and hidden, Alix began to suffer from a touch of the blues, and from a sense of isolation. She thanked goodness for the TV in the sitting room, which kept her in touch with the world, while the iPod she had brought with her filled her ears with music and kept the deafening silence at bay.

*   *   *

One morning, to her amazement, she woke to bright sunlight blazing across her curtains. She leapt out of bed and went to look out, moving from room to room to gaze from the windows, astonished at the transformation. All around, a blue sky smiled over steeply sloping hills where dying brown bracken flecked the green of grass. And the trees—oh, the trees! They were as lovely as any in New England, rowans aflame in scarlet, while oaks and birch had mellowed into shades of gold. The big copper beech by her gate, which had loomed so dark in the mist, now blazed bronze and crimson, contrasting with the red and yellows of the woods that spread out from the Glenwhinnie gates and down a gently sloping hillside to circle the loch. And along the drive the aspens shimmering their glorious pale yellow leaves. Alix could hardly believe her eyes. Glenwhinnie in sunlight was glorious!

Throwing on a pair of jeans and a sweat-shirt, she hurried to make breakfast. She couldn't wait to be out in the sunshine, though as yet she planned to avoid the village—it was still too soon to risk meeting people.

The trees whispered as she went out by the main gate and crossed the lane to where beneath bright autumn leaves a rough path led down to the loch and along by the water. Turning away from the village, Alix followed the loch shore until it met a narrow river in spate, with a plank bridge spanning the fast-flowing peat-brown water. After the recent rains the stream had flooded the small bridge, making it impassable. However, a side path turned up beside the stream, to where the lochside lane crossed it at a sturdier road-bridge, and on the other side of the road the rough path continued, enticing Alix to follow the course of the water as it tumbled down from the hills.

At first arching trees sheltered the way, but after a while the going grew steeper, the river tumbling in a series of waterfalls and pools, and the trees gave way to rocky hillsides patched purple with ling and heather. Alix found herself coming to a rough stony slope where the worn path petered out. Shade and sunlight flowed across the land as clouds drifted on a brisk breeze.

A few sheep ambled away as she climbed on, ignoring the ache in legs unused to such exercise. Slowly the view opened out and she was surprised to see how far she had come, and how high she had climbed. A mile or so away, the glen road snaked off to disappear between dark, pine-forested slopes, while below, beyond a shoulder of hillside, the chimneys of what must be Glenwhinnie House lifted among a glory of deciduous woods painted with autumn, against a backdrop of more hills, flowing off into hazy distances. A smaller knot of trees hid the lodge where she was staying, and beyond it the loch stretched out, glinting deep blue to mirror the sky, with the village clustered around its nearer shores. Across the water a rugged hill lifted its head to touch small drifts of cloud. What had Catriona called that hill? Ah yes, Ben Lachan. How grand it looked, towering over loch and village, though in blue distances Alix made out even higher mountains. The Scottish

Highlands, she thought with a spurt of wonder.

The river had brought her by a long, meandering route, so she decided to head back in a more direct line. She must get some walking boots if she hoped to wander around like this; her city shoes were not made for rough grass and heather and bracken, all uneven and strewn with rocks and boggy patches. As she strode, head down to watch her footing, a large bird flew up with a harsh cry. Alix stopped, startled, watching the speckled bird clatter away to circle with outspread wings and land at a safe distance. Was it a grouse?

In the distance, she noticed a vehicle heading down the long decline of the glen road. Could the driver see her? Probably not—she was wearing clothes that would blend in with the scenery. She almost crouched down behind a rock, then next second chided herself for an idiot. So what if someone saw her? She had a perfect right to be out walking. Did she plan to turn into a recluse? What, for the rest of her life?

The vehicle vanished behind a rise of ground as she strode on, short hair tousling in the breeze. She headed straight toward the road. Tarmac would make the walk home easier. At least, that was her idea.

A faint rushing sound slowly grew louder, resolving itself into the music of fast-flowing water. A cleft in the ground abruptly opened before her, worn by a peat-brown stream that flowed fast and deep, churning over rocks, barring her way. Alix calculated the odds of leaping the cleft. She could probably make it—the stream was only around three feet wide. But its banks were uneven, undercut by rushing, swirling water that looked pretty deep. She didn't fancy getting soaked and battered out here all alone.

Above the noise of the water, she heard an engine approaching and she realized that the narrow hill road was only fifty yards or so away. The yellow dot she had seen far away now revealed itself as the workmanlike Range Rover which so often came and went along the Glenwhinnie drive. As it came nearer, it pulled off the road and came bumping towards her, stopping only a few yards away, on the other side of the stream. She recognized the driver when he climbed out— the Glenwhinnie factor, the man Catriona called Drummond.

Alix had to concede that the man did have a certain rugged appeal. Dishevelled dark hair framed a tanned face that, though not exactly handsome, might be considered personable. Attractive, even. To some women, maybe. Not to Alix. No, Alix was not planning to get into any sort of relationship, least of all the romantic entanglement kind: she had enough on her mind without inviting yet more complications. Still, she could see why an air-head like Catriona might fancy this man. He had the build of an athlete—over six feet tall, fit and well-muscled, with shaggy dark hair tousled by the wind. Casual working clothes of blue roll-neck sweater and black cords seemed to emphasize his height and lean fitness as he strolled unhurriedly down the shallow incline and stood with folded arms, smiling at her.

That smile was not a kindly one. In fact, that smile made her feel a total idiot. Why didn't he just laugh outright and have done with it?

'Having some trouble?' he enquired, projecting his voice above the stream's clamour.

'Depends if my wings work,' Alix quipped back.

He glanced at the turbulent stream, mentally measuring the gap, then gathered himself and with maddening ease leapt across to land beside her as graceful as a gazelle. 'So what's the problem?'

'No problem,' said Alix crisply. 'All I have to do is grow my legs a few more inches and it'll be a cinch.'

He took a considered, appreciative look at her jean-clad legs. 'They're long enough. Come on, I'll catch you.'

Another huge, bouncy stride took him safely back across the stream, where he turned and held out his hands, his smile throwing out a challenge that stung Alix's pride. She glanced again at the three-foot gap edged with wet heather and clumps of tough grass, took a few backward steps, and launched herself into a flying leap.

She made it, but caught her foot, slid on the wet grass, stumbled. For a second she thought she was going to fall backwards into the water, but Drummond stepped up to catch her and she clutched handfuls of his blue sweater, momentarily breathless. Just a few more steps and she was safely away from the chasm. 'Phew!'

'Next year, the Olympics,' he said, his deep voice rich with laughter.

Pleased with herself, but flustered to find him so close, she backed off a little, running a hand through her shockingly short hair. 'Yeah. Piece of cake.'

'Bet you wouldn't have done it if I hadn't been here to catch you.'

Piqued, she looked up into eyes that brimmed with amusement—eyes that she now saw were a startling deep blue in his tanned face. 'That's all you know! But thanks, anyway.'

'The pleasure was mine,' he said, with a slow smile that for some reason reminded her of his arms locked around her waist. 'Can I give you a lift?'

'Oh—no, don't trouble. The exercise is good for me.'

'Independent lady, are you?'

'Every inch.'

Slanting an eyebrow at her, he shrugged and started back to the Range Rover. 'Suit yourself. Oh, by the way . . .' He stopped and turned to look back at her. 'We solved the mystery of how we came to assume you were male. Apparently Sir Anthony referred to you as 'my young friend', and with a name like Alix . . . What's it short for—Alexandra?'

She seemed to remember that Catriona had already told him her name was Alexis, but probably he hadn't taken much notice. In fact, the name on her birth certificate *was* Alexandra, but . . . No point in risking complications.

'Alexis,' she said, and held her breath in case the name rang any bells for him.

Apparently it didn't. All he said was, 'That's unusual.'

'My mom . . .' She stopped herself, shrugged in a you-know-what-mothers-are way. 'Anyhow, does my gender make any difference to anything?'

Again he looked her over in a frankly approving way, blue eyes gleaming. 'Depends who's looking, I suppose. I mentioned it because, when Dame Janet came home and discovered you were a girl she was a bit concerned about your being alone at the lodge. She's a wee bit old-fashioned that way.'

'I can take care of myself. It's been a long

26

time since I considered myself a "girl".'

'Noted,' he replied with a twitch of his lips. 'Anyway, don't be surprised if she calls in to see you, to make sure you're OK.'

'I look forward to meeting her,' Alix said.

He turned away, laying a hand on the Range Rover's door handle, then paused and again looked round at her. 'Are you a friend of the McKenzies?'

'Who? Oh . . . you mean Sir Anthony?'

'And his daughter.'

'Catriona? No, I never met her until the other day. Why?'

'Just wondering.'

Alix felt she ought to explain, at least a little. It might help to stop speculation since people in a small place were bound to talk about a newcomer in their midst. 'Sir Anthony is . . . an old family friend. When I needed somewhere to work in peace, he suggested Lachanbrae. He arranged it all for me. He was supposed to bring me here himself, but the day I arrived he was too busy. So he sent Catriona. That's it.'

'You're here to work?' he asked, frowning. 'Doing what?'

'I'm writing a book. About New York. Actually, it's a commission, kind of. I have to produce a text, and if the editor likes it he'll get a photographer to take the pictures. Why, what did you think I was doing?'

He shrugged. 'Hadn't given it much thought

27

until now. I suppose I assumed you were on holiday. Anyway . . . are you sure about the lift? It's further than it looks. And in those flimsy shoes . . .'

'I'll be fine,' Alix said firmly. 'I came out for some air, and for a walk now the weather's improved. Thanks for your help, though. Hey . . . what do I call you? Drummond? Is that a first name, or . . .'

He stopped her with a sharp look from those blue eyes, his lips twisting in an odd, bitter smile. 'Drummond is my surname. What *you* call me, please, is Niall.' He pronounced it "Neil" and, as if it was important to him, spelled it: 'N-I-A-L-L—that's the Irish version.'

'Niall.' She spoke it carefully, saying it the way he did. Obviously she had inadvertently touched a nerve.

'Good.' He didn't explain; he simply opened the door of his vehicle, swung up to the seat and, without another glance at her, drove away.

Alix stared after him, a hand raised to shade her eyes from the sun. What was all that about? Why did Catriona refer to him by his surname? Was it a lovers' thing, a name that only Catriona used? Alix's memories of that first day were hazy, but she did remember the red-head showing her claws and giving out 'keep off' signals whenever Niall Drummond came into the conversation. The man himself, however, didn't seem to realize he was spoken for. Or maybe he was still playing the field despite his relationship with Catriona. Was that why he had asked if Catriona was a friend of hers?

Alix didn't know either of them well enough to come up with any answers. Not, she reminded herself firmly, that any of it made the least difference to anything. The very last thing she intended was getting involved here in Scotland—with anyone at all.

*   *   *

After lunch, Alix was attempting to light the fire—she had yet to master that chore, peat not being a common fuel in Greenwich Village New York—when a sharp knocking sounded at her front door. The caller proved to be an elderly, angular woman dressed in caped tweed, with cropped grey hair beneath a deerstalker hat. She leaned heavily on a walking stick, but her eyes were bright, inquisitive, a clear Celtic blue against sharp, lined features.

'I'm Janet McDonald,' she announced gruffly. 'And you must be Alix Grant. Delighted to make your acquaintance.'

'I'm glad to know you, Dame Janet.' Alix took the offered hand, finding it twisted and gnarled by arthritis but still with a firm grip. 'Please come in. The place isn't very tidy, I'm afraid. I'm not much of a housekeeper.'

'Och, not to worry, not to worry.' Waving the excuses aside, Dame Janet stumped into the sitting room, where she viewed the litter of crumpled newspaper and sticks in the hearth with a, 'Hmph!' of amusement. 'Used to central heating, I suppose. Or was it air conditioning? Here, let me show you the trick.'

Without more ado, she got stiffly down on her knees and set to work. In a very short time, it seemed, bright flames licked up among squares of dried peat.

'You'll soon get the hang of it,' the old woman said, accepting a hand from Alix to regain her feet. 'I'll just wash my hands, if I may.' She made for the kitchen, rinsed her hands and dried them on the towel Alix offered. 'So,' she said briskly, with a birdlike tilt of her head. 'How're you settling in?'

'Pretty well, I guess.' Bemused, wondering quite who was the hostess here, Alix followed her visitor back to the sitting room. 'May I fix you some tea?'

'Haven't forgotten my lunch yet,' said Dame Janet, grunting with effort as she lowered her aching back into one of the rust-velvet armchairs. 'Just thought I'd pop in and say hello.' She fixed Alix with bright eyes. 'We were expecting a man, y'know.'

'Yes, I'm sorry about that. I don't believe Sir Anthony would intend to mislead you.'

30

'Oh, I'm sure he didn't.'

'And it really needn't make any difference. I'm used to being on my own. You don't have to worry about me.'

'Glad to hear it,' said Dame Janet, though her expression said she still had doubts. 'You're a writer, I gather.'

'I'm trying. I've been commissioned to do a travel book and . . . I needed somewhere quiet where I could concentrate.' It wasn't entirely true—not the whole truth, anyway—but it wasn't exactly a lie, either.

'And when you're not working?'

Alix sank into the second armchair by the fire. 'Oh, I . . . I like to read—you've got some interesting titles on the bookshelves here. At home, I play tennis, and swim. I like to sketch a bit—landscapes, mostly. Music, too. Listening to it, and . . . my guitar should arrive with the rest of my things.' She watched the fire, seeing the flames beginning to burn into the peat, causing it to glow, but her mind was far away, back in her loft apartment in Greenwich Village. Had the lawyers found someone reliable to pack up her belongings? They were supposed to be coming by sea, directed to a central collecting address in Edinburgh. Anyone looking for her by means of her belongings would find the trail went cold at that point. Or so the plan went. Sir Anthony had arranged to handle everything with the utmost discretion. Pity he hadn't extended that to his daughter.

Dame Janet was saying something about her tennis court having gone to weed. 'But there's plenty of goodly scenery for sketching hereabouts, and some fine walks, and when you've read the books here there's a whole library up at the big house . . .' She chatted on, friendly and amusing, all the while watching Alix with those shrewd blue eyes, and eventually adding without change of tone or expression, 'Your father was a Scot, so I believe.'

All Alix's defences went up, her scalp tightened and goose-bumps prickled on her skin. Dame Janet's curiosity was natural, in the circumstances, but even so Alix knew she must be wary. 'That's so,' was all she said.

'And your mother?'

'She was American. From the mid-West. Kansas.' True, but hopefully misleading.

'Was?'

'She died a while ago. And you? Have you always lived here in Glenwhinnie?'

If Dame Janet noted the unsubtle change of subject she was too canny to show it. 'Glenwhinnie has always been my home,' she amended. 'Family's been here nigh on three centuries. But my career took me away a good deal. I was a musician—concert pianist. Oh, not famous, just a jobbing musician, steadily working. In my younger day.' A rueful grimace indicated the gnarled hands that she briefly lifted. 'Now . . . well, now I'm home again, and here, I suppose, I shall stay.'

There was, Alix noted, no wedding ring on those thin, twisted fingers. 'You never married?'

'I'm wed to Glenwhinnie.' A sharp note in her voice warned that she did not wish to explain, but a second later her eyes softened and she sighed. 'Aye, the estate. It's been both a headache and a heartache. But it's been in McDonald care too long for me to desert it. It's my heritage.' Her eyes had turned inward, onto bleak thoughts that tightened her mouth. 'And I'll fight to keep it so!' she said fiercely. 'To the last breath in my body, if that's what it takes.'

Did some threat hang over the estate? Alix wondered, but before she could say anything Dame Janet heaved herself to her feet and reached for her walking stick. It was made of wood, the handle beautifully carved.

'It's yew,' the old woman said, seeing Alix's interest and displaying the stick for her to admire. 'The clansmen used to plant yew trees, to grow wood for their bows. It's very supple. Well . . . I'll not disturb you any longer. I'll be on my way.' And she stumped to the door, where she paused to say, 'You busy tomorrow evening? No? Then come up to Glenwhinnie House and we'll have dinner. Don't bother to dress.' On her way out, she stopped herself again, looking round to add dryly, 'And that doesn't mean come naked. Murdo Gordon would *not* be amused. Mind you, Murdo Gordon disapproves of most things, the old Calvinist. Muttering already, he is. Single girl living all alone at the lodge? Sinfulness setting in! Whatever next?'

Laughing, Alix said, 'What does he imagine I'll be doing?'

'Corrupting all the young men for miles around,' Dame Janet said with relish. 'But, as I reminded him, I've lived all alone for years without corrupting anyone—more's the pity. See you tomorrow. Around seven?'

*   *   *

Alix went early to bed that night, still trying to adjust her body clock to the new time zone. But for the first time since leaving New York she slept long and deeply and, much to her own surprise, woke feeling refreshed. So far, everyone she had met in Glenwhinnie had accepted her at face value, as Alix Grant, a writer in need of a peaceful hideaway in which to work. Perhaps it was going to be all right. Perhaps she could stop worrying.

34

TWO

Morning mist rose with the sun, leaving a few strands to float across the face of Ben Lachan as Alix set out to walk the mile or so to the village. Breathing deeply of the crisp air, she strode out briskly along the lochside road. The water looked navy blue that morning, fringed with trees of flame and rust and gold, with the sage and brown hills rising all around. The wonderful good-to-be-alive morning encouraged her growing sense of safety and optimism.

Passing a stone-built village hall, she reached the outskirts of Lachanbrae. Soon she would have to encounter people. Her feet wanted to falter, but she kept her head up and strode on, beside pretty cottages and bungalows set on a slope above the lane, fronted by stone walls and flagstone pathways crossing neat front gardens where bronze and yellow chrysanthemums bloomed beside dahlias of all shapes and colours. A couple of small children went by on tricycles, their pet dog leaping alongside and mother and grannie following more slowly. The adults nodded and eyed Alix curiously. She made herself smile, 'Hi. Good morning,' and passed by, heading into the centre of the village where four trees stood sentinel over a patch of grass with a seat or two at the edges. Around the green stood more cottages, a white-washed inn with a disused petrol pump beside it, and beyond that a small convenience store-cum-post office.

Making for the store, Alix heard the bell jangle as she stepped inside a bright, modern interior with crammed display shelves, cold cabinets along the side wall, wire baskets stacked handy by the door.

A youngish woman with a face like a red apple, mouse-brown hair cut to fall softly round it, came swiftly. 'Can I help? What is it you're needing?'

She proceeded to guide Alix round the shelves to find the provisions she wanted, recommending this brand, suggesting additions, her plump hands darting out to select the item and place it in Alix's wire basket. And all the time she chatted: 'You'll be Miss Grant, staying in Glenwhinnie Lodge. Och, news travels fast in Glen Lachan. A new neighbour's always an excitement. You're a writer, so I hear.' Her name, she said, was Maggie Gillivray—*Mrs* Maggie Gillivray, she emphasized proudly, been wed two years now. She was a crofter's daughter. 'A croft? Och, that's a small farm in the hills,' she explained. 'A crofter mebbe runs a wee flock, mebbe a few hens, and grows vegetables for the pot. That sort of thing. It'll not make you rich but it's a living. Mostly. That's what my dad says.'

Other customers had followed Alix into the shop. They lingered around the shelves, listening, observing, occasionally adding a remark. Alix was aware that their interest was caused by nothing more sinister than curiosity about a stranger, but even so it made her edgy.

To protect herself from questions, she was the one who kept asking, prompting an eager flow of information about Lachanbrae and Glenwhinnie. The estate covered thousands of acres, including the scatter of far-flung crofts, the pine forest, a Home Farm and most of the village. All were owned by Dame Janet McDonald, who was obviously loved and respected by her tenants—as was Mr Drummond, the factor.

'A fine man,' said Maggie Gillivray.

Another woman muttered darkly, 'But not even he can work miracles.'

Maggie sighed. 'That's so. The Lord knows what will happen when Dame Janet goes to her reward, though please God that won't happen for many a long year. She's hale and hearty yet.'

Dame Janet, it seemed, had enjoyed a brilliant and highly successful career as a concert pianist—winning a Damehood, a DBE, from the Queen. When crippling rheumatoid arthritis forced her to retire, with the fortitude of her breed she had come home, opened up the big house—which had

37

been closed since her father's death—and settled down to do her best for her employees and tenants.

'It's as well for us it was her and not her brother that inherited,' said Maggie. 'It would have been sold off long ago if yon shiftless John McDonald had outlived the old man.'

The other women murmured agreement. By now they had given up all pretence of shopping and were grouped around Alix prepared for a good old a gossip.

'I had no idea Dame Janet had a brother,' Alix said.

'Och, he died years ago,' said Maggie. 'Of the booze and the women, so they say.'

She glanced aside as a loud male voice from somewhere at the rear of the shop called, 'Maggie, are you doing any work today?' The other shoppers drifted away, but Maggie paused to add in a low voice, 'But if rumours are true, the next generation may yet put a shine on John McDonald's tarnished shield.' With which mystic allusion she bustled off duty-bound while the other women murmured, 'Aye, that's so,' and other impenetrable comments.

Amused, Alix completed her purchases.

By that time Maggie was busy behind the post office counter, the shop being guarded by a small, balding man who stood by the till and whose only interest was in the flow of money. He was Maggie's father-in-law, owner of the shop. His son Jim, Maggie's husband, worked as a forester on Glenwhinnie estate, apparently.

By the time Alix had walked back to the lodge, the morning mail lay on the mat. It comprised a large envelope containing a letter from Sir Anthony McKenzie and a couple of communications he had redirected for her, from her lawyers—he had offered to field her mail, trying to keep her whereabouts a secret, at least for the time being. Well, it seemed to be working. Alix felt cheered by her uneventful trip to the village. What had she been worried about? No one here had the least suspicion of who she really was.

*   *   *

For her dinner engagement at Glenwhinnie House she chose a plain blue, figure-skimming dress and added a white jacket, a minimum of plain gold jewellery, with her hair . . . how she regretted the fear-driven impulse that had shorn her of her hair! The red streaks had washed out, thank goodness, but the rest was still dyed raven-black and there wasn't much she could do about the pixie cut, even if it did give her a rather appealing gamine look when her eyes were big as saucers in a thin, pale face. As she fixed a final gold stud ear-ring she met those huge grey eyes in the mirror and discovered she was shaking. Tonight she might have to face personal questions. How much did she dare to tell Dame Janet?

The sun had gone and the last daylight was fading over the western hills as she went on foot down the Glenwhinnie drive. Shimmering aspens stood sentinel either side of a strip of badly-worn and uneven asphalt that made Alix watch her step and regret her high heels. An occasional soft yellow leaf drifted down through the dusk and from the hillside sheep bleated as she passed between ornate wrought-iron gates and into the courtyard, following the flagged pathway across to the main porch. The clipped yews seemed to crouch like cloaked figures, while the house opened its granite arms in welcome, light showing behind several curtained windows.

A lamp over the porch shed light on the bright carmine leaves of a Virginia creeper. It also illumined the great oak door and its bronze lion's-head knocker, though Alix chose to use the modern bell-push, which elicited a distant ringing somewhere inside the house.

What she had expected she couldn't afterwards have said. A butler, perhaps? Murdo Gordon? A comfortable housekeeper, or a maid? Certainly she had not expected the door to be flung open by the tall, formally-suited figure of Niall Drummond.

His broad smile mocked her surprise. 'Welcome!' he greeted with a deliberately theatrical bow. 'Please . . . come in.'

Alix stepped inside, glancing around the oak-panelled hallway, noting a fine old staircase, pictures in ornate frames on the walls, a big display of bright yellow chrysanthemums in a polished copper bowl sitting on an antique chest . . .

'This way.' The factor ushered her into a sitting room softly lit by standard lamps, with deep cream walls and a deep rose-printed carpet. Old settees and chairs of worn leather, tossed with tasselled throws and soft cushions, stood around a long low coffee table made of a single broad plank of well-varnished wood— from the estate, Alix guessed, probably made by a local carpenter. In one corner a grand piano stood closed and silent, providing a stand for another bowl of yellow chrysanthemums from the garden.

Taking her jacket, the estate manager laid it across the piano stool and invited her to sit somewhere comfortable. 'Dame Janet won't be long. What would you like to drink? Sherry, whisky, gin?'

'Scotch, please. Just a dash. Lots of water.'

She sank into a corner of one of the settees, watching as he poured scotch from a crystal decanter which reposed, with other bottles and glasses, on a tray on top of low bookshelves. What was he doing here? Did he live here? Was this where he entertained Catriona on nights when she slept over?

41

Surely not!

Curious about the man, she studied him more closely. The well-cut dark suit set off his broad shoulders and long legs, the blue shirt emphasized the colour of his eyes, the tie was a splash of red and pink and aqua blue— signalling a touch of the rebel? Catching herself admiring the sheer maleness of him, Alix both envied Catriona and was glad that the red-head existed. Here was one complication that, hopefully, wouldn't arise.

He turned and found her watching him, which made her flush and him smile as he came over bringing two glasses, toasting her, *'Slainte mhath!'*

'Slarnger . . . what?'

He laughed. 'It means good health. Cheers. *Slainte!'*

Alix lifted her glass. 'You too,' she returned, and sipped the drink, pleased to find it very weak, as she had asked.

'I hear you were in the village today,' he said, dropping into an armchair. 'So you're finding your way about all right?'

'Just fine. Grapevine pretty active, is it?'

'Faster than broadband,' he laughed.

She was grateful that he hadn't sat down beside her. In some errant, instinctive, female part of her mind she noted the way his shoulders filled out that elegant jacket while the dark wool of the trousers revealed the contours of athletic thighs. He had had his hair trimmed, but it still fell in thick, springy waves above straight dark brows, an appealing contrast against those amazing sky-blue eyes. There was nothing soft about Niall Drummond. Physically, anyway. She had yet to learn about his personality.

He was engaged in a silent scrutiny of his own, making her conscious of her too-short, too-dark hair and of her slim curves and long legs. The mutual interest was a force running strong and irresistible between them, and both of them knew it.

As a defence, she found herself chattering about the people she had met that day. 'Does Maggie Gillivray have the second sight?'

Niall's eyes gleamed at her. 'What makes you say that?'

'Something she said. Something about Dame Janet's brother. He let his shield get tarnished but the next generation will shine it up again. Something like that. You know what she meant?'

His expression didn't change but he seemed to have gone still, like a wildcat surprised in mid-prowl. 'If I were you,' he said quietly, 'I wouldn't mention that in front of Dame Janet. Her brother—' The ringing of a phone interrupted him and he got up to answer it, with an alacrity that said he wasn't sorry for the distraction. But before he could reach it the phone stopped ringing. Niall paused, then shook his head. 'Dame Janet must have taken

43

it. There's an extension in her room.'

He returned to his seat amid a lengthening silence that he eventually filled with, 'I'm sorry she's taking so long, but apparently she was busy writing letters and forgot the time. She was still in her old gardening clothes when I arrived. Gets distracted at times. And she has problems dressing. Her hands don't work properly, as you may have noticed. So that slows her up, too.' He glanced at the slim steel watch on his wrist, checking it against the grandfather clock in the corner. 'Sir Anthony's late, too.'

'Sir Anthony?' Alix felt her eyes widen with surprise. 'Sir Anthony McKenzie?'

Niall gave her an odd, sidelong look that she found hard to interpret. 'Didn't Dame Janet tell you? That's why I'm here—to make up a foursome.'

'I had no idea! Then . . . you don't live here?'

It was his turn to be surprised. 'Here? In Glenwhinnie House, you mean? Good Lord, no. Whatever made you think that?'

'You did answer the door-bell.'

'Well, yes, I did, but only because—' He glanced beyond her at the door, rising to his feet. 'Oh, there you are!'

Dame Janet was coming in, dressed in a skirt suit of heather purple bouclé over a paler lavender blouse, leaning on her stick, gruff as ever. 'Excuse me, please, leaving you in the

44

lurch like this. Damn fingers are all thumbs tonight. Alix . . . I'm so sorry. Forgot the time, as Niall probably told you. Must be getting old.'

'Drink?' Niall asked, making for the drinks tray.

'My usual. Thank you.' The old woman chose to seat herself on the settee near Alix, subsiding into its cushions with a sigh. 'That was Sir Anthony on the phone. Sending his apologies. He's been performing emergency surgery all afternoon and has only just got out of the operating theatre, so he won't be coming.'

'Oh, that's too bad,' Alix said, meaning it. But she wondered what prompted the sharp look that Niall flung at her as he handed Dame Janet a drink. What had she said?

In odd quiet moments as the evening progressed, Alix began to notice things that not even soft lighting could entirely conceal: the carpets in the fine old rooms were shabby, faded, patched in places. Going up to use the bathroom, she noticed cracks in the plaster, chips in the gesso frames of huge portraits, woodworm holes in the panelling. The place had an air of worn, faded grandeur. Someone worked hard to keep up appearances, but the toll of years was winning. She recalled the conversation in the village shop, which had implied some financial problem here at Glenwhinnie.

45

During dinner, served in the draughty dining room by Murdo Gordon's wife, Ailie, the lady laird talked about her career as a concert pianist, telling anecdotes with a dry, self-deprecating humour. Later, back in the sitting room, the conversation turned to Scottish history, tales of Robert the Bruce, tragic Queen Mary Stuart, bold Rob Roy McGregor and the old enmity between the McDonalds and the Campbells. Lively arguments between Niall and Dame Janet, over the details of a legend or the exact date of a battle, amused Alix. She was intrigued by what she was learning, not only about local history but about the relationship between the lady laird and her factor. Obviously they liked and respected each other, but at times a prickly undercurrent swirled between them.

At one point, speaking of the highland clearances, Dame Janet remarked, 'Many Scots emigrated because of that, and others have wandered away for various other reasons—to Canada, and to other countries across the world. Including America, as you'll know, Alix. But some are irresistibly drawn home again. Aren't they, Niall?' She afforded him a cool, direct stare, which made his mouth go grim.

'Not all of them entirely from choice,' he said flatly, and changed the subject, leaving Alix to wonder what lay behind that brief thrust and riposte. She did not feel inclined to enquire. Keeping the conversation impersonal was fine with her.

Around ten thirty, when Dame Janet began to look tired, Alix decided it was time to leave. 'It's been great, but I'm starting to flag. Still haven't got my body-clock adjusted properly.'

Dame Janet struggled to her feet. 'Of course, my dear. Niall will run you back to the lodge, won't you, Niall?' Alix began to protest but the old woman brushed her off with a flip of the hand. 'Nonsense, of course he will. He's going that way anyway, and it's horribly dark down that drive. We don't have streetlights here, you know. But first let me choose you out some books. Where's the girl's coat, Niall?'

He fetched it and while Alix slipped into her jacket Dame Janet peered along her bookshelves, picking out a title here and there. 'Those should start you off in the right direction.'

So Alix had her arms full of books—five or six weighty tomes that promised weeks of reading—when she left Glenwhinnie House.

Outside in the cool late-September night the moon had risen, a rusty orange disc brightening as it lifted over the hills. But the shadows it threw were black and Alix was glad not to have to pick her way on foot down the uneven drive. Even so, being alone with Niall Drummond made her a tad edgy. All evening, sexual awareness had been sparking between

47

them. She must at all costs avoid the complications that could so easily arise.

'I'm sorry you have to settle for me as a chauffeur,' Niall said brusquely as he settled beside her in the Range Rover and flicked the engine into life.

Clutching the books to her bosom, Alix considered his averted profile, mystified. 'In the absence of Bonnie Prince Charlie, you'll do fine.'

He negotiated the archway and headed down the drive, flicking her a look. 'I wouldn't have thought I was much of a substitute.'

'For Bonnie Prince Charlie?'

'For Sir Anthony McKenzie.'

'I'm sorry?'

'Well, presumably you were expecting to have *him* drive you back.'

Alix seemed to have lost the thread of this conversation. Maybe she had drunk too much wine. 'I'm sorry?' she said again, and, 'You'll have to explain. What makes you think . . . ? I had no idea Sir Anthony had been invited. Why would I . . . ?'

'Forget it.' He frowned down the bright tunnel created by the car's headlamps. 'Maybe I got it wrong.' To his evident relief, they were almost at the lodge. He slowed the car, bringing it to a stop by the gate, switching off the engine and saying much too cheerfully, 'Well, here we are. I'll just see you safely inside and—'

'No, hold it,' she broke in. 'I want to know what you meant. What's this about Sir Anthony and me?'

He glanced at her, but with the engine off and the lights out she couldn't read his face. 'I asked you to forget it, Alix. Obviously I got my wires crossed.'

'You thought there was something . . . something *personal* between Sir Anthony McKenzie and me? Such as what—that we were an item? That he'd set me up in a cosy little love-nest hideaway and . . . and had his *daughter* bring me over?'

Now that her eyes had adjusted to the faint glow of moonlight, she saw Niall's mouth twist before he turned away and reached for the door handle. 'Put like that, I agree, it's fairly ludicrous. But it's what some of the locals have been speculating, him being a widower, rich and successful. I know he's a lot older than you, but . . . Well, some women go for older men, don't they? Not,' he added hastily, 'that I believed it myself.'

'So why bring it up?'

She thought he would refuse to reply. He climbed out of the car, but paused and bent again to peer in at her. 'I wanted to know the answer,' he growled, slammed the door, and began to march round to the near side.

Burdened as she was, Alix had little choice but to allow him to help her with the awkward, slipping books, though his proximity made her

49

self-conscious and clumsy. She was glad when he snapped, 'Oh, for heaven's sake! Here, I'll take them all. You go ahead and unlock the door.'

Opening the gate, she brushed past the untamed leaves of the copper beech and fumbled for her keys, horribly aware of Niall Drummond not far behind her. Would he expect to be invited in for a coffee? Not wise, she decided. Better make it absolutely clear that she was not in the market for romantic liaisons, however fleeting. All thumbs, she fiddled with the keys, unable to find the lock. Then to her relief the key slid in, turned, the door opened. Thank heaven.

'Thanks for your help,' she muttered. 'And for the ride home. I'll just take the books and—'

In her attempts to avoid touching him, she nearly dropped the books. One big volume slid from between two others and thudded to the path. 'Oh, no!' Alix breathed. 'Dame Janet's precious—' She bent to retrieve the book. So did Niall. Their shoulders connected and she was caught off-balance, clutching at the other books to save herself from dropping them all, half falling into a bush. Two more volumes escaped and fell. A cry of pure exasperation escaped her.

His hands fastened around her upper arms, straightening her and pulling her upright. 'Just stand still,' he said between his teeth. 'Let *me*

50

get the books.'

The situation struck her as ridiculous. They were both behaving like fools. She made herself take a couple of deep breaths as she watched him rescue the books, brush off the worst of the dirt, and carefully add them to the pile in her arms.

Alix heard herself say, 'Why don't you come in and have a coffee?'

'I thought you were feeling tired.'

'I said that because I thought Dame Janet was starting to look a bit weary.'

'Yes, she was.'

'So . . . coffee?'

The silence lengthened as he considered her upturned face with eyes made inscrutable by hazy moonlight. 'I don't think it would be a very good idea,' he said evenly. 'Do you?'

'Why not?' She knew why not, but some demon seemed to have hold of her, egging her on to madness. 'Because the Glenwhinnie factor has to be careful of his image?'

'What?'

Alix shrugged. 'Something Catriona said.'

A frown dug lines between his dark brows. He stepped closer, lifted his hands to cup her face, and kissed her full on the mouth. She knew she ought to do something to stop him, to put up a show of resistance, but her arms were full of books and she didn't want to risk dropping them again, and anyway the touch of his lips on hers was doing wonderful things to

51

parts of her she had almost forgotten existed. All her senses came alive to the slight roughness of bristle against her skin, the faint tang of aftershave, the softness of his suit and the firmness of muscle beneath . . .

He drew away slowly, scanning her face with eyes that asked questions as much of himself as of her. He started to speak, but had to clear his throat and even then his voice was gruff. 'Don't believe anything Catriona says,' he advised. 'See you,' spun on his heel and strode back to the waiting Range Rover.

*   *   *

September became October, fading the jeweled leaves, while gales and rain helped to strip the branches. As time passed and no hint of harm disturbed her haven, Alix felt the tension lifting like black clouds from her mind. When the weather allowed she went walking in the hills, exploring and becoming familiar with her surroundings; other days she dipped deep into several of the books Dame Janet had loaned her; she visited the village hair-dresser and had her crop restored to its normal colour—she had the fair skin of a natural blonde and no way was the raven Gothic look ever going to suit her. But most of the time she applied herself to work, not only writing about the delights of New York State—the mountains, the Finger Lakes, the

52

ski resorts and the wineries—but starting a novel about a girl from the mid-West thrown suddenly into city life. It was her own story, not intended for publication but solely for herself. Perhaps by writing it all down she might begin to comprehend the forces and emotions that had made her flee from the States in such turmoil, though she doubted she could put into words how it had felt to discover that her whole life had been a lie.

Occasionally Dame Janet joined Alix on her walks, or invited her up to the big house for tea, which was always served by the plump and friendly housekeeper, Ailie Gordon. Ailie's husband, however, continued to disapprove of Alix. Every time she encountered him, Murdo Gordon managed, by word or look, to remind her that in his eyes it was unnatural, if not downright sinful, for a single young woman to be living all alone in a house set in relative isolation at the end of the Glenwhinnie drive. His scowling face and narrowed eyes made him look like a gargoyle.

Of Niall Drummond she saw little. The Range Rover came frequently up or down the drive, but when she bumped into him at the big house, where he kept his office, he was unfailingly pleasant and polite but offhand, in a hurry and too busy to stop. Presumably he too regretted the momentary madness of that moonlit night, though when they did come face to face the look in his eyes told her he

53

had not forgotten, any more than she had. The memory still disturbed her far more than was sensible. It was, after all, just a kiss. Just one brief kiss. One of dozens she had shared since boys first became objects of desire rather than disdain. She should forget it. She told herself so at least ten times a day. But at night the memory kept repeating itself in her dreams.

*   *   *

On a clear cold day in November, when all the deciduous trees had been left skeletal by a scouring wind and when the loch looked like a sheet of steel, Alix went to the village to order more bags of peat. At the door of the shop she almost ran into Maggie Gillivray, who was brandishing a purse left behind by a recent customer.

'It's Maura's,' Maggie explained, distressed. 'Och, she'll be so upset when she finds she's lost it. Poor wee soul, things like that get her into a proper state. But I can't leave the shop, I'm here by myself the day.'

'I'll take it to her,' Alix offered, and set off in pursuit of the retreating figure, a woman dressed in a blue anorak, stumping along with her head down into the wind. She wasn't walking very fast so Alix soon came within hailing distance. 'Miss Drummond! Miss Drummond, wait!'

Maura Drummond was Niall's older sister. Over the past weeks Alix had seen her about the village and learned something about her story from Maggie. Maura was 'slow' but harmless. She lived in Lachanbrae with her father, Fergus, who was confined to a wheelchair after an accident some years before.

'He was gamekeeper over to Ardmuir,' Maggie had confided. 'There was a big shoot on and someone wounded a deer that got away, so Fergus had to go after it, to put the beast out of its pain. A huge beast, they say. A stag in full antler. It turned on Fergus. Attacked him. Threw him across a rock. Broke his back, poor soul. When he came out of the hospital he and Maura took a cottage here, to be closer to young Mr Drummond, the factor.'

Now, running along the wet lane in her sturdy all-weather shoes, Alix called again, 'Miss Drummond! Wait! Your purse. You forgot your purse!'

The stocky figure stopped and looked round. Beneath a knitted blue tam-o-shanter her face was broad, unlined, covered in soft down like a peach, and her hair was greying blonde, cut straight about an inch below her ears. Alix could never see any resemblance between the tall, athletic Niall and this slow-moving, slow-thinking woman who was a good ten years his senior.

Maura stared at Alix, then glanced down into her shopping basket as if expecting to find her purse there. 'Why . . . I must have left it in the shop,' she said at last, adding shyly, 'You're Miss Grant, are you not? Will you come and have a cup of tea with us? My father would like to meet you. Niall's told us all about you.'

'Has he?' Alix was surprised.

'Oh, he tells us all the news. My father doesn't get out a lot, you know, but he likes to hear what's going on.'

The Drummond cottage lay down a lane where stone dwellings stood behind small gardens walled with hill-stone. As they walked, Maura talked about Niall, saying how good he was to her and their father, visiting them often, bringing them good things to eat and small gifts to please them. Obviously she adored her younger brother.

'He doesn't live with you, then?' Alix observed.

The notion made Maura look blank. 'With us? No, of course not. He lives in the factor's house on the estate.' She added proudly, 'He works for Dame Janet, you know. Her right-hand man, she calls him.'

A glass porch protected the Drummonds' front door, which led into a sitting room warmed by a roaring fire. The room seemed cramped with furniture, probably because a good deal of space was taken up by the

56

wheelchair in which Fergus Drummond spent most of his time. He was watching horse racing on television.

'This is Miss Grant, from the lodge,' Maura informed him, flicking a shy smile at Alix. 'I'll put the kettle on.' Making for the kitchen, she passed close to the television.

'Switch that thing off while you're there,' her father bade, and as the racing commentary cut off in mid-sentence he wheeled his chair so that his back was to the window, from where he could see Alix more clearly. 'So you're Miss Grant. Well, sit ye down, lassie. Sit ye down and welcome.'

He must have been a big man once, like his son, but illness and inactivity had made him gaunt and lean. Shaggy white hair was brushed back from an angular face with a hawk-like nose and dark eyes that assessed Alix intently, though the stare was softened by a deepening twinkle.

Afterwards, Alix always recalled that first visit as a friendly occasion. She soon felt at home with the Drummonds. Fergus had a wicked sense of humour, chaffing his daughter for her 'daftness' in leaving her purse behind, and teasing Alix about being a 'transAtlantic Sassenach'. Despite his addiction to TV, he didn't appear to connect Alix with any sensational news stories that he might have viewed that summer.

Maura made tea very strong, so that Alix

could only drink it loaded with sugar, but drink it she did, warmed both by the fire and by the friendliness of Niall's family. She envied him his childhood, with loving parents and an older sister who doted on him. That childhood was enshrined, along with Maura's, in photographs around the room. One snap in particular caught Alix's eye—a colour shot of a younger Niall with his arm around a petite brunette. Neither of them could have been much more than twenty.

Despite her efforts, her eyes kept straying to that picture until eventually Maura noticed and picked up the photo, bringing it to show Alix. 'That's Niall and Barbara, soon after they met. In Canada.' Her stubby fingers stroked the glass lovingly. 'She was pretty, wasn't she?'

'Beautiful,' Alix agreed, glancing to Fergus for help.

'She was . . . Niall's wife,' Fergus said slowly.

'Was?'

'They'd been married . . . it would be about two years, when she died. It was a skiing accident. Some lads in one of those ski-sled things, went off the track and . . . Barbara was badly hurt. She died two days later.'

Having assumed Niall Drummond to be a bachelor, Alix was taken aback by this news. How had the tragedy affected him? She moistened dry lips, managing, 'I'm sorry,' and

58

handed the photograph back to Maura, who sadly polished the glass on her cardigan sleeve before replacing it on its spot among the rest.

The sound of a vehicle outside made Fergus ease his chair round so that he could peer through the net curtain. 'Talk of angels,' he said. 'Here's Niall now.'

Alix got to her feet, looking round for her coat. 'I'd better go.' All at once she felt like an intruder, but before she could do anything the door opened and Niall was there, carrying a plastic bag with something heavy inside it. His vibrant presence uncurled a strange warmth inside Alix.

The cheerful greeting died on his lips as he saw her there and twitched a dark eyebrow in surprise. 'Miss Grant! What are you doing here?'

'We've been having tea,' Maura answered. 'Now you're here, I'll make a fresh pot.'

'No, I can't stay.' He handed her the plastic carrier. 'Take care of that, Maura. It's a fresh salmon. Cut it into steaks and put them in the freezer, there's a good girl. Several suppers there for you and Dad.'

'You won't have tea?'

'No, I have to get back to the office. Sorry. Perhaps I can give you a lift, Miss Grant?'

'I have to go to the shop,' Alix demurred.

'Fine. There are a couple of things I need myself. If you're ready to go, that is.'

Alix hesitated but, unable to think of any

excuses, agreed to go along with him. She didn't want to outstay her welcome at the Drummond cottage and, anyway, the temptation to spend a few minutes alone with Niall proved too strong. Saying thanks yous and farewells, she went with him out to the yellow Range Rover and climbed up into the passenger seat.

Feeling that the situation demanded it, she explained, 'I was just going into the shop when Maggie Gillivray found Maura's purse, so I went after her to return it, to save her being upset, and she invited me in for tea. I could hardly refuse.'

'Who said you should?'

'Well, nobody. I just didn't want you to think . . .'

Niall slanted her a satirical glance. 'Found out all you wanted to know, did you?'

'No!' The fact that her motives *had* included curiosity made her defensive. 'You make it sound as if I was spying!'

'Weren't you? Just a little?'

'No, I most certainly . . .' About to launch into hot denials, she stopped herself. 'OK. I admit I was curious. But that doesn't mean I had ulterior motives. Just because you want to know a little bit more about somebody . . .'

'I'm flattered!'

'I was talking about Maura and Fergus!'

'Oh. Sorry.'

'You surely don't think—' She stopped,

60

aware that she was digging the hole deeper with every word, especially when he slid her one of those disconcerting wicked-blue looks. But thankfully they had reached the shop and when he pulled up she jumped out at once and sought sanctuary among the tinned peas and cabbage.

Niall followed her and stood flicking through a boating magazine while Alix ordered her fuel. Maggie chatted in her usual garrulous way, obviously curious to see them together, but Niall made a point of explaining that he was simply giving Alix a lift, least he could do after she'd been so good as to return Maura's purse, etc, etc.

Alix lost track of the conversation at that point. Her entire being had focused on a picture and headline on the front page of a tabloid newspaper lying with others on the counter. The picture was a studio glamour shot of late movie star Claudia Cantrelle and the headline beside it screamed: *"CLAUDIA'S MAID TELLS ALL Full story on Pages 4, 5, 6 and 7"*.

Alix picked up the paper and, as casually as she could, tossed it onto the counter. 'I'll take one of these, too. How much is that?'

She escaped while Niall bought his boating magazine and a packet of mints.

Back in the Range Rover, she clutched the rolled-up newspaper in nerveless fingers, wanting to open it and read the worst.

Presumably some journalist had finally offered more money than Claudia's housemaid could resist. Why should Alix be surprised?

'I wouldn't have thought that scandal sheet was your sort of reading,' Niall remarked as the vehicle moved off in fading afternoon light.

'I wanted the TV programmes. Anyhow, I didn't know *you* were into yachting!' Her voice sounded strained and Niall flung her a puzzled look.

'I used to have a boat once,' he informed her. 'Sometimes I look at that loch and think . . . a man can dream can't he? Want a mint?'

'No.'

'Are you all right?'

'Fine.'

'You don't sound it.'

Change the subject, she thought frantically, blurting, 'I didn't know you'd been married.' Oh, good grief! What a stupid thing to say!

'The subject has never come up, has it?' he said levelly. 'And what else did Dad and Maura have to tell you about me?'

'Nothing! If you think I was deliberately dangling for information then you're wrong. I'm not interested. Except academically. Saves me going completely stir-crazy!' Jangled nerves made her turn her head away so he couldn't see the tears that suddenly stung, hot and bitter. Stop it, Alix, don't go to pieces now, girl! What was wrong with her? Was it the story in the news, or being so close to Niall, or everything so mixed up and mad . . .

A chill November dusk had gathered among the trees around the lodge as the vehicle pulled up by the gate. As she made to open the door a warm, strong hand on her other arm made her freeze. She could feel the electric current running between them—even through her padded coat his touch made her skin tingle. She daren't look at him.

'Have I upset you?' he asked. 'What did I say, Alix?'

'Nothing!'

She tried to wrench away but he only held tighter, leaner closer and trying to see her face. 'Are you crying? For heaven's sake . . . tell me! What's wrong?'

She twisted to face him, anger her only defence. 'What do you care? You ignore me for weeks, and then—'

Wrenching free, she flung herself from the vehicle, almost falling in her hurry to get away. Oh, God! Why had she said that? What must he be thinking? She had made it sound as though she wanted to see him, as if she was lonely for him. And that wasn't so. It wasn't him in particular she needed, it was just . . . just someone. Anyone. She felt so horribly alone . . .

Alix ran for the lodge and shut herself into its quietness, tears trickling down her face.

Tears of self-pity. How she despised herself.

*   *   *

With the forest-green velvet drapes drawn to shut out the night, the lamps aglow and the fire sending out its comforting peat glow, Alix sat and read every word of the story which had been bribed out of Rosalia, her mother's Mexican housemaid. It told lurid details of life in the Beverly Hills mansion, of drink, drugs, lovers, wild parties, mad extravagance . . . and of one particularly florid evening when Claudia Cantrelle, darling of the screen, known for her raven locks allied with ice-cool grey eyes, much-married but still achingly glamorous at the age of thirty-six (read forty-four, thought Alix bitterly), and midway through a multi-million-dollar movie of which she was the star, had drunk herself into a feverish crazy mood, gone out in her Rolls Royce convertible, and driven straight over a cliff. Her body was found amid the wreckage next day.

The story described again the funeral that had turned into a circus, and the revelation that some little nonentity from New York—a young woman named Lexie Marisco, who had always believed herself to be Claudia's niece—was in fact Claudia's only daughter, product of an early, secret relationship that had ended in tragedy.

64

Well, the gist of it was true.

It came over like a B-movie melodrama. Something Joan Crawford might have starred in. The writer didn't pause to consider what a terrific shock the whole thing might have been to that 'unknown young woman' who had suddenly found herself the centre of attention for the world's media, sought by newsmen, cameramen, paparazzi from more countries than she had known existed.

One consolation was that the two pictures of herself that accompanied the story bore no resemblance to the way she looked now. Alix had always hated having her picture taken: when she was young her teeth had been crooked, and in later years she'd been forced to wear horrible ugly braces to correct the fault. Her father, and her younger brother, had taken perverse pleasure in assuring her that she was plain Jane, unlikely ever to win a beauty pageant. So she had avoided cameras. Consequently the only pictures the press had to work with were an old one from her schooldays, complete with braces, puppy fat and pony-tail; the other was a still taken from a piece of video film shot as she left her flat, caught unawares before she fully realized the storm that was about to break around her. On that hot day last July she had been wearing a sunhat pulled low on her brow, fishing in her bag for her sun-glasses. As the cameraman called, 'Lexie!' she had looked up, throwing

65

up a hand to shield her eyes—this was the shot everyone now used—then she had turned away in panic, shoving her sunglasses on, hailing a cruising cab and away . . . The memory made Alix feel chilled. From that moment she had felt like a fugitive.

In the text, of course, she was referred to as Lexie Marisco—the name she had for most of her life believed to be her own.

Sickened, she tore the newspaper to shreds and threw it on the fire, watching it turn to ashes. Hopefully—please God!—no one in Lachanbrae would latch onto this latest revelation. Only the most avid, sharp-eyed celebrity-watcher, surely, would be likely to connect their quiet neighbour, reclusive Miss Alix Grant, with this piece of trash journalism.

THREE

Next morning Dame Janet phoned and asked Alix to drive her to Auchinveray, the nearest town. Murdo Gordon, who usually acted as driver, was otherwise occupied, and the lady laird thought Alix might enjoy a change of scene. She was wrong there—all Alix wanted to do was hide away at the lodge until everyone had forgotten about the sensational news story that was seemingly told and re-told on every bulletin and every paper review on both radio and TV. Luckily more important stories had kept it down the list and hopefully it would drop out of public consciousness in a day or so, when the next celebrity slept with his children's nanny, beat up a barman, or announced her pregnancy.

'I don't have an international licence,' Alix objected.

'You don't need one. Your American licence will serve you here, for a whole year. We checked on the internet.'

Unable to think of another quick and convincing excuse, Alix found herself agreeing to play chauffeur. Cunningly trapped into it, she felt.

'Whose idea was this?' she asked as she accustomed herself to the right-hand drive of the big grey Volvo, and the left-hand orientation of the road. Fortunately the car had automatic gears, which made things easier, but thank goodness they had a few miles to go before they met any busy roads!

'Why, mine, of course!' Dame Janet replied briskly. 'Who else would it be?'

'I wondered if Niall had suggested I might need an outing. I was uptight yesterday. Lost my cool. Did he mention it?'

'He . . . may have done,' the old woman conceded.

Which meant he had. 'I suppose he was the one who checked about the driving licence, too.'

'Well, I'm hopeless with computers, as you know.'

Between them, it seemed, the lady laird and her factor had decided that Alix needed a break. She was vaguely miffed at being manipulated, though it was kind of them to care about her wellbeing. Diplomatic, too—Dame Janet didn't once try to press Alix to talk about her reasons for being edgy the previous day.

Auchinveray lay about half an hour from Lachanbrae, along a scenic route among the colourful autumn hills, an impressionist landscape of purples and bronzes and pine-green. The houses of the town clustered round an ancient and impressive bridge that spanned a broad river. 'Good salmon fishing,' commented Dame Janet.

While the lady laird attended to her business appointments, Alix explored the shops, buying some new winter clothes and other essentials. An electrical store lured her in to enquire about the possibility of improving her TV reception and she was momentarily startled to see a picture of herself—the one with the hat and shading hand—appear on a bank of screens. But to her relief the salesman took no notice. He had such a way with him that she emerged from the shop having rented a new set, complete with video and DVD recorder. An engineer would come and install the machines, check the aerial and replace it if necessary.

'Well, and how was your morning?' Dame Janet enquired as they met for lunch at the large and luxurious Bridge Hotel.

'Just great,' said Alix.

'Spot of retail therapy never did any harm, eh?'

The trip to Auchinveray provided a boost to Alix's confidence, welcome after the shock of the newspaper story. She was glad she had decided to come to Scotland, to spend time regaining her balance. The past few weeks had been good. Too soon yet to go back and face the problems that waited, but more and more she was starting to believe she had nothing to fear. Not while she stayed here in the Highlands, anyway.

* * *

The new TV equipment was installed a few days later, the aerial realigned to catch the strongest signal, though reception might be affected by the weather, and by the mountains, so the helpful engineer informed her. But at least Alix was once more in touch with the outside world without constant hissing and snowing on the screen.

It was ironic that, just as her TV cleared, real snow threatened: a cold north-easter brought ominous clouds and that evening the weather girl announced the arrival of Siberian winds, with blizzard warnings for the Scottish Highlands.

Next morning Alix woke to find the glen transformed yet again, brilliant white beneath a sky of hurting blue. Just as well she had bought those warm winter clothes, and good boots. Getting to the village for her weekly groceries turned into quite an adventure, though the children weren't complaining. School, it seemed, was out for the day. Maggie Gillivray said that the road round Ben Lachan was blocked, so the school bus couldn't get through to take the children to Auchinveray. The curriculum today consisted of building snowmen, sledding, and having snow fights. Great fun.

Trudging back through the drifts, swaddled in thick coat, hat, scarf and gloves, Alix had just reached her gate when the Glenwhinnie Range Rover drew up and Niall Drummond leapt down from it, warmly clad in a padded stone-coloured jacket over a thick white sweater. 'Morning!'

'Hi,' said Alix, determinedly offhand. There was no reason why her heart should lurch and start to race the way it had. Unless it was from the exertion of struggling through the snow. And if her face was glowing the cold had caused it. That was all. That was definitely all.

Shuddering expressively, Niall blew on his hands and rubbed them together, remarking unoriginally, 'Strewth, it's cold!'

'I think it's the weather,' said Alix with irony. 'I'm about to indulge in a hot chocolate. Want some?'

She half expected him to make an excuse, but instead he nodded, 'Thanks,' and helped her transfer her shopping into the lodge. He would have helped her stow the food away too, if she hadn't shooed him off, telling him to, 'Go get warm by the fire. Put some more peat on.' Sheer self-consciousness made her add punningly, 'For Pete's sake.'

'You should do stand-up,' said Niall, and returned to the sitting room.

Fact was, the kitchen had felt much too small with him in it.

As she put away the groceries and made coffee, Alix lectured herself about playing it cool. Remember you're only here temporarily. No point in getting involved. Besides . . . he's involved with Cat McKenzie and you wouldn't want to get wrong side of that lady. Much too volatile.

Even so, when she took the mugs of chocolate through and found him standing on the hearthrug warming his back she'd have had to be made of wood not to feel happy he was there. She did feel lonesome, at times, and Niall was appealing company. He had removed his thick jacket and the white sweater he wore beneath it suited him well. He looked tall and solid and oh so very desirably, warmly masculine.

Saying, 'Was this a social visit, or what?' she chose a fireside chair rather than the settee which might have offered an invitation.

'I came to make sure you're coping in this weather. Have you got everything you need? Managing to keep warm?'

'M-hm. Especially since I worked out how to keep the fire burning, and when to switch on the other heaters. Thermal underwear helps, too. And hot water bottles in the bed.' Oh Lord, why had she mentioned the bed?

Niall dropped into the near end of the old sofa. 'Dame Janet's concerned about you.'

'I know. Sweet of her, but I'm used to being alone.'

'I don't suppose you're used to being quite as isolated as this,' he argued. 'Lanachbrae's a bit out-of-the-way, off-the-beaten-track, compared to New York City.'

Alix flinched. How did he know she came from New York—because of those news reports about Claudia's runaway daughter? Panic made her mind go blank. 'Why do British people think New York's the only city in the States?!'

'I wasn't aware that they did. I thought Dame Janet mentioned . . . No, it was you— you mentioned writing a book about New York.'

'New York State! It's a big place.'

'So where do you call home?'

Good question, Alix thought. What was the

72

answer? She could name places where she had lived, but as for Home . . .

'Dame Janet also mentioned Kansas, come to think of it,' said Niall. 'I expect areas of the mid-west can be pretty remote.'

Totally fazed, Alix jumped to her feet and went to the window, wishing she'd simply told the plain truth and not got herself into such a fix. She daren't start talking about Kansas, there was no telling where it might lead. 'I live in New York. Manhattan. The Village. Greenwich Village, you know?' Her hand clutched in the velvet drapes at the window. It was snowing again, thin flakes driving across the view of the small front garden and the snowy road and trees beyond. She could feel the cold lapping in through the single glass. No double-glazing at Glenwhinnie Lodge.

Niall's silence told her he was wondering at her jumpiness. Stupid, Alix, stupid! Now you've given him reason to wonder.

The battered red pickup went by, pulling out to avoid the yellow Range Rover whose bright colour made it so visible and so easily recognizable. 'There's Murdo,' she said with a sharp laugh. 'Wonder what he'll make of that? Your vehicle outside my gate for all the world to see. He already thinks I'm a harlot, living on my own, waiting to ensnare every passing male—including Sir Anthony McKenzie, of course.' It was meant to be a joke, but to her horror the words snagged in her throat and

73

brought tears to her eyes.

'Murdo's a miserable old puritan.' His soft, deep voice came from right behind her and the hands on her shoulders urged her round to face him. 'What's wrong, Alix?'

'Nothing!' Not wanting him to see her tears she kept her face averted, but he lifted her chin and studied her face with concern.

'You want to talk about it?'

She shook her head, croaking. 'No. No, I'm just . . .' She couldn't bear that sympathetic look on his face. Fresh tears came hot, dazzling her.

'Hey, now,' Niall murmured, and folded her into his arms as if it were the most natural thing in the world, cradling her as if she were a child. Alix couldn't help herself. All her loneliness and despair welled up in a huge sob and burst free in a flood of misery. She clung to Niall Drummond as if he were a lifeline, knowingly only that he was someone to lean on when she needed a friend. But oh he was so sturdy and warm, his sweater so soft and cuddly, his smell so clean and male and comforting . . .

She had not cried until now. Not properly. The tension of months seemed to be finding a release at last. The lost child in her heart welcomed the chance to let go. But the adult in her head knew it was all wrong. She had planned to keep to herself, to fend off the world and all its questions. What was she doing letting herself give in to self-pity and her need of human warmth? She wasn't here to get involved.

After a while, when the storm began to subside, she eased away, not looking at him, drying her face on a handkerchief he pushed into her hands. Her make-up would be streaked. Oh, what did it matter?!

'I'm sorry,' she managed thickly. 'Didn't mean to do that. Don't know what came over me. Just . . . like you said, I get lonely. When Maggie said the Ben Lachan road was closed, I guess I felt . . . cut off.'

'They'll get it open soon enough,' he assured her. 'Alix . . . Look, I know you said you had come here to work in peace and quiet, but . . . There's more to it, isn't there? Some reason you needed to escape for a while? Some man . . . ?'

She didn't answer. She couldn't. If she began she might not be able to stop.

Niall said, 'I can understand that. I've been there, believe me. And I'm not going to ask about it—I know how unwelcome that can be, too, however well meant. But if ever you need a friendly ear, I'm a good listener. And if I'm the wrong person then Dame Janet would certainly be ready to help. She's more worldly-wise than you may think. She's concerned about you. We both are.'

'I know.'

He let the silence lengthen, perhaps hoping

she might say more, but Alix stood with her back turned to him, wiping her face in an effort to minimize the damage to her make-up. Belatedly she noticed the smears on the square of white cotton.

'I've made a real mess of your hanky.'

'It'll wash.'

'I'll do it.' She half turned, glancing at him for the first time in minutes. 'Do you have another?'

Niall was watching her from across the room with sombre eyes, a furrow of puzzlement between his brows. 'I have a whole drawerful.'

'I meant do you have another hanky with you? In this weather . . .'

'Box of tissues in the car.'

'Oh.' Finding the eye contact unbearable, she let her gaze roam. 'There's mascara on your sweater, too. Oh, God, Niall, I'm sorry! I'm not usually the weepy type. What must you think?'

'I think . . .' he said quietly, stepping to where he had thrown his coat over a chair, 'that I had better get back to work. You're right about leaving the Range Rover outside here too long. If Murdo comes back and sees it still there he may haul us both off to face the minister and we'll find ourselves sitting on the penitents' stools in the kirk with the whole congregation throwing rotten tomatoes.'

Alix managed a half smile. 'They still do

76

that?'

'Only when the wind's in the north.' He was shrugging into his stone-coloured parka, zipping it up, all the while watching her with speculative eyes. 'Are you OK now?'

'Fine.'

'Sure?'

'Sure as shootin'! Or will be. Niall . . . thanks.'

He crooked his lips in a rueful smile. 'We aim to please. Don't forget what I said. Don't hibernate here all on your own feeling miserable. There are friends around if you need them.'

Friends . . . Yes, maybe she could risk that much. Everyone needed some human contact, after all.

'You have the office numbers on your list by the phone,' he reminded her. 'If no one's there, the answering machine will be on. You've only to pick up the phone, or send an e-mail, and someone will come.'

Only after he had gone did she notice that he hadn't even touched his hot chocolate. Nor, she realized, had he offered her his home number, or his mobile. Maybe he was as reluctant to get involved as she was. Well of course he was! Any decent man would avoid getting mixed up with an emotionally needy female when he already had a hot relationship going. Had Alix completely forgotten all those unsubtle warnings from Catriona McKenzie?

*　　　*　　　*

Snowclouds continued to loom behind the white heights of Ben Lachan and often the view was obscured by freezing mist or fresh falling snow. Alix spent hours hunched over her laptop, often working with numbed fingers because the storage heater, even augmented by an electric fire, hardly took the chill off the front bedroom. She might have worked in the living room by the real fire, except there was no convenient power point, besides she preferred to keep her work separate from her relaxing hours. Or so she told herself. Even in her own mind she refused to admit that the real reason she endured that icy room was because it was the only place from which she could watch the main drive, where Niall's Range Rover was a frequent sight.

Niall . . . he was a bright thread woven through the drab fabric of her life, a memory of strong arms and sweet kisses that got into her dreams at night and distracted her thoughts during the day. Every time she saw the Range Rover she hoped it might stop at her gate. He might call in for a coffee, or bring some message from the lady laird. Just five minutes would be enough.

But he never did stop by.

However, on occasions when Alix was sunk in gloom the phone would ring and Dame

Janet would demand that she come up to the big house for tea. Sometimes on these visits she ran into Niall, if he happened to be at the big house discussing business, but they never said more than a few words. Oh, he was cheerful and friendly, but always in a hurry to be elsewhere on some urgent errand. Or he might appear at an upper window in the side wing, where his office lay, and they'd exchange a wave and a smile. He wasn't exactly avoiding her, she decided. But he wasn't going out of his way to meet her, either.

Well, that suited her fine. At a distance he was no threat. In the same room . . . in the same room he had a strange effect on her equilibrium, in a way that she didn't care to analyze.

*　　　*　　　*

After two weeks of winter, when the weather seemed to be the main topic on the news— 'Could this be another side-effect of global warming?'—the temperature liftcd, the winds switched from north-east to south-west and within three days most of the snow had gone from the valley. The hilltops and distant mountains retained their white icing, jagged and bright against a backdrop of clear blue sky, but real winter had not yet arrived: it had merely sent an outrider as a warning.

The thaw made trips to the village easier.

It also brought Catriona McKenzie back to Glenwhinnie.

Hearing a vehicle slow to turn in at the gates, Alix glanced up from her work. It didn't sound like Murdo's pickup, or the Range Rover—by now she knew the sound of those two vehicles all too well. Then she glimpsed the scarlet colour of the car through bare branches and her heart seemed to contract. Of course it might not be Catriona's car . . . but the thought had hardly formed before it died, stabbed through by the clear sight of the Fiat pulling up at her gate, with the red-head behind the wheel. Until that moment she hadn't realized how she had for ages subconsciously been anticipating Catriona's return. Anticipating it, and dreading it.

Catriona must have seen Alix at the window. She jumped out of the car, waving gaily, shouting, 'Come down and give me a hand! I've got your things!'

The car turned out to be laden with boxes containing most of Alix's belongings, shipped from New York to an accommodation address organized by Sir Anthony. Alix had authorized her lawyers to pack her possessions and send them on, settling with her landlord for what she owed on her room. It had been done in panic. Now it seemed like burning bridges. She no longer had a place to return to.

'We could have had them brought by a parcel carrier but I thought it would be quicker if I brought them myself,' Catriona chatted as they hauled the boxes from car to lodge. 'I'd have been over before, if it hadn't been for the weather. Drummond and I have had to make do with phone calls and texting. E-mails, too, only I don't like e-mails for intimate communications, do you? Too impersonal.'

'It's a shame you're so far apart,' Alix muttered through lips stiff with insincerity. 'Anyhow, thanks for bringing my things. It was good of you.'

'No problem.'

While Alix began to open some of the boxes, to make sure nothing was damaged, Catriona surveyed the results with interest. 'Looks like you're intending to stay for quite a while.'

'Until spring, I thought.' She was glad to see her old belongings again. With special delight she opened a black instrument case and found her precious guitar in one piece. She had always found strumming a great way to relax. The guitar would help to beguile away a few lonely hours.

'You play that?' Catriona asked.

'After a fashion.' Realizing she was being a poor hostess, Alix laid the instrument away. The rest of the unpacking could wait until Catriona had gone. 'You want coffee?'

'Oh—no, thanks, I'm not stopping.'

'Not even for a coffee? You can't drive all

that way back without—'

Catriona's sharp laugh cut her off. 'I'm not going back to Edinburgh tonight, don't worry. No, I'm on my way to Glenwhinnie House, to get the keys to Drummond's cottage. I'm going to cook a steak dinner for him, warm his slippers and so forth.'

'Well, great!' Alix said with as much warmth as she could muster. 'That'll be nice for you both.' Needing something to do with her hands, she knelt down and began to attack another of the sealed boxes with a pair of scissors.

Seeming in no hurry to be gone, Catriona perched on an arm of the settee, swinging a high-heeled, booted leg. 'Drummond says you're a bit of a recluse,' she remarked. 'He says he doesn't see much of you.'

'No reason why he should,' said Alix with studied indifference. 'Is there?'

'No! No, not at all. I just . . . My jealous mind, I suppose. I'm away in Edinburgh, and he . . . He's a very attractive man. Don't you think so?'

'I guess.' Alix shrugged her shoulders, flicking through a copy of 'Tender is the Night' that Claudia had given her one Christmas. On the fly leaf it said, *To my favourite niece, darling Lexie, from your loving (Aunt) Claudia.* She had always written the 'aunt' in parenthesis, being 'too young to have a niece your age'—at least, that had been her joking excuse.

'. . . enigmatic and intriguing,' Catriona was saying. 'I mean, you must have noticed.'

Alix looked up. 'Sorry?'

'All that Celtic gloom!'

'Who?'

'Drummond!' Frowning, Catriona stood up, straightening her jacket. 'How often *do* you see him?'

'Once in a while. We sometimes run into each other up at the big house when I go to visit Dame Janet.'

Catriona's green eyes narrowed in speculation. 'And that's all?'

'What else did you expect? You made it pretty clear he was spoken for. And anyhow . . .'

'And anyhow,' Catriona concluded for her, 'you're not the type to try to steal another woman's man just because you're here and I'm miles away.'

'Exactly so,' Alix lied. 'Not even if I was interested in him. Which I'm not.' She was struck again by the other girl's naivety. Catriona might believe she had an exclusive right to Niall Drummond's attentions, but the man himself didn't seem particularly hampered by any notion of commitment.

Fastening her jacket, Catriona came across something in her inside pocket—a bulky envelope which she now produced. 'Nearly forgot. This came for you, too. From your lawyers, by the looks of it.'

The envelope was emblazoned with the name and logo of a firm of Los Angeles legal eagles—Claudia's lawyers. 'Thanks.' She laid it aside, having no intention of opening it with Catriona there, despite the avid curiosity on the other girl's face.

Realizing she was not going to discover what lay inside the envelope, Catriona made to leave. 'Oh, something else—Daddy wants to know when you're coming to Edinburgh. He's dying to meet you at long last.'

'I'll try to make it soon. I want to get the next section of my book finished and then I plan to take a break.'

'We'll look forward to it.'

Alix saw her out, then, shutting out the cold, went back to the window to watch the Fiat head away up the drive, bound for the factor's office. She sat down at the table near the window to open the lawyer's envelope and take out a wad of documents, but she had hardly begun reading them when the Fiat returned, sounding a couple of triumphant toots on its horn as it passed, through the gates and away up the glen. Catriona had evidently obtained the required keys.

The factor's cottage, as Alix had been told by someone or other, lay at the end of a side road off the main valley. Not that she had ever been there. Nor ever expected to.

Forcing her mind away from Niall

84

Drummond, she smoothed out the legal papers and began to read.

In gist, the papers informed her that she was becoming a very rich woman—amazingly rich, as it turned out, even after taxes. Until that moment, Alix had had no real idea of the extent of her mother's wealth in property, investments, insurance . . . not to mention cash in bank accounts. Hadn't really thought about it, she supposed. Been too shocked and upset even to imagine . . . But now in black and white she saw it confirmed. Film actress Claudia Cantrelle, born Mary Jane Sanders, had left everything to her only daughter, Alexandra Mary Sanders, also known under the adoptive name of Alexis Marisco—the child she had never, while she lived, acknowledged by word, deed or hint. How much did it amount to? The lawyers had summarized the estate, reaching an estimated total of . . . *How much?* The figure was augmented by a hefty insurance amount which had come due when Claudia's death was declared an accident. It looked absurd. It couldn't be real. Certainly not as real as the sound of Niall's Range Rover, passing by on its way up the glen, heading to the cottage where Catriona would be waiting to welcome him home.

That night Alix lay in bed trying to come to terms with the fact that she now had more money than she had ever dreamed of. What on earth would she do with such a sum? Her imagination spun off in all kinds of wild directions—helping the poor and needy, buying a home on a Caribbean island, an apartment in Trump Tower, a Lear jet—but all of that was just smoke and mirrors, obscuring the real scenes her mind could not help but conjure—a cottage at the end of a small valley, a bedroom where a red-haired girl and a dark-haired man lay entwined, white limbs against tanned flesh, soft femininity against an athlete's firm muscles . . . No amount of money could buy off the green-eyed monster that haunted Alix's dreams.

*   *   *

Naturally, this being Lachanbrae, where a chimney couldn't smoke without the whole place discussing whether it was peat or coal you were burning, everyone knew that Catriona had visited. Her red car and her red hair had been observed by many a canny eye.

'Did you have a visit from Miss McKenzie?' Maggie Gillivray asked the next time Alix was in the shop.

'Yes, she looked in at the lodge,' Alix said carelessly. 'Maggie, do you keep sugared almonds? I have a yen for some.'

From some obscure corner, Maggie produced a packet of the requested candied nuts, but the hunt didn't deter her from her chosen subject: 'I hear she was up to the big house, too, looking for Mr Drummond.' She glanced around the shop, though it was empty apart from the two of them, and lowered her voice. 'Mrs McNab told me. La McKenzie was after the key to his cottage, so it seems.'

'Really.' Alix privately considered that as estate secretary Mrs McNab ought to have better things to do than gossip about the factor's private business. 'Oh, and I'll take a bottle of your best liqueur whisky. For Dame Janet. It's her favourite. She needs a bit of pampering. She has a nasty cold.'

'Yes, I heard she wasn't well,' Maggie Gillivray said.

Maggie Gillivray heard *everything!*

Taking her gift up to Glenwhinnie House, Alix strode across the courtyard deliberately avoiding a glance at the upper window of the factor's office. But as ill-luck would have it she encountered Niall in the panelled hallway of the main house. He had apparently just left Dame Janet.

'She's a bit down today,' he confided with a nod at the sitting room door. 'Try to cheer her up, will you? She always feels better after seeing you.'

Avoiding meeting his eyes, Alix replied, 'I'll do my best,' and brushed past him, only to have him catch her arm and mutter her name. 'Alix . . .'

An odd, indefinable note in his voice made

her look at him directly. Big mistake. Even in the gloomy hallway his eyes burned blue, heavy with . . . what? Guilt? Regret? Of course he knew she knew he had spent the previous night with Catriona. How could he not? And why did she care?

Alix kept her own face coolly neutral. 'So?'

His hand relaxed on her arm, fell away. He shook his head as if to clear it. 'Nothing,' he muttered, shrugged, grimaced, and was gone.

Damn. Damn! What was wrong with her? Why did this one particular man have the power to . . .? No, she daren't explore it enough to put it into words. It was impossible. She was going to conquer it come hell or high water.

Squaring her shoulders, she walked to the sitting room door and, as she had been instructed several times, knocked briskly and went in.

Dame Janet, suffering from a thick head cold, was ensconced in a chaise longue by the fire, covered in shawls and throws and with a small table loaded with proprietary remedies beside her. She was in querulous mood, snapping at poor Ailie Gordon, who was spooning medicine and trying to persuade the old lady that she might feel better if she were properly in bed.

'I hate lying in bed!' Dame Janet snorted through thick sinuses. 'I get so stiff and achy. I'm perfectly all right here. I'm not ill. Not *ill*

ill! For heaven's sake, woman, stop fussing. Go and make some tea.'

Giving Alix a look that told a whole chapter, Ailie departed kitchenwards.

'Better not come too close!' the lady laird snapped at Alix as she approached. 'Don't want you catching my germs.' Briefly, a touch of her old humour softened the dour lines of her face. '*Or* the sharp edge of my tongue, though poor Ailie's had the worst of that, I fear. Sit down, child, if you can bear with me. I never did make a patient patient. I hate being a nuisance.'

'You are not a nuisance,' said Alix, placing the tissue-wrapped bottle in the old woman's lap. 'You should have the grace to let us all fuss over you once in a while.'

'Oh . . . blether!' came the retort. 'And what's this?' Her gnarled hands unwrapped the tissue to expose the label, which made her eyes gleam. 'Really! This is wickedly extravagant. I can't accept it.'

'Well, it's no use to me,' Alix said. 'I shan't drink it.'

Beneath her bluster, Dame Janet was touched by the gift, and after a while her usual good humour asserted itself. They enjoyed each other's company despite the differences between them, having a mutual love of music, history and people. Dame Janet might have spent a fairly sheltered life, mainly among musicians and in concert halls, with no

89

husband or children to widen her horizons, but she was aware of human faults and foibles, and empathetic toward her fellow man. Alix would have loved to ask what the old lady knew about Catriona and Niall, but she hadn't the nerve to raise the subject and if Dame Janet did know anything she was much too discreet to mention it.

*　　　*　　　*

After that day, for a while, Alix called frequently at the big house to check on Dame Janet's health and on almost every occasion she seemed to bump into Niall. But now *she* was the one in a hurry, too busy to talk. She virtually cut him dead every time they met. Best that way, she assured herself. If you didn't get involved you didn't get hurt.

Even so, she formed the distinct impression that something was troubling both the factor and his employer—something to do with the estate, she inferred. But when she probed, ever so gently, Dame Janet refused to be drawn.

'Just a few financial hiccups,' she said with a wave of the hand. 'Just temporary. No reason for you to trouble yourself, my dear. Now, how about a game of Scrabble?'

*　　　*　　　*

The weather continued unseasonably mild, often calling a heavy mist to clothe the valley in damp cobwebs. When the skies cleared, fresh snow gleamed on the highest tops, visible in the shortening hours of daylight as the year turned to December.

Sir Anthony phoned, to enquire after Alix's wellbeing and to invite her again to visit him when she had the time. Aware that, out of courtesy, she ought to make plans for a few days in Edinburgh, Alix still found reasons to delay. The journey was complicated—bus to Auchinveray, then the railway train, then a taxi. It would be easier if she had a car, but it would be silly to make that financial commitment when, as she kept telling herself repeatedly, she was not planning to stay very long. Nor was she keen on having to socialize with Catriona and, inevitably, have her chatter about her lover, 'Drummond'.

Deep down, however, she knew that all of these 'reasons' were actually excuses to cover her real reluctance, which was sheer funk— she was still hiding away like Bambi in a dappled thicket, thinking every shadow might mean a tiger on the hunt.

While she was still vacillating, Catriona McKenzie visited Lachanbrae twice more. Or so Alix learned in the village. She pretended she knew of these visits, though the fact was she saw nothing of Catriona and could only guess that the little red Fiat would be parked away out of sight on the back road leading to the factor's cottage. Did he go home earlier when Catriona was waiting? It certainly seemed that way to Alix.

Obviously Niall wasn't lonely any more.

The thought made Alix irritable. As a result, she quit her table by the upper window and set up a working space in a corner of the sitting room, where it was much warmer. She still heard the Range Rover go by, most times, but at least she didn't find herself staring from the bedroom like a lovesick teenager, watching for the vehicle and aching with loneliness every time it didn't stop at her gate.

Her work was not going well. The words on the page seemed pudding-like and plodding. She couldn't seem to capture the places she was trying to describe in their true colour, sound and scent, despite the copious notes she had made when travelling round the state, augmented by sketches and photographs as extra *aides memoires*. New York had begun to seem unreal, as if it was fading from her memory, leaving Glen Lachan the only reality.

Trying to counteract her growing depression, she went for a long and vigorous walk, avoiding the village and most of the roads. Not a good idea, as it turned out: the temperature had dropped and some of the stony places were treacherous with ice. By the time she returned within sight of the Glenwhinnie gates she was near frozen. All she could think of was getting warm again all through.

Happily, the fire heated a back boiler which provided enough hot water for a reasonably deep bath. She let it thunder into the tub, added a good dose of foaming essence and as scented steam filled the air she went along to the bedroom to strip off her clothes and pull on a warm rose-coloured robe. By the time she returned to the bathroom the water was starting to run cold, so she bent to shut off the flow, twiddling the antiquated taps. And that was the moment someone chose to start knocking loudly at her door.

Oh, darn it! Alix finished turning the taps and looked at the door indecisively. If she answered the caller, the water might go cold before she got back. It would take ages for the boiler to heat up again. Besides, she was hardly dressed for visitors.

She had almost decided to ignore the interruption, but the knocking turned into an insistent hammering. Distantly she heard a male voice calling her name. It sounded like Niall. Was something wrong? Not Dame Janet—!

She sped down the stairs in a panic of anxiety, yelling, 'I'm coming!' when he called her name again. Snatching the front door open, she clutched her robe to her throat and gasped, 'What's wrong?'

'What?' He seemed not to understand her.

A swift glance took in her dishevelled hair, her robe, bare feet . . . 'That's what I came to ask *you*! Is everything all right? You're not ill?'

'Ill?'

'You look as though you've just got out of bed.'

The cold outside sent fresh shivers through her, not improving her temper. 'At three o'clock in the afternoon?' She almost explained herself, but decided he didn't deserve it. 'What the heck do you want, Niall? Is Dame Janet OK?'

'Yes, of course. Still got a bit of a cough, but—'

'Then what's so urgent? You come banging on my door like there's a fire or something . . .'

He had the grace to looked chagrined, hunching into his coat. 'I just . . . I've been worried about you. You haven't been at your window recently. I wondered if you were ill. When I called earlier there was no reply. And no one in the village had seen you.'

'You went checking on me?!'

'Well, no. Not exactly. I just . . . I was concerned, is all.'

'Well, I wish you'd stop being concerned! I'm good! I don't need a nursemaid. For Pete's sake . . . Go away, Niall!'

She closed the door on him and turned the key, knowing he would hear the lock snap. How could he pretend he gave a hoot about her when he had Catriona warming his bed at frequent intervals? Alix didn't have that comfort. All she had was the hope of a hot bath.

But as she lay soaking in the blissfully hot water, it occurred to her that if Niall had noticed her absence from the upper window that must mean that he watched for her just as she watched for him. As if that made any difference to anything!

*   *   *

That evening, when the phone rang, Alix answered it cautiously, half expecting to hear Niall's voice apologizing. Instead, the voice belonged to Sir Anthony.

'My dear girl!' The eminent surgeon sounded especially hearty. 'We wondered if we could persuade you to join us for Christmas. Won't be anything fancy, just Catriona and myself, and a few friends staying over. Might do you good to meet a few people.'

Alix demurred. The last thing she needed was to be exposed to a house full of strangers all curious about her relationship with the McKenzies. She could just imagine Catriona throwing hints and arch looks. But she couldn't immediately think of a good excuse so she hedged, 'May I think about it? I'll let you know . . .'

Happily, only a few days later, on one of her regular visits to Glenwhinnie House, she had a far more welcome invitation from Dame Janet, who asked her to spend the holidays with her: 'The Gordons will be away for a few days, with their daughter in Glasgow. And Niall will be with Fergus and Maura, naturally. Since you and I will both be alone I thought it might be nice to get together. Unless you had other plans?'

'I'd love to come,' Alix said simply, meaning it.

Dame Janet's blue eyes sparkled with pleasure. 'Come on Christmas Eve, and bring your guitar. Ailie will leave everything prepared in the freezer for us. I'll ask her to air the spare room. I shall so enjoy having you here, Alix.'

As Alix was leaving, the old lady gave her a bulky envelope file, asking if she would be kind enough to drop it off at the office. 'Give it to Niall personally, will you, if he's there? If not, leave it on his desk where he'll find it at once when he gets back. It's got some rather confidential letters in it and, good as Mrs McNab is, I sometimes suspect she talks a little too freely. Niall and I have learned to keep certain things strictly between ourselves. Go through the house. There's a passageway . . .'

Flattered to be trusted, Alix followed directions, through an inner hallway and into

96

a shadowy passage beyond, where a looming figure made her pause in momentary alarm. It was only Murdo Gordon, but the stone-faced steward always made her feel like a misbehaving schoolgirl.

'And what'll ye be doin' here?' he demanded, barring the way.

'Dame Janet sent me,' Alix replied, indicating the file in her hand. 'I'm to give this to Mr Drummond. Am I going the right way?'

'Aye, though it's no' our usual practice tae allow strangers to wander freely aboot the hoose. Go through the door at the end and turn right. You'll find the office doon there.'

'Thank you.' Alix edged past, stung by that remark about 'strangers'. That was not the way Dame Janet thought of her, she was sure.

'And mind ye dinna keep Mr Drummond bletherin'!' Murdo called after her. 'He's a busy mon.'

It was good to escape through the end door and close it behind her, leaving Murdo Gordon on the other side.

Light glowed down the next passage and she soon recognized the lobby she had entered with Catriona when she first arrived. And here was the office, brightly lit against the oncoming evening. Through the window, an edge of the light picked out a corner of the yellow Range Rover parked close outside, so Niall must be in the office above.

The reception office was staffed by estate

secretary Joan McNab, a small, mouse-like person in her fifties, mainly memorable for the perfectly-coiffured jet-black hair which didn't match her aging skin, and the owlish red-framed glasses of a style that went out years before. The photographs of children were her addition to the décor—she had five grandchildren on whom she doted but who were, sadly, scattered about the globe. Maybe that was why Mrs McNab liked to pry, to fill her empty life.

When Alix revealed her mission, the secretary leapt to her feet, crying, 'I'll take that up, no need for you to bother.'

'No, it's all right.' Alix clutched the file to her sweater. 'I, er . . . I want to have a word with Mr Drummond anyway.' It seemed the most tactful way of dealing with the problem.

Except that Joan McNab's look, magnified behind huge lenses rimmed with red, turned speculative, running over Alix assessing her clothes and figure. 'You'd best go up, then. First door on the left.'

The carpet on the stairs was worn thin and stained with the years. At the top, another corridor led into the depths of the house. The door to the left bore a hand-carved notice saying, 'Factor's Office' which looked as though it had been there for more years than Niall Drummond had been born. Staring at it, Alix had to brace herself for her first meeting with the man since she ordered him away from her door. She stifled a sigh. Why was life so complicated?

'Come in,' Niall's voice answered her knock. His office was unlit except for an angular lamp spotlighting the accounts books over which he was poring with head bent. He looked up, frowning against the shadows for a moment, surprised when he identified his visitor. 'Alix?'

'I brought you this,' she said, laying the file on a clear area of the desk. 'Dame Janet said I was to give it to no one but you.'

'She did?' He peered at the label on the file, only to shake his head, none the wiser. 'Well, thank you.' He seemed disconcerted by her presence in his office.

'Welcome.' Feeling uncomfortable, Alix made for the door.

'Wait!' The order made her stop, her nerves on edge, and when she looked round again he was on his feet, though still behind the desk. 'Must you rush off?'

'Murdo Gordon warned me not to keep you "blethering",' Alix informed him, wishing there was more light: now that he was standing up all she could clearly see was his patterned sweater. 'I can see you're busy.'

'Not too busy to take a few minutes' break.' He gestured at the books lying open on his desk. 'These figures are driving me crazy.'

'Can't you use the computer?'

Niall hesitated, and when he spoke his

voice had gone several degrees cooler. 'Modern technology *has* reached us, even here in the backwoods. And, yes, I am entirely computer-literate. Unfortunately Dame Janet likes to see it all written out in the ledgers, too. For posterity. In case the machines seize up on us.'

'I didn't mean to imply . . . Oh, never mind.' She turned away, irritated, anxious to escape, but before she could open the door Niall said: 'Actually . . . Actually, I've been hoping to see you. I wanted to apologize for intruding the other day. I called at a bad moment, for which I'm sorry. But my only intention was to make sure you were OK. I've got used to seeing you up at that window and—'

'So I should have stayed there, freezing to death?' she snapped. 'That bedroom's like an ice-box, so I moved my work station. I guess I'm free to do that? Or do I need your permission?'

The office sang with silence. After a moment Niall said slowly, 'I've said I'm sorry. I was only concerned in case you were ill, and when I mentioned it to Dame Janet she—'

'Then I wish the both of you would get off my case!' Alix flung at him. 'I'm not your responsibility. I'm a grown woman, perfectly able to look after myself. It was my own choice to come here, to be on my own. I *like* being on my own. Get that? I wish . . . I wish you'd stay out of my life!'

Another long moment passed, then, 'That,' he answered, 'is exactly what I've been trying to do, in case you hadn't noticed.'

She could find no answer to that. Actually his motives for that ill-timed visit had been commendable. He wasn't to blame for the fact that he had to keep driving past the lodge, constantly reminding her of his nearness—and his unavailability. Still, it irked her to know he had had to consult Dame Janet first before calling.

Niall stuffed his hands into his pockets, saying, 'I hear you're going to Edinburgh for Christmas?'

'*What?* Who told you that?'

'Cat McKenzie did. At least, she said her father had invited you.'

Her head seemed about to explode. Catriona, Catriona, always Catriona, laughing and lively and somehow sly. 'So he did. And I said I'd think about it. But as it happens Dame Janet has asked me to come and spend a few days here instead. She'll be on her own and I'd prefer to be with her. I'm not so keen on spending the holidays with people I don't know.'

'I'm sure she'll be glad of your company.'

'I shall enjoy hers, too.' Her back felt rigid with defiance and hurt pride. Suddenly the room felt airless. She choked, 'I'll let you get back to work,' and clawed blindly for the door handle. This time he didn't try to detain her.

Alix almost ran down the stairs and out into the cold twilight. What on earth was wrong with her? She could never seem to act naturally around Niall Drummond.

FOUR

On Christmas Eve Alix took an overnight case and went up to Glenwhinnie House where the guest room had been made ready for her. She helped Dame Janet trim her small tree, then the following morning they drove to the small kirk in the Volvo. Niall was at the service, with Maura, and Fergus in his wheelchair, and many of the other folk whom Alix had come to know. Everyone wanted to have a word with the lady laird and, by association, with her American tenant. With Niall himself Alix exchanged no more than a token, 'Happy Christmas,' but even that brief contact left her feeling depressed until after she and Dame Janet had returned to the big house. There, she made herself busy putting the finishing touches to a traditional Christmas dinner largely prepared in advance by the super-efficient Ailie Gordon.

As a gift for her hostess, Alix had bought a large box of whisky liqueur chocolates and a glorious poinsettia, which seemed to delight the old lady. In return she presented Alix with a book of Scottish folk songs, which amused them both as Alix fingered the chords on her guitar and attempted to get her tongue round the dialect and Gaelic. After a dram or two of Drambuie (a gift from Niall, it seemed), Dame Janet even felt up to joining in the music on her piano, though it was obvious that her arthritic fingers frustrated her and she soon closed the lid on the instrument.

Returning to her seat by the fire, the lady laird turned nostalgic, telling tales of the house as she recalled it in her youth. 'My parents used to give wonderful balls. My nanny allowed me to sit on the gallery and watch, sometimes. Oh, you'd never believe it, seeing the ballroom the way it is now, but in those days . . .' Her eyes grew misty as she gazed back into her memory. 'It was beautiful—the music, the lights, the ball gowns and jewels, the men in their kilts . . .'

The descriptions of the way the house had looked in its heyday remained with Alix as she said good night and went up to the guest room, with its worn carpet and faded green velvet drapes and bed-hangings, and the old radiator gurgling as if with indigestion. She lay awake, trying to imagine how it would have been forty or fifty, even a hundred years ago, when the estate was prospering and the laird in residence with his family. She also found herself wondering how Niall Drummond had passed his day. Presumably he had spent it

103

with Fergus and Maura, but no doubt he had also found time to contact Catriona. He made no secret of his close relationship with her. Why, then, hadn't they arranged to be together over the holiday? Something about those two puzzled Alix. She couldn't quite figure out what it was, but something didn't sit right. Was it a genuine love affair, or just a physical thing?

Annoyed by her train of thought, she turned over and snuggled down into the newly-bought duvet. Niall Drummond was none of her concern. Nor did she want him to be. He made her feel unsettled and she didn't care to feel unsettled. Away from him she longed for even a glimpse of him, but when they met everything went haywire. She never said what she intended to say, and he never reacted the way she expected. He was like a breeze—a highland breeze that skimmed along, whipping her skin into goose-bumps and flirting in her hair but refusing to be captured and held still even for an instant.

Which was ridiculous, she told herself. She didn't want to catch Niall Drummond. She would not be here long. She would be flying away, come spring. Nothing that happened here could be permanent. Glenwhinnie was a stop-over, a sheltered harbour that had no connection with the broad and uncertain sea that was her real life.

*　　*　　*

After lunch next day, Dame Janet decided they both needed some air. The weather was cold but clear, with sunlight lying along the hills, and the old woman set a vigorous pace, swinging along lopsidedly with her walking stick, heading up through the woods behind the big house. Leaves edged with frost crunched under foot and brown bracken rustled as they brushed by.

Eventually, as they came to a saddle of land between russet hills, Dame Janet paused to point with her stick.

'Look there, see?'

Her keen eyes had spotted a stag in full antler, scenting the wind in a corrie not far away, while below him, camouflaged against the brown land, the rest of the herd grazed peacefully. Down in the valley, Glenwhinnie House and its woods commanded attention, its grandeur etched in blue shadow. It blended into the setting, slumbering among its hills as the brief midwinter day faded.

'Ah!' said Dame Janet, pointing again with her stick to where, just visible in a fold of land towards the sunset, a slate roof nestled among bare branches, smoke writhing thinly from its chimney. 'Niall's at home, then.' She pushed back her coat sleeve to examine her watch. 'Time's getting on. We'd better start back if we're to have dinner ready. I told him seven thirty for eight.'

'You mean . . .' Alix faltered, 'he's coming to dinner? Niall is? Tonight?'

Blue eyes wide with surprise gazed from beneath the brim of a tweed hat with a jaunty feather. 'Didn't I tell you? Damn. Sorry. Getting forgetful in my old age. Yes, he usually dines with me on Boxing Day. Tradition, you might say.'

'Who else is coming?'

'No one else! Good heavens, d'you think I could cope with extra guests, with Ailie away? No, it'll be just the three of us. I expect you'll be glad of someone of your own generation to talk to after two days with a boring old fogey like me.'

Ignoring Alix's protests, the old woman set off back down the slope.

Ailie Gordon had, of course, left everything prepared, and Dame Janet had thoughtfully removed items from the freezer to defrost while they were out walking. There was home-made venison pate, a duckling casserole with cherries, and a flan case which had to be filled with bottled fruits and decorated with whipped cream. Between them, Alix and her hostess made final preparations and laid the large table in the dining room with the best silver, cut-crystal wineglasses, and slim red candles in a heavy silver candelabrum decked with holly.

Later, bathed and groomed, wearing a

suitably warm magenta sweater and black velvet pants—comfort being preferable to glamour since she had no intention of making an idiot of herself by getting dressed up for Niall Drummond—Alix considered her reflection with critical eyes. She hardly knew the heavy-eyed young woman who stared back from the long cheval glass. The lodge contained no full-length mirrors and she usually just threw on some comfortable clothes, bundled up with coat, scarf and hat when she went out. It was some while since she had paused to examine herself. She had lost weight—too much for her liking; she had never liked the skin-and-bone look affected by model girls. The local hairdresser had gradually removed all the dark dye from her hair, returning it to its normal golden-blonde, and it had grown long enough to curl round her ears and into her neck. It would take a long time to grow back to the mane she had been so proud of only a few months ago, but maybe she would keep it shorter. It suited her well, made her look more sophisticated. Not that she felt very sophisticated. She felt as gauche and unsettled as a teenager, her stomach in knots and her brow in a sweat.

'You look lovely. Very understated,' Dame Janet approved when they met in the sitting room. 'Oh, bang on time. Here's Niall.' Lights swept across the closed curtains and a car engine purred to a stop outside. 'Go and let him in, will you, my dear? I'll pour us some drinks.'

In the panelled hallway, Alix paused to take a long breath and assemble an air of cool dignity as if it were armour. When the bell rang, she opened the door and gestured an invitation, avoiding Niall's eyes. 'Good evening. Come in.'

He was wearing that well-cut charcoal suit again, looking tall, broad, elegant—she refused to add 'attractive', though he undeniably was. In one hand he carried a bottle of wine, and beneath his other arm was a parcel wrapped in shiny red paper and done up with lacy gold ribbon.

A glint of wetness on his sleeve made Alix say, 'Is it raining?'

'It's more like sleet,' Niall said. 'Oh—this is for you. Merry Boxing Day.'

Her reflexes acted faster than her brain and she found herself holding the shiny parcel, staring at it blankly. 'For me? But—'

'Open it,' he suggested.

After one bewildered glance at him, Alix fumbled with the gold ribbon and the sticky tape holding the red paper. Her fingers encountered the softness of wool, light as down, the colour of purple heather. She shook it out and discovered it to be a pashmina shawl, finished with a long silky fringe.

Instinctively, she draped it round her shoulders, bending her cheek to enjoy the

108

softness against her skin. 'It . . . it's lovely!' she breathed. 'And such a beautiful colour.'

Niall reached out and adjusted the fall of the pashmina. 'She said it would suit you.'

She? She didn't say it aloud but the question must have been sharp in her eyes as she shot a look at him. Had he consulted Catriona?

'Maura came with me to choose it,' he said. 'She has quite an eye for that sort of thing.'

Maura. Not Catriona. Alix allowed herself to be thankful for that as she luxuriated in the feel of the shawl. Eventually, she made herself meet his eyes, her own gaze wide and wondering. 'I don't understand you. Why—'

'You're not required to understand,' he said, bending to brush a brief kiss on her cheek before making for the inner door. 'Is Dame Janet in here?'

He was not a highland breeze, Alix thought—he was a cyclone. Every time they met he had a cataclysmic effect on her emotions. Why had he gone to the trouble of buying her a gift? Such a thoughtful gift, too.

Dame Janet admired the shawl. She was equally pleased with the wine Niall had brought, and the silver ear-rings he produced from his pocket, gift-wrapped in tartan paper and curling scarlet ribbons.

On the surface, it promised to be a convivial evening.

When it came to serving dinner, Alix played

109

hostess and listened to her companions exchange small-talk, often with that subtle undercurrent of cut and thrust that she had noticed before when the lady laird and her factor got together. She wondered if Dame Janet might be equally aware of the sub-text between herself and Niall, a lightning force that accompanied the meeting of their glances or the occasional fleeting contact of sleeve or fingers, though overtly the conversation remained light and bantering.

The meal over, Alix suggested that the others should retire to the sitting room while she cleared away. Dame Janet said, 'Oh, leave it until the morning,' but Niall decided he would help Alix, 'While you, Dame Jay, go and pour us some more drinks and get yourself settled.'

Niall had his way, somewhat to Alix's dismay since it meant being alone with him and at times in close proximity. She was able to bury her discomfort under a display of brisk efficiency until the job was almost done and all that remained was to stack the dishwasher and put the cooking pans to soak.

'I can manage the rest,' she told Niall. 'You go and talk to Dame Janet.'

'Trying to get rid of me?'

When she dared a glance at him his face was bland, deep blue eyes dancing under a dishevelled lick of dark hair. 'Yes,' she replied evenly. 'You're getting under my feet. Scoot!'

'Thought so,' he said, and turned away before she could interpret the expression on his face.

Relieved of his unnerving presence, Alix took her time about the chores, even to scrubbing the pans clean before leaving them to drain.

As she finally crossed the inner hall to rejoin the party, she was horrified to hear an argument in progress. They weren't speaking loudly but the door stood ajar and the tension in both of their voices was plain.

'I shall ask him!' Dame Janet was saying furiously. 'It's time. High time.'

'You're not to!' Niall replied, his voice quiet but laced with anger. 'I absolutely forbid it. You made me a promise, remember?'

'Of course I remember, but—'

Embarrassed at being obliged to eavesdrop, Alix cleared her throat, kicked a chair leg in passing and swore loudly. Waiting a heart-beat or two to make it appear she had been further away than she actually was, she walked into the sitting room, saying, 'Sorry for the language. That darn chair was lying in wait to bushwhack me.'

The silence hung keen as a new-honed knife. Dame Janet sat erect, her whole demeanour forbidding, and Niall's face was darkened by a scowl as he wrenched himself to his feet and made for the drinks tray. 'What can I get you, Alix?'

111

'I'll have a mineral water, thanks,' she answered, sinking down into an armchair. Aperitifs and wine were already having an effect on her thought processes: more alcohol might be unwise at this juncture.

Niall glanced at his employer. 'Something for you?'

'I've had enough,' the old woman answered, and struggled to her feet. 'I think I'll get to bed. That walk today tired me. Haven't got the energy I once had. No need for you to hurry off, though, Niall. Stay and keep Alix company. Show her the house, why don't you? It's still an interesting old pile despite its decrepitude.' She pulled a wry smile at Alix. 'Much like its mistress, I dare say. Good night, my dear.' In passing she laid an affectionate hand on Alix's shoulder, blue eyes asking forgiveness. 'I'll see you in the morning.' And she made for the door, adding as an afterthought, 'Good night, Niall.'

'Sleep well,' he answered evenly.

Hobbling badly, yet with enormous dignity, the old woman went out to the hall, closing the door behind her. She left a singing silence in the room.

Niall handed Alix a glass of sparkling water clinking with ice. He stood beside her staring down into his own drink, swirling the amber liquid round and round so that it washed around the glass in jerky swirls, threatening to spill.

'Am I allowed to ask what all that was about?' Alix ventured.

'Yes.'

She waited for him to go on and when he said no more she prompted, 'Well?'

He looked across his shoulder at her, face grim as granite. 'You may ask. That doesn't mean I'm obliged to answer.' Another moment and his face twisted. He shook his head, went to throw himself into Dame Janet's vacant seat, sprawling there and taking a long swallow of whisky. 'I'm sorry. I shouldn't take it out on you. Where's your guitar? Play me something. Dame Janet says you've got quite a talent for it.'

'Dame Janet exaggerates,' said Alix. She herself sat tensely upright on the edge of the chair, wondering why he was in such a black mood. Evidently it had to do with the quarrel he had had with Dame Janet, though just as evidently he didn't plan to share it with Alix. The pashmina he had given her lay across the back of her chair, its colour attracting her glance. She reached to stroke the soft wool, grasping at a fresh subject. 'This shawl is beautiful. I never expected a Christmas present. I didn't get one for—'

'Forget it. It was a spur of the moment thing. Maura said it would suit you, that's all.'

'It was kind of her. And of you. Thank you.'

Niall made no reply, only watched her through veiled eyes, reminding her of

113

something Catriona had said about 'Celtic gloom'. Then as if the tension inside him needed release he emptied his glass in one swallow and got to his feet. 'Let's do something. We have Dame Janet's permission, so why don't I show you the house? Come on, I'll give you a guided tour.'

As she had begun to suspect, the house was a maze of passageways, rooms and stairs, with an air of sadly neglected grandeur. It must have been a wonderful place when every room was used, every piece of furniture polished, every picture dusted and every ornament cared for. Today, the side wing where the offices lay was used mainly as a store, rooms containing tea chests full of bric-a-brac, pictures stacked against walls, all under dust sheets. Lamps of the lowest wattage shed a faint, tawdry light and in some passageways the bulbs had blown.

'Whole place needs rewiring, apart from anything else,' Niall sighed, picking at a piece of loose plaster. It came away from the wall, bringing a palm-size piece to flake on the dirty floor.

'It's so sad,' Alix said. 'Sad that it has to be this way.'

'I couldn't agree more. We'll go through here. Mind the bottom stair, it's higher than it looks.'

In the upper part of the main house they crept past Dame Janet's room and the head of the stairs, coming to the door of the guest room which Alix was using. Beyond it lay antiquated bathrooms thick with dust, without a vestige of heating, and more bedrooms shrouded in old sheets and curtains to protect valuable antique furniture. Niall showed Alix some of the best pieces—Georgian chairs and tables, magnificent mahogany wardrobes, a Queen Anne cheval glass, a black oak chest from the time of the first Queen Elizabeth, a few long-case clocks, all of them stopped. Like Sleeping Beauty's palace, Alix thought, shivering a little.

'The time is coming when we shall have to start selling off some of the treasures,' Niall said. 'Dame Janet's dead set against parting with anything—every piece has its own place in McDonald history, she says. It all belongs here, it mustn't be sold to people who won't understand. But if she's going to carry on here she may have to accept some huge changes. Empty the big house, sell off most of the stuff, move into the lodge . . .'

'Oh, she couldn't!' That would hurt the old lady badly, perhaps even lead to her early demise. Dame Janet clung fiercely to her heritage, to the stories this house could tell— she had regaled Alix with many of those stories.

'She insists that she'll die first, but if things

go on as they are . . .'

'Is that what you and she quarrel about?' Alix asked.

Niall stopped and looked fully at her for the first time since the tour had begun. About to answer, he stopped himself and, after a second, said, 'Yes, it is, mostly.' But in the dim, uncertain light from a dangling bulb she couldn't read his eyes.

'You really care, don't you?' she observed softly.

'If this place goes, so does my job,' he reminded her, and moved on.

Shivering in the unheated air, Alix began to wish she had brought her new shawl, or maybe even her outdoor coat.

In the upper passageway, past her room, one of the doors had been nailed shut with batons of wood. A notice fixed there read: *'Do not enter. DANGER'*.

'It leads onto the gallery above the ballroom,' Niall told her, 'but the gallery's not safe and the stairs are lethal. This part of the house has been shut up for years. Since before the last laird died.'

'Is there another way into the ballroom?'

'Of course. Downstairs. You want to see it?'

'Sure! Dame Janet was telling me, just yesterday, about the parties they used to have there.'

He twitched a sceptical eyebrow, shaking his head. 'That was a very long time ago. Now,

116

I warn you, you wouldn't want to hold a wake in there. It's a mess. We'll have to go back. This way.'

He reached for her hand, pausing to look at her in the meagre light. 'You're cold.'

'My hands are always cold.'

'We'll get back to the fire in a minute,' he said, taking a firmer grip, as if trying to warm her with the heat of his own strong hand.

The comfort was welcome. Alix decided to enjoy it.

Quietly back down the stairs they went, past the big kitchen and on along a corridor towards a part of the house which Alix had seen only from outside, at a distance. The unused ballroom wing. Opening a door, Niall snapped a switch and revealed a largish, square room with an ornate plaster ceiling badly stained by damp. The carpet had been rolled and covered with a dust sheet, while more sheets covered humped shapes of furniture. Footsteps sounded intrusively loud on the bare floor, making Alix tip-toe.

'This is the ante room,' Niall said. 'The ballroom's through here.'

In the far wall, a set of large double doors stood closed. Niall opened one of them, creating a cold draught, and switched on a set of dim wall-lights which revealed the expanse of the ballroom littered by a jumble of crates and ends of wood which gathered dust on the filthy floor. A once-grand staircase, now

117

supported by more lengths of wood and with tape slung across to prevent anyone from climbing it, led up to the balcony-style gallery that spanned the room.

'They were about to repair the stairs when the builders' boss died,' Niall said, closing the door behind them to stop the worst of the through-draught. 'The work stopped, and nobody came back to finish it. Probably just as well. They had to wait ages to be paid for the work they'd already done. It was before my time, but it's all there in the books when you look for it. Sad sight, isn't it?'

'Desperate,' Alix agreed sadly. Despite his warning, she had not been prepared for such delapidation. What a waste!

He was still holding her hand. She wondered if he were aware of it. She didn't want to be the one to break free, making it look as though the contact bothered her—in fact, it was sending hot messages along all her nerves, making her want to cling closer. Trying to ignore the urge, she looked around the desolate ballroom, remembering Dame Janet's tales of the parties she had enjoyed here in her youth. Once, couples had danced beneath chandeliers where now cobwebs hung festooned like lichen, the grime of years dulling the gleam of crystal drops while filth and plaster debris lay thick on a dance floor which must once have shone with French polish.

An idea sparked in Alix's head—a wild, crazy idea that scurried into the back of her mind when Niall unexpectedly turned to her, lifting her hand to shoulder height as he bowed to her like the prince to Cinderella.

'Would you care to dance, ma'am?' Without waiting for an answer, he swept his free arm round her waist, drew her close and began to waltz very slowly, taking her with him in widening circles across the dusty, sticky parquet.

Alix had never learned to waltz, not properly, but she let her feet go with the flow, her limbs and body responding easily to his lead. Closing her eyes, she gave in to the magic of the moment, no longer caring about past or future. This moment, this man . . . it was all she desired.

'We're crazy,' she said after a while.

'Yes, I know,' he replied on a sigh, folding her more closely with his cheek on her hair. 'Look.'

Alix opened her eyes. They had come near an expanse of windows whose smeared, grimy surface showed an indistinct reflection of the scene in the room—the dreary yellow light, the debris of years of neglect, and the tall man in the dark suit with his arms around a skinny young woman in black pants and warm pink sweater.

'Will you come with me to the Hogmanay Dance?' he asked.

Startled, Alix lifted her eyes to his. 'What?'

'The Hogman—' he stopped himself and, with a slight smile, translated, 'The New Year's Eve Dance. In the village hall.'

'I know what "Hogmanay" means!'

'Fine. Then would you like to go with me?'

'I—' Her throat had seized up. She managed to swallow, licked her dry lips. 'What will Catriona have to say about that?'

She felt him go still, his arms loosening around her though he didn't entirely release her. 'Alix . . .' he said sombrely, 'didn't I tell you already? Whatever you may have heard, I am still a free agent. What about you? Someone back in the States waiting for you?'

She shook her head, too entranced to do anything but answer with the truth. 'No-one who matters.'

'Then what about the dance? It's nothing fancy, just the village letting its hair down. Everyone will be there.' He drew her close again, his eyes saying things that made her head spin. 'Let me take you. Please?'

She felt herself drawn irresistibly by the force that had existed between them for so long. So strong was its tide that it drowned all her common-sense objections before they had fully formed. He doesn't love Catriona, was all her heart could sing. He doesn't love Catriona. Oh joy, oh delight. 'Yes, I'd like that,' she whispered.

The smile faded from his eyes, giving way

120

to a gleam that was almost ferocious as he dropped his head and captured her mouth, holding her against him with arms like steel bands. Her stomach jolted as if it had hit the bottom of a rollercoaster, then went soaring, up and up to where there was nothing in all the world but Niall and the need to hold him, touch him, have him go on kissing her.

Her fingers wove into the thick silky softness of his hair and worked down to the warmth of his neck, but as she touched his bare flesh he drew a sharp breath and lifted his head, catching her arm. 'Your hands are like ice! Put them under my jacket.'

Willingly, partly for warmth but mostly for the sheer pleasure of touching him, she let her hands slide inside his jacket, against his shirt. She leaned her cheek on his chest, feeling him cradle her tightly, bent round her to warm and protect her.

'You're like a little iceberg,' he breathed, his lips moving against her temple. 'Why didn't you say?'

'I'm OK,' she murmured, nestling contentedly against his warmth.

Near her ear, his voice came gruff. 'You make me feel so . . .' His arms tightened in a demonstration that made her gasp and as she lifted her head to make a token protest he added fiercely, 'You know it, don't you? You know exactly what effect you have on me.'

Whatever she might have replied was lost

121

as he kissed her again, his mouth possessing hers. She responded gladly, emotion swooping through her, weakening her knees and making her lean helplessly against him. His lips traced a warm pathway across her face, caressing her eyes, her brow, her earlobe . . . 'Good grief, girl, you're half frozen!' he muttered, lifting his head to look at her.

As he did so, with a silent thud the lights all went out.

'Oh sh—'!' said Niall with feeling, then: 'You'll recall I did say this place needed rewiring. I only hope we haven't fused the lot. We'd better go back to civilization.'

'I guess,' Alix sighed, reluctant to end the moment.

She felt his face brush hers and his breath was a warm whisky-scented zephyr against her skin. 'It's hardly the ideal place, anyway,' he said ruefully, finding her mouth again in the darkness. Their lips clung briefly as they finally drew apart.

He took her hand, beginning to edge his way across the coal-black ballroom, occasionally pausing to guide her round an obstacle and once cursing furiously as he crashed into something. Wood went clattering with deafening effect.

'Hurt yourself?' Alix enquired anxiously, crowding close to his warmth. Now she was really shivering, wondering how they had ever come to be kissing in this bleak, forsaken place that felt like a freezer.

'My shin!' Niall said through his teeth. 'Watch yourself.'

Eventually she heard a door-handle rattle and welcome light flooded out from the damp-ridden, dust-sheeted ante room, forlorn and musty under a low-watt bulb.

'Thank the Lord for that!' said Niall with feeling. 'It's just the ballroom phase that's blown. Murdo can look at that in the morning. You all right?'

'Just cold,' she said, shuddering.

Their eyes met for a long moment, questioning and half shy over what had passed between them. She must have been out of her mind, she thought. Now the warning bells were ringing loud and clear: Don't Fall For Him, was their song. But the message came far too late.

'We'd better get back to the sitting room,' Niall said, his hand still locked firmly round hers, his thumb stroking her fingers. 'A hot toddy might be in order.'

'Sounds good to me.'

The warmth of the sitting room gathered them into its glow and while Alix sat on the settee letting the fire's warmth melt the ice in her bones, Niall busied himself preparing the hot toddies he had suggested. Alix wasn't sure what he put into the mixture, but it smelled good, tasted better, and sent welcome heat curling inside her.

'Great!' she murmured, relaxing against the soft cushions of the settee. 'Thank you.'

'My pleasure. Special Drummond recipe.'

He came to sit beside her, elbows on knees as he watched the fire and sipped at his drink. A fresh pine log crackled and spat as flames licked round it, and the old grandfather clock in the corner ticked ponderously. For a few minutes neither of them spoke. Alix felt utterly content, reluctant to break the mood, simply enjoying the warmth and the quiet companionship—and the memories of a brief interlude in a cold, filthy ballroom. If it had been madness, it had also been unbearably sweet.

It was Niall who ended the silence. 'You've got me confused,' he informed her frankly.

'Me, too. But . . . let's not analyze it, Niall. Let's just enjoy it, while it lasts.'

'You mean until you fly away with the spring?' He turned to look at her with searching eyes.

Alix took refuge in staring into her drink. By now she knew that she wanted this— whatever it was—to last much longer than springtime. But it was too soon to say so. She remained unsure of the wisdom of getting involved. And embedded in with her own doubts was the lingering shadow of Catriona. 'Niall . . .'

'Hush!' He laid a long finger across her lips to stop the words. 'You're right. We should take it a step at a time. Maybe we both had too much wine at dinner. Maybe I made these toddies too strong. I think I ought to go home, before we say or do things we might regret.'

He was leaving?! 'Oh, but—'

Putting his glass aside, he relieved her of hers too, and then he kissed her, slowly and thoroughly. Just as Alix feared she might melt with delight, he drew away, gave her an odd little smile, said, 'Good night, Alix,' and made for the door. She was too stunned to do anything but sit there and let him go. Confused . . .? That didn't even begin to describe it.

That night, cosy beneath the duck down duvet in the guest room, Alix dreamed of the ballroom brilliant with light, with an orchestra playing, men in evening dress and women in gowns with wide, romantic skirts. Among the whirling couples, Niall and Catriona danced together, his dark head bent to touch her red hair, while Alix was outside in the freezing night, staring through the huge and cobwebbed French windows. Though she knocked, called and wept, no one appeared to notice she was there.

She woke to find that the duvet had slipped. No wonder she felt cold! That was soon remedied, but still she lay awake, while frosty moonlight poked silver fingers between her curtains. The dream stayed with her. Maybe it was prophetic, telling her that she had no

125

place at Glenwhinnie. She was an outsider and would always remain an outsider.

*   *   *

Over breakfast next morning, she and Dame Janet somehow began talking about birthdays and to their mutual surprise they discovered that they shared a date—both of them had been born on 24 June, Midsummer Day, but with fifty years between them.

'What a coincidence!' Alix exclaimed.

'It's not so surprising. They say that you only need a few people together to find that two of them share a birthday.'

'Well, I reckon it's an omen. A good omen.' She hadn't intended to start on this but all at once the moment seemed right. 'Dame Janet . . . tell me to keep my long Yankee nose out, if you want, but it's obvious you're having some problems here at Glenwhinnie. What happens if you can't keep the estate going?'

The old lady looked ready to rear up and defend herself. Her spine had stiffened and her eyes had narrowed. 'What has Niall been saying?'

'Nothing! Not about your private business. You know he wouldn't do any such thing. But I have eyes. Seeing the house last night brought it home to me. Believe me, I have good reasons for asking. The way it looks . . . the way things are going, you may have to sell up and leave at some time not too far off. Am I right?'

The old woman took a deep breath, her mouth compressed as if to stop its trembling. Eventually, she admitted gruffly, 'Yes. Yes, you're right. No point in denying it. It doesn't bear thinking about, but it may have to come to that, before too long. Unless we can find some way of making the place profitable it may end in the bankruptcy court. Niall has plenty of good ideas, but all of them would take huge amounts of capital, which we don't have.'

'So one answer might be to go into partnership with someone who does have capital. Someone who could help you modernize the estate and—'

'Someone fool enough to throw money down the drain,' Dame Janet grunted. 'And whether or not it was a success, I'd probably lose Glenwhinnie anyway. No enterprising businessman would want an old woman like me hanging around for long.'

'How about an enterprising business *woman*?' Alix reached for the coffee pot and poured herself another cup, aware that Dame Janet was frowning at her.

'What?'

'Someone like me, for instance.'

'You!' The word came out on a bark of laughter. 'My dear child . . . You don't know what you're talking about. It would take thousands. Hundreds of thousands. If not more. Where do you imagine you could you get your hands on that sort of money?'

Setting the coffee pot back on its mat, Alix lifted her eyes to the lined face with its frame of iron-grey hair. 'Through my bank account.' Seeing amazement widen the old woman's eyes, she added swiftly, 'Oh, we'd do it properly, naturally. Signed, sealed and witnessed to everyone's satisfaction. A business arrangement. My lawyers would not approve anything less, and they'll want to handle the legalities themselves, but—'

'Your *lawyers*?!' Dame Janet choked. 'My dear girl . . . do you know what you're saying?'

'I know very well. It's true I haven't had much business experience, but even so I didn't just fall off the Christmas tree. Fact is, I . . . I recently inherited . . . well, a lot of money. Now I need to find ways of using it. Investing it. In worthy causes like Glenwhinnie estate. I'd like to help you, if I can.'

'Charity, you mean!'

'No. You don't expect to make a profit from giving to charity.'

Dame Janet leaned a gnarled wrist on the table, her blue eyes intent. 'You heard me arguing with Niall last night, didn't you? Did he tell you what we were arguing about? Is that why—'

'I've already told you,' Alix broke in. 'Niall hasn't mentioned anything to do with the estate—except to confirm what I could see for myself. Nor does he know that I'm in a position to do something about it. And I'd prefer you don't tell him quite yet—I'll do that myself when I'm good and ready. But I mean what I say. I want to help. If only to stop you from worrying about it and save you having these constant spats with Niall.'

For a long moment narrowed blue eyes stared into clear grey, wordlessly asking and answering a host of questions. Then the old woman shook her head. 'No, Alix. You're very kind—extraordinarily kind—to even think of it. But I could never take your money. Never.'

'And why not? Isn't my money as good as any other? This is not an altruistic offer, Dame Janet. Let's call it a long-term loan, an official business deal between the two of us. No one else need know where the funds came from. Or would you prefer me to join the jet-set, living in idle luxury, fighting off all the sharks and fortune-hunters, getting into drink and drugs, ruining my life, never knowing who my real friends are? Is that what you want for me?'

The old woman pursed her lips, her eyes sparkling with shrewd humour. 'That's verging on emotional blackmail, my girl. What would you get out of it, pray tell?'

'Satisfaction,' Alix said at once. 'The knowledge that I'm helping my friends—all of my friends in this area, because it would bring in jobs and make all kinds of differences. And it would give me a link with the glen, an excuse to keep in touch, to come back now and then and see you all. You've been so kind to me, Dame Janet. Won't you let me do something in return?'

'No,' the answer came at once. 'It's out of the question. Absolutely impossible. We shall say no more about it. Though . . . there is one thing you can do for me.'

'Anything.'

'Will you please stop calling me "Dame Janet"? It makes me sound like an old fossil. My friends—my very closest friends—call me Jay.'

FIVE

Though Alix didn't fully understand how it had happened, that Christmas proved to be a turning point. Suddenly she felt more confident, more in control of her destiny, and she determined to have her own way over the loan to Glenwhinnie estate. She put through a call to her lawyers to set wheels in motion: one way or another she would persuade Dame Janet—Jay—to agree.

If only she could feel as sanguine about her relationship with Niall Drummond things would be just peachy. As it was, despite all her efforts to stay cool and rational about it, she anticipated the Hogmanay Dance with as much nervous excitement as she had anticipated her first real date at the age of fifteen.

Anxious to blend in for the occasion she asked Dame Janet's advice what to wear and between them they selected an oufit of a long, embroidered skirt and strappy top with a lacy cardigan for warmth—plus the soft pashmina Niall had given her. Since the temperature had plummeted again, a thick coat was de rigeur, too, with a warm scarf she could wrap round her head if necessary. But she refused to compromise on the glamorous high heels. Boots were great, but not for dancing. And she did hope to be dancing, most of the night, warm in Niall Drummond's arms.

Hearing the Range Rover arrive, she went out to the hall and took a last glance in the mirror to check her make-up before opening the door.

Niall was well-bundled too. 'It's freezing, I warn you,' he informed her. 'Still, it'll get good and warm in the village hall before the night's out. Oh—and I promised to pick Maura up on the way. Hope you don't mind.'

'It'll be good to see her,' Alix said brightly. Having Niall's sister along as a fifth wheel was not her idea of a romantic arrangement, but she mustn't be selfish.

At the Drummond cottage, Fergus waved

131

from the window as Maura came hurrying out to the car. Her smile and her excited face made Alix feel mean for wishing, however briefly, to rob her of this outing. Maura was evidently thrilled by the thought of the evening ahead.

Outside the village hall a clutch of cars stood on the gravel, with more arriving every minute. Their lights cut swathes through the darkness, picking out fine flakes of falling snow. Not far away the loch lay still and black, and across the water Ben Lachan's bulk bit a slice out of a sky glittering with cold stars.

The noise of the party spilled out as the door opened. Inside, people gathered at seats set around tables while others joined in a reel to the tune of bagpipes and fiddles. Niall led Alix through the paces of a traditional dance that proved quite easy once she had mastered the pattern of steps, and then he escorted Maura onto the floor, much to her delight, while other partners claimed Alix.

Around ten thirty, everyone gathered round the buffet and as supper progressed various villagers took the floor to provide a cabaret with party pieces—a ritual that evidently occurred annually. 'Oh, not "Wee Dock and Doris", please!' someone groaned as constable Wullie Carr stepped up. Then a trio of middle-aged ladies performed the song 'Sisters' to much hilarity. One old man told hair-raising tales of ghosts; a young girl sang sweetly in Gaelic; another man told jokes in an accent so thick that Alix understood less than half of it; then a teenage boy and girl executed a lively sword dance to the skirl of pipes played by their father—he was Jock Moray, a shepherd from up the glen, so Niall told Alix, with an intimate glance and a smile that compensated partly for the way he had shared himself round all evening, leaving her often to be entertained by others. She caught herself remembering what Catriona had said about the factor needing to 'preserve his image'. Tonight, after all, in Dame Janet's absence, he was representing Glenwhinnie.

Before midnight, someone looked out and announced that it was snowing. 'Jings!' another voice exclaimed. 'It's a blizzard!'

'Blether!' someone else replied. 'It's just a wee flake or two.'

Evidently the weather had deteriorated, enough for Jock Moray to hustle his off-spring away despite their chorus of disappointment at missing the actual turn of the year. Their croft lay way up the glen on a road that might easily get blocked should the snow continue.

Back in the hall, the dancing resumed and soon midnight approached. It was a moment Alix always hated and that year she felt more choked than ever. But as she and Niall exchanged kisses and seasonal wishes other emotions over-rode bitter memories, and then other people were gathering round to claim kisses and warm handshakes, men and women alike, before they all gathered in a circle to sing 'Auld Lang Syne'.

Finally, much to Alix's relief, the awkward moments had passed. She went to find her purse, needing a kleenex to dry her eyes, while behind her some of the more boisterous party-goers elected to go first-footing. But as they piled energetically into the lobby a blast of cold air swirled round the hall, accompanied by cries of both glee and dismay.

'It's a white-out!' someone shouted.

The snow must have been falling for some while, growing thicker and thicker. The wind had piled it in drifts, here an inch or two, there a foot deep, and more was steadily coming down, adding to the piles. Those who lived further afield made a dash for their cars, hoping to make it home before the roads grew impassable. In the few short hours the party had lasted, deep winter had returned to Lachanbrae.

Wrapped warm in coats and scarves, Alix and Maura and Niall made their way to the Range Rover, Alix regretting her flimsy shoes with their high heels. Her feet were soon freezing, and then cold and wet. During the drive through the village, Niall had to go slowly to avoid the car sliding, and occasionally drifts of deep snow threatened to bar the way. But eventually they arrived at the Drummond cottage. Maura invited them in for a hot drink, but her brother refused, anxious to get Alix and himself home while the way remained relatively open.

As he turned along the loch road, heading for Glenwhinnie, a white swirl all but choked the wipers. The wind came straight from the North Pole, piling the drifts higher with every minute. Even the sturdy Range Rover had problems coping, and Niall began swearing under his breath as he wrestled with the wheel.

'Now you know why Jock Moray left early,' he muttered. 'We ought to have done the same.'

'But it's not far,' Alix said, trying to be reassuring.

'It's far enough in this weather!'

Snow flashed dizzyingly across the beam of the headlamps, but for a while the tyres crunched on through deepening drifts. Then a wall of snow, strung between low hedges, barred the way. Niall attempted to drive through it but not even the Range Rover could cope; it ground to a halt, wheels spinning uselessly.

'I'll see if I can dig us out,' he said, opening the door. 'Slide over here and keep the engine running.'

'Niall, don't!' She caught his arm, stopping him. 'Look at it—it just gets deeper ahead. It's not that far to the lodge, is it? I can walk the rest of the way. You go back to Fergus and

Maura.'

'You must be joking! It's just as bad behind us. Besides, d'you think I'd leave you on your own? How the hell can you walk through this lot—in those stupid shoes?'

'Well, what do you suggest? That we stay here all night and freeze?'

His only answer was to shake her hand from his arm and climb out into the crisp deep snow to assess their situation. With the headlamps half buried in snow it was difficult for Alix to see what was happening through the darkness and the driving white flakes. She dimly saw Niall make for the rear of the vehicle, open its back flap and search around for something which he appeared to find. A spade, maybe?

No, not a spade. When he reappeared at the door he was wearing a padded weatherproof jacket, with another for her tucked under his arm, in one hand a hefty torch and in the other a large pair of wellington boots which he tossed onto the driver's seat, saying, 'Get those on. I'm afraid we shall have to go on foot. And don't argue, Alix! Of course I'm coming with you. You surely don't think I'd let you go alone in this lot?'

In its way, that walk was a weird kind of fun (or seemed so when she remembered it afterwards), frozen as they both were before long, heads down into the wind and the

136

blinding snow. Thank heaven for those big warm jackets he kept in the car! Niall forged ahead to make a path for her, occasionally stopping to help her along when she stumbled in the clumsy, oversize boots that gathered snow with every step she took. It melted on her legs and slid down to puddle round her feet, but Niall was still in his ordinary shoes, she knew. His feet and legs must be numb with the cold. But he made no complaint, only concentrated on helping her get through.

To her relief, before too long the torchlight showed up the familiar gateway. Beyond it, down the Glenwhinnie drive, the wind had swept the snow around until only a few inches remained. They were soon entering the lodge, shucking off their snow-covered coats and shivering their way into the living room where the fire had burned low

Exhausted, she reached to flick two inches of snow from the front of his hair. 'One thing's for sure—you're staying here tonight. I won't take an argument, Niall.'

'You're not getting one,' he replied through clenched teeth.

'There are towels in the kitchen. Help yourself. I'll go fix myself up upstairs.'

She hardly knew how to climb the stairs: her feet were cold and wet, her skirt soaked, the scarf round her head coated in melting snow. With little heat in the back bedroom she managed with numb hands to undress herself and rub some life back into her limbs with a rough towel. Then, wrapped in her thick pink angora robe—a present from 'Aunt' Claudia last Christmas—she took some blankets from the airing cupboard and went down to the sitting room.

Niall had made himself at home, dried himself off and taken off his shoes and socks. He had made up the fire so that it blazed beautifully, roaring in the chimney. He even had hot chocolate waiting for her, just the way she liked.

'My Galahad!' Alix sighed, tossing the blankets across the settee.

Niall eyed the pile of bedding doubtfully. 'Could be I'm more like Lancelot. This may not be a good idea.'

'Who's to know?' Alix asked, avoiding his eyes. 'No one will come by before morning.'

'It wasn't gossip I was thinking about,' Niall said quietly.

That electric current was running between them again, both of them equally aware of being alone together—totally alone and cut off from the rest of the world, at least until morning. Keeping the robe well round her, Alix sat in an armchair by the fire, drinking her chocolate and warming herself while Niall sat on the hearthrug and made conversation.

'You've got it nice in here. What are those shells? . . . Did you enjoy the dance? Maura had a great time, didn't she? . . . What did you think of Wullie's performance? He always has to do "Dock and Doris" . . . The Moray youngsters are talented, though. They did a turn at the Highland Games this year—last year, I mean . . .'

The small talk gave Alix time to finish her drink, by which time she was feeling warmer, and tired. She threw a hand to her mouth to cover a yawn.

'Yes, it is late,' Niall said with a rueful twinkle. He got lithely to his feet and drew her out of the chair, holding both her hands. 'You looked lovely tonight. The belle of the ball. Thank you for coming.'

Could he feel that she was trembling? Maybe he would think it was from the cold. 'Thanks for taking me. I had a great time.'

'I'm glad.' He bent and kissed her gently on a corner of her mouth. 'Go to bed, Alix. I'm so tired I may sleep until noon.'

'Me, too,' she said, edging away. 'Good night.'

After all, it was as simple as that. She was grateful to him for not making the situation more awkward than it had to be. However, his presence had distracted her from her routine—she had forgotten the hot bottle she usually took to warm her bed.

She lay huddled in the duvet, still wearing her wrap, but she couldn't get properly warm. Her feet felt like lumps of lead, her nose was numb and her teeth started chattering uncontrollably. Eventually she threw back the duvet, climbed out in darkness reaching frozen toes to find her slippers, and went down the stairs, feeling her way, not switching on lights for fear of disturbing Niall. The hot water bottle hung in its usual place, a hook on the back of the larder cupboard door. Alix laid it on the draining board while she fumbled for the kettle, which—naturally—needed filling.

'What on earth are you doing?' Niall's voice said from the doorway behind her.

Shivering, she managed, 'I'm too c-cold to sleep. I came to g-get a hot-water b-bottle.'

'Then why not put the light on?' The light snapped on, blinding her. She threw up a hand to guard her eyes and stayed there, shaking uncontrollably.

'To hell with hot bottles,' he said in a low voice, swooping with outstretched arms to gather her inside the blanket he was wearing draped over his underwear. He was blessedly warm. But then she had discovered that once before, hadn't she? 'Lord, girl, you *are* cold! Not enough flesh on you, that's the problem. You obviously don't eat enough porridge. Come on back to the fire. It's cosy on the settee.'

The glow from the hearth spread out like a blessing, bathing the roomy settee where they huddled together, both of them wrapped in the same blanket. Her head rested on his shoulder while he talked softly about winters he had known as a child, and her eyelids began to droop. Nothing seemed more natural than to lie down beside him, encompassed in his sturdy warmth, from her toes to her hair.

That was all she remembered.

*   *   *

Surfacing from dreams, she was aware of Niall at once. He lay half across her, feathering kisses on her cheek and the tip of her nose. It was still dark as her lashes lifted and she looked into smiling eyes touched by an edge of red light from the fire.

'Good morning,' he whispered, and kissed her willing mouth, sending sparks of delight to flood her being and bring her entirely awake.

'Niall . . .' Was it a protest, or was it an invitation? She never knew. Nor did she much care. She wanted this man. And he wanted her. Nothing else mattered. Not right then.

But they both became still as the phone intruded into their private world, bringing a sharp reminder of reality. Niall lifted his head, moving away from her. 'You'd better answer that. It's probably Dame Jay, anxious about you.'

Gathering her wrap securely round her, a flushed and dreamy Alix padded barefoot across the carpet, a hand holding her tumbled hair. 'Hello?'

'Alix!' Dame Janet's relieved tones came

down the line. 'Thank goodness you're there. I was worried . . . When I saw the snow I just had to make sure you'd arrived home safely last night. Are you all right? No problems there?'

'No problems. I'm good, Dame Janet, don't worry. How are *you* managing?' She glanced round to where Niall sat on the floor by the settee watching her. He tilted an eyebrow, shook his head, said softly, 'Told you so. Mother hen syndrome,' and got up, reaching for his trousers.

The lady laird chatted on, but Alix hardly heard her. She was conscious of Niall moving about, getting fully dressed, tidying up and folding the blankets, going into the kitchen to fill the kettle. Evidently their romantic interlude was to be curtailed. When eventually she managed to end the conversation, he came to lean in the kitchen doorway, smiling a rueful smile.

'Saved by the bell, wouldn't you say?'

'Couldn't you have gone on "stand by"?'

The smile turned crooked. 'Maybe. On the other hand . . .' He rasped a hand across his stubbled chin. 'I need a shave. And it's after nine already. I'd better start clearing snow. You get yourself dressed. Make breakfast. Large pan of porridge. Eggs. Toast. Hot, strong coffee.'

'So what did your last servant die of?'

'OK—*I'll* make breakfast and *you* clear

142

snow, if you prefer.'

She had a feeling he was capable of letting her do it, too; so she batted her eyelids at him, cooing, 'Oh, but you'll do it so much better, macho man!'

'Hah!' said Niall. 'Thought so. Now, where did you leave my wellies? Ah, here . . .'

After he had gone out to make a start, Alix ran up the stairs to her arctic bedroom and threw on some warm work clothes. She had started to feel crazily happy. Just being with Niall, having him take care of her, made her feel kind of fuzzy inside. She regretted the abrupt end to their lovemaking, though. If the phone hadn't interrupted . . .

What *would* have happened if the phone hadn't interrupted?

She stood at her window watching as he shifted snow with a spade taken from her shed, wearing his bulky yellow and blue waterproof workcoat, working smoothly and efficiently to clear a path from her gate to the Glenwhinnie entrance. Was it her imagination, or had he been glad of Dame Janet's untimely intervention? He, not Alix, had made the decision to call a halt to their intimacy. He was the one who had got dressed and tidied away the blankets. Was he still determined to keep her at arms' length, mentally and emotionally—and physically too if that were humanly possible? Why?

As usual, he had her dangling. Every which

143

way but loose, as they said.

Toward the big house, the snow lay less deep for maybe thirty yards, tarmac showing through in places before the smooth whiteness piled again into undulating drifts to block the driveway. A red sun had risen beyond Ben Lachan, turning to gold as it eased higher and blazed white across the snow, beneath a sheer blue sky. Blue as Niall's eyes. He was a chameleon, too. Just like the place where he belonged. Glenwhinnie never looked the same two days running. The weather changed, or the light changed, daily and hourly. Niall was the same—an enigma. But with every day that passed she grew more determined to solve the puzzle.

Preparing breakfast, she laid the small table by the bow window in the sitting room. When she called Niall in to eat he came at once, declaring himself starving. The sight of the table, laid with bowls of steaming porridge, seemed to surprise him.

'My, aren't we domesticated? That porridge looks quite edible, considering you're only half Scots. And here's me thinking you were a dedicated career woman.'

'They call it multi-tasking,' said Alix. 'You want cream? Or do you take it with salt?'

The back-chat continued throughout breakfast, eventually turning to discussion of how he was to rescue the Range Rover from the deep drift where they had abandoned it.

The task required a deal of hard digging.

'I'll lend a hand,' Alix offered. 'I can use the coal shovel.'

'You certainly can *not*! I'm not having you straining yourself.'

'I'm as fit as you are!'

'It's not a question of fitness, woman, it's about muscle power.'

'You calling me a seven-stone weakling?'

He got up from the table, slanting her a sceptical look. 'All right, Mighty Mouse. Please yourself. But if you split your difference don't say I didn't warn you.'

Piqued, Alix went to clothe herself suitably and put on her old boots, then went out to the shed only to find that Niall himself had appropriated the big coal shovel. He was working away with it, leaving the smaller spade by the gate. She went to join him and after one sardonic glance at her he continued working on the car-wide swathe he was cutting through the snow. Alix also set to work, glad to find that the crisp fresh snow shifted easily. Soon she was comfortably aglow, though trying to ignore the ache that was starting in some of her less-used muscles.

Beyond a deep drift that filled the road, they came across an area where swirling wind had kept the fall shallow. But the next drift piled even higher, part of the windshield of the Range Rover showing through the mounded snow.

145

It took them maybe half an hour to clear a path for the vehicle. Niall climbed in. The engine started second try. Alix stepped aside, watching as Niall drove slowly by, parking at last near the hedge around the lodge garden.

'At least it'll be off the road,' he commented as he climbed out. 'It will give the snow plough an easier job. When it comes.'

'How long will that be?'

He shrugged. 'Depends. Why? Planning to go on a trip?'

'Matter of fact, I was hoping to visit Edinburgh pretty soon.' She stretched her aching back, leaning against the yellow vehicle for support.

'I warned you you'd wear yourself out,' said Niall with a gleam. 'Won't be told though, will you, Miss Stubborn? So . . . what's the attraction in Edinburgh all of a sudden?'

'It's not sudden. I've been meaning to go for weeks. Just never got around to it. But I need to talk to Sir Anthony McKenzie.'

'About what? Or shouldn't I ask?'

'You can ask,' she replied, echoing a conversation they had had once before. 'I don't have to answer.' But, seeing the barb go home, she relented. 'But I will. Truth is . . . recently I found out that Sir Anthony knew my father, and since I know very little about my father I want to ask his old friend about him.' She gestured about her, adding, 'That's one reason I came here.'

Niall's attention sharpened as he regarded her with narrowed eyes. 'You mean . . . your father came from Lachanbrae?'

Puzzled by the sharp edge in his voice, Alix said, 'Why . . . no, I don't think so, though . . . I guess it's possible.'

'I thought his name was Grant, like yours.'

'It was. Leastwise . . . that's what I've always been told. Only I'm not sure how true it is. Seems I've been lied to, by lots of people, for lots of reasons, most of my life.'

'Surely your mother knew?'

She fixed him with wide grey eyes that told of her inner pain. 'I never had a chance to ask her, Niall. See . . .'

On the verge of telling him at least part of the story, she stopped as a distant, 'Halloo!' came clear on the air and they saw Murdo Gordon waving from midway along the main drive. He had cleared a path from the big house and as they watched he completed the job, breaking through to the clearer area leading to the lodge. Stamping gobbets of snow from his boots, he strode over to them.

'So you're here, Mr Drummond,' he greeted, taking in the scene with suspicious eyes and drawing obvious conclusions. Murdo always thought the worst.

'So I am,' Niall answered dryly. 'That's observant of you, Murdo.'

The dour-faced man merely gave him a baleful look. 'Dame Janet's been trying to

147

reach you. No answer at your cottage, or from your mobile.'

'Probably because I haven't been home and my mobile's switched off. As I'm quite sure Miss Grant won't mind my telling you, I spent the night on her settee. Scandalous, isn't it? Right. If you'll hop into the car we'll get up to the big house and see what's to be done.' Turning to Alix, he rolled his eyes expressively, said, 'Thanks for the shelter. And the breakfast. See you.'

And he was gone. Glad to escape? She often wondered about that in the days that followed—days when Niall made no attempt to contact her.

*   *   *

More snow fell, but after a while a snow-plough cleared the glen road and life continued much as normal. Occasional parties of skiers appeared on the hills and a tractor hauled bales of feed up for the sheep and the deer. Once again the Range Rover came and went, but to Alix's increasing bafflement it never so much as slowed down when it passed the lodge.

She applied herself to work, completing the text for the travel book and packing it off to her publisher. For now, it was out of her hands. And so she turned to the novel she had been working on in spare moments—the

148

novel about the girl who suddenly discovered that very little of what she knew about herself was the truth.

It was proving more of a challenge than she had imagined. What *was* the truth? Every time she sat down to work she found her thoughts straying, remembering incidents from the past which now took on new significance—why Art Marisco, the man she called 'Pop', had seemed so cold at times, why her younger brother Tom had been the undoubted favourite, why her family had hardly ever mentioned her mother's sister, movie star Claudia Cantrelle. Over and over again she read the letter Claudia had left, in which she made excuses for her behaviour, telling only half the tale in her efforts to deny her own culpability and try to stave off any ill-feeling Alix might harbour.

Her efforts were vain. Alix still despised Claudia Cantrelle.

More and more she knew that she must talk with Sir Anthony McKenzie if she were ever to solve some of the mysteries.

And when those bitter musings tailed off her mind automatically returned to the subject of Niall Drummond, like a CD stuck on Repeat Track. At New Year they had been so close. What had happened? Oh, why had Dame Janet had to phone at just that moment? Another half hour or so and . . . What difference might that extra time have made? Perhaps no difference at all. Niall Drummond remained as much of a mystery as he had ever been.

Eventually, unable to stand the waiting and wondering any longer, she phoned the office and asked to be put through to Niall. When he answered, she invited him to supper. Niall demurred. He had extra work to do, problems caused by the weather. He couldn't talk, he had someone with him. He would call her.

He didn't call her.

Baffled, Alix waited a couple of days and tried again, with similar result. He was sorry, but . . .

'Then maybe you'll call *me*, if you ever do have a minute spare,' she said with asperity, and slammed the receiver down. She believed she had got the message. Boxing Day night and New Year's morning had meant nothing to him. Presumably with a few drinks inside him he'd make love to whichever female happened to be nearest.

No, she didn't entirely believe it, but getting mad at him was her only defence.

*   *   *

Conveniently enough, Sir Anthony McKenzie phoned and invited her to spend a few days in the city with himself and his daughter. 'We were sorry not to have the pleasure of your company at Christmas,' he told her in his precise Edinburgh accent. 'But now we've got the holidays over Catriona would enjoy showing you round.'

Alix wondered how true that was: she had always felt Catriona to be a covert enemy. But she accepted the invitation, anyway. She needed to talk with Sir Anthony.

Dame Janet thought the visit would be, 'A jolly good thing. Nice break for you, my dear. Just be sure not to let Catriona lead you astray. I gather she has a wild streak.'

'Oh, I can handle her,' Alix replied. 'And, while I'm in the city, is there anyone I might see—to talk about this loan? Your lawyer, perhaps? Or your bank manager?'

'Absolutely not.' Dame Janet donned her mulish face, folding her hands in her lap. 'I shall talk to them myself—*if* I decide to look into the possibilities, and it's a very big "if", I remind you.'

'You haven't . . . discussed it with Niall, have you?'

'I have not. Not when you asked me not to. Besides . . . I know what he'll say.'

'He'd turn my offer down.'

'He would. And I would have to agree with him. Well, so you're away to Edinburgh. When were you thinking of going?'

Wryly noting the unsubtle change of subject, Alix said, 'Wednesday. There's a bus from the village that connects with the late morning train out of Auchinveray, so—'

151

'Och, you don't want to be rattling about on the bus! Niall generally goes into town mid-week. He can give you a lift.'

Alix felt her face stiffen. 'There's no call to trouble him.'

'Why should it be any trouble if he's going anyway?'

Only then did Alix begin to realize . . . 'Are you playing matchmaker?'

'Certainly not! The very idea!'

'But you do keep trying to get us together. Any excuse to make me go to see him, or him to give me rides here and there . . .'

'Nonsense!' came the snort. 'Would I do any such thing? I'll hear no arguments now. Of course Niall will take you, it's the obvious solution. There's no more to be said.'

*   *   *

That Wednesday morning, Niall duly turned up and carried her case out to the Range Rover, being polite, helpful, and about as reachable as the sky. Alix bore it until they had passed through the village and were climbing the road around Ben Lachan, which ran like a wet black ribbon through snow-covered countryside. As Niall regaled her with some lengthy tale about Murdo's eccentricities, she could no longer contain her annoyance.

'So New Year's morning was just a

152

temporary aberration, was it?'

His sudden silence told her he knew exactly what she meant. After a while he slid her a veiled glance. 'A mistake, shall we say? We were both half asleep. We'd had a few drinks.'

'That's what you said on Boxing Day, too.'

'It was a fact. I wouldn't want to stand accused of taking advantage.'

Furious, and deeply hurt, she stared out of the side window, turning up the collar of her coat as if it could provide a barrier. 'If you're worried I might tell Catriona that her boyfriend has trouble controlling himself when she's not around, think again—kiss and tell was never my style.'

Another few seconds of silence ticked by before he said through his teeth, 'I thought I had told you, quite clearly, that I'm under no obligation to Catriona.'

'I know what you said, but in my innocence I misunderstood. No obligation. No strings. No ties. Just sex.'

She hoped he would deny it. Instead, he said, 'That sort of relationship suits Cat, too. She's not big on commitment.'

Choked with incredulity, she flung him a wide-eyed glance. 'Oh, great! I suppose I should be grateful you didn't add *me* to your list of casual conquests!'

'Damn it, Alix! . . .' Now he was angry, too. 'You're not being fair. I'm trying to explain . . . Oh, what the hell! It doesn't matter. Believe what you like, it's of no importance to me. Like the man said—frankly, my dear, I don't *give* a damn!'

They drove the rest of the way in stony silence.

At the train station in Auchinveray, Niall pulled up at the entry, climbed down to remove her case from the back and dumped it on the pavement.

'I won't hang around,' he said when she joined him. 'I've got an appointment.'

'Fine by me. You want me to pass on some message to your girlfriend? She's sure to ask after you.'

Blazing blue eyes spitted her with cold fire. 'Yes—say that I sent her my fondest love,' he grated, spun away to climb jerkily back into the vehicle and drove away without another glance in her direction.

Damn the man!

All the way to Edinburgh in the train Alix wrestled with her hurt, fury and self-disgust. Why did she let herself care about that impossible Scot? She was delighted to be getting away from him for a few days.

*   *   *

Catriona and her red Fiat waited at the station in the capital to take Alix on a tour through streets of tall grey houses dominated by the walls and towers of the castle on its craggy

154

rock, high above the famous Prince's Street. The windows of large department stores glittered in the fading winter light, their displays beckoning Alix to enjoy some more retail therapy during her stay. Heavy traffic moved slowly through streets crowded with pedestrians and cyclists, an invigorating bustle of life after the quiet of Lachanbrae. But in some ways the city felt empty. Here there was no chance of seeing Niall.

She hardly heard anything of Catriona's inconsequential chatter until a familiar name sharpened her ears.

'And how's Drummond? I suppose he's busy, as usual.'

'Never stops.'

'That man is so conscientious it's sickening,' Catriona said, slanting Alix a wicked grin. 'Lovely with it, though, eh? And still keeping his distance, I trust?'

'He drove me to the station in Auchinveray,' Alix admitted. 'And he said . . . he said I was to tell you that he sent you his fondest love.'

'He *what*?!' The exclamation jerked out of Catriona as she turned to stare at Alix in astonishment, only recovering herself when a horn blared and she narrowly avoided a collision. Watching the road again, she burst into laughter.

'Is it funny?' Alix felt perplexed.

'Hilarious!' Catriona choked. 'Is that really

155

what he said?' She went on laughing, leaving Alix to wonder what the joke was. Before she could ask, they were arriving at the McKenzie house.

It stood on a broad avenue lined with horse chestnut trees whose bare branches spread like lace above cars parked along the kerb, with piles of snow lining the sidewalks. Catriona pulled the Fiat on to a half-circle of drive in front of a large, double-fronted Georgian-looking house with a garage added to one side.

'Daddy promised to be home in time for dinner,' she informed Alix. 'Come on in and make yourself at home.'

The house was roomy, filled with antiques and comfort. In the hall, glass cases displayed the cups Catriona had won for horse-riding. There was also a portrait of a gently smiling, titian-haired woman. 'My mother,' Catriona said. 'She died five years ago. This way. We've put you in the Rose Room.'

The guest room lived up to its name, roses blooming on curtains, bed-linen and towels, with more pictures of roses hung against pale pink walls.

Being a widower, Sir Anthony employed a middle-aged couple to care for himself, his daughter, his house, garden and cars. Catriona herself worked in a travel agent's office, though to judge from her tales of foreign holidays she spent more time taking breaks abroad than selling them. She and Alix sat over aperitifs, neither of them entirely at ease. When Sir Anthony finally arrived, Catriona leaped up and went to greet him as if she were pleased to be relieved of playing hostess.

At last Alix met the man who had known her parents a quarter of a century before, when all of them had been young. He was now a consultant surgeon, much lauded in his field, a neat, distinguished-looking man who looked older than his years—she assumed him to be in his late forties, but he looked nearer sixty. Perhaps that was partly because of the grey hair and the half-moon glasses over which hazel eyes smiled appraisingly at her.

'You're welcome in our home,' he said, holding her hand between both of his own. 'Very welcome, my dear. And so like your father . . .'

That surprised her. 'Am I?'

'Oh, yes. Oh, yes, indeed.'

Having so much to say that must be kept private, neither of them raised the subject of Claudia over dinner. Catriona, it seemed, knew only a few basic facts: she wasn't interested in details. However, when the meal was over she took her leave—she had promised to meet a friend for a drink. 'Unavoidable, I'm afraid,' she excused herself with a smile, a shrug, and palpable insincerity.

Her absence allowed Alix and Sir Anthony to talk more freely.

157

Settled in the comfortable sitting room over cups of coffee, Alix made a start on the dozens of questions she needed to ask—about Sir Anthony's memories of Claudia, her mother, but mostly his recollections of Duncan Grant, the father she had never known.

'He was real, then? He did exist?'

'Of course he did! Did you doubt it?'

'I doubt everything anyone tells me lately,' Alix said wretchedly. 'The letter Claudia left . . . It wasn't very coherent. It was mostly about herself—how sorry she was, how bad she felt, how different her life would have been if she'd opted for love instead of a career. It read like a script from some old melodrama. At times . . . At times I've even thought she might have lied about his name. It occurred to me that *you* might . . .'

'I? My dear, you flatter me. A bright butterfly like Claudia would never have looked twice at a dull chap like me, whereas Duncan . . . Duncan was a fine, handsome chap. Tall, strong, fair as Apollo. A dedicated doctor. With an irrepressible lust for life. Until Claudia destroyed him.'

' "Destroyed"?' The word startled her.

Whatever he read in her face made him uncomfortable. He rose abruptly. 'Excuse me a moment, I've been looking out some things for you.'

When he returned, he presented her with a

158

monochrome photograph of a good-looking young man in his early twenties, with a shock of wavy fair hair and an engaging, disarming smile. 'This is your father, Alix. As he was when your mother knew him. My very good friend Dr Duncan Alexander Grant. He was twenty-three when that was taken.'

Alix stared down at the picture, stroking the likeness with tender fingers, aware of a lump in her throat and tears tugging behind her eyes. So this, at least, was true. He had been real.

'How well did you know him?'

'Very well indeed. We were at medical school together—though I was a few years his senior. Later we worked at the same hospital, I as a surgical registrar, he as a houseman. That was when he met Claudia. She was here making a film. She was eighteen then, and quite, quite, stunning. For him, a least, it was love at first sight. The love of a lifetime. This bright meteor flashed across his sky, lit up his life. Consumed him, you might say. He would have married her then and there, but she didn't see herself as a doctor's wife living in Scotland. No, she was young and very ambitious. She wanted her career. She went away and he never heard another word from her. He never recovered from it. Never forgave her, I'm afraid. He eschewed women from that day on. Dedicated his life to medicine. Helping others.'

Alix looked up through aching eyes. 'She didn't tell him about me?'

'It seems not. When I met her again recently—when she told me of your existence—she said that she had been afraid Duncan would insist on being involved with the child. She couldn't have that. She wanted a clean break from him. No complications.'

'You met Claudia "recently"?' She could hardly believe it. 'How recently?'

'About two years ago now. She was in London for a première. There was a reception at one of the big hotels. We were both guests. I rather boldly went up and introduced myself. Naturally she asked after Duncan. And I had to tell her that he had died, in Africa, where he was working with the AIDS prevention programme.'

Appalled, Alix looked again at the smiling young man in the photograph. 'Is that what killed him? AIDS?'

'No. He died of malaria. He neglected his own health. He was thirty two.'

The fact of his death came as no surprise, but the circumstances of it were new and painful to her. Thirty-two . . . The same age as Niall was now.

'Your mother was distraught when I told her,' Sir Anthony added. 'I thought she was going to faint. Her minders whisked her away. Later she telephoned me, asked for my contact details. We remained in touch, off and on. She confided that she had never forgotten Duncan, had hoped he was happy. Still loved him, in fact. Then last year . . . It would be in April, I seem to remember. Yes, April. She e-mailed and asked me if I would be prepared to help you, if you should need it. As an adviser, she said. I had no idea what she meant by that. Then of course when I learned what had happened I began to understand.'

Last April Claudia had made her final will. Had she known she was going to die? Some people had speculated whether her death had been accident or suicide. Had she killed herself—because of her guilt and grief over Duncan? The questions hung unspoken between them.

'And so you see,' Sir Anthony went on after a while, 'when you telephoned to ask for my help, I was not surprised.'

Alix lifted her head, unashamed of her tears. 'I was out of my head. I'm sorry to have thrown it on to you but you were the only person I could think of who the press wouldn't know about.'

'It was my pleasure, my dear. I was very fond of your father. He was like a younger brother to me. And I had a feeling you might enjoy Lachanbrae. Dame Janet is a wonderful lady. I knew she would take you under her wing.'

Later, when he had told her what she needed to know about her natural father, they

161

talked about Dame Janet. Alix mentioned her hopes of helping to restore Glenwhinnie's fortunes, if only the old woman would allow it. Sir Anthony seemed concerned by her wish to invest a large sum of money in the estate, but as they talked and she explained the ideas for business expansion that Dame Janet—and her factor—would be able to put into practice given the chance, the surgeon agreed to do what he could to smooth the way. He and Dame Janet used the same solicitor, who was a personal friend of Sir Anthony's. Perhaps the two men might try their powers of persuasion on the lady laird.

*   *   *

During the next few days, thanks to Sir Anthony, Alix met the solicitor, Ian Blair, informally over pre-dinner cocktails and then in more businesslike mode in his office. Phone calls with Dame Janet succeeded in establishing a figure for the projected loan, and transatlantic connections set Alix's New York lawyers to work on details.

Meantime, along with Catriona and her friends, Alix played tourist by day and party-animal by night. Several of the young men in Catriona's circle would have liked to get more closely acquainted, but Alix fended them off. She had never been entirely happy to indulge in casual relationships—her Presbyterian upbringing, probably. Besides, none of the men she met in Edinburgh stood a chance of impressing her. By then Alix knew for sure that she was hopelessly in love with Niall Drummond.

Over breakfast one morning—after a long night at a club, which would have been followed by yet more partying back at someone's flat had not Alix decided to summon a cab and return alone to the McKenzies' house—a bleary-eyed Catriona slumped over a mug of black coffee, demanding, 'What's wrong with you, anyway? I suppose you know they're calling you the Snow Queen?'

'Better than the girl from Easy Street,' said Alix. 'Sorry. Been there, done that, got the T-shirt. And decided it's not for me.'

'Born-again virgin!' Catriona sneered.

Alix was not about to get into a slanging match. 'You and Niall Drummond must have a pretty open relationship. Does he know you sleep around?'

Mention of Niall made Catriona narrow her eyes. 'What's that to you? He's mine. When I'm tired of him, I'll let you know.'

'But you're not serious about him?'

Harsh laughter exploded from Catriona. 'I'm deadly serious. But if you mean will I do something stupid like marrying him . . . You've got to be joking! Can you see me living in that scratty little factor's cottage?'

'Then why . . .'

'Because I'm not ready to let him go just yet.' Catriona leaned across the table, eyes contracted to slits. 'He fascinates me. Most men are so boring. You can read them like a book. But with Drummond . . . I never know what's going on in his mind and I find that infuriating. One day I'm going to *force* him to unlock those doors.'

Since Alix herself had had similar thoughts, she could hardly blame the girl for finding Niall Drummond an attractive enigma, though she had a feeling that if Catriona ever did break through his reserve she would immediately lose interest. Catriona didn't really *care* what motivated him, it just maddened her that he refused to succumb to her wiles. Whereas Alix . . . Alix was beginning desperately to regret the things she had said to Niall. He was right—she had not been fair. Imagine accusing him of having no self-control, when as she knew all too well he had far more control than was good for a man. The more she rewound the memory of their quarrel on the way to Auchinveray, the more she winced at the sharp words she had flung at him. She hadn't meant it. She had been hurting and lashed out without thinking. She would tell him so, the minute she got back to the glen.

Catriona pushed away from the table. 'You stay away from my Drummond, you wide-eyed little pip from the Big Apple!'

'And if I don't?'

'If you don't . . .' said Catriona nastily, leaning over her, 'If you don't, I might take it into my head to phone one of the tabloids and tell them exactly where they can find Claudia Cantrelle's missing daughter, Lexie Marisco, a.k.a. Alix Grant.' She straightened, her mouth twisting in triumph as she saw Alix's dismay. 'See. I did warn you I had claws.'

SIX

The confrontation with Catriona soured Alix's visit to Edinburgh. She made excuses to leave the next day. Oddly enough, the threat of exposure no longer had the power to reduce her to panic. Given the choice, she would prefer to remain incognito for a while yet, but if her cover should be blown, for whatever reason, she felt strong enough to face it and fend off the press. Quite how she would explain it to Dame Janet—and to Niall—she had no idea. Best not to think about that until it happened.

She spent her final day in the city shopping, for clothes and for a gift for Sir Anthony—a painting by a local artist, since he enjoyed such things. She also went to a used-car dealer's and selected a neat white Mazda, having confirmed that she could drive in the UK on her American licence for twelve months. The transaction took less than an hour.

That evening Catriona didn't put in an appearance but sent excuses and apologies. Alix spent a pleasant evening with Sir Anthony and his guests, local solicitor Ian Blair and his wife. Ian was now officially Alix's legal representative in Scotland and thanks to his help the loan to Glenwhinnie was going through.

Catriona stayed away all night. In the morning Alix rose early, breakfasted with Sir Anthony and took her leave of him.

'Call me if there's anything more I can do,' he told her. 'And feel free to come and stay whenever you like. You're always welcome here.'

Which was kind of him, but, as she drove away, Alix was fairly sure she would never stay in that charming house again.

*   *   *

By dint of frequent stops to consult the maps she had bought, she made her way back to Lachanbrae, where the snow still lay deep across the fields and hills but the roads were mostly clear. Dame Janet would be surprised by her unannounced return—during one of their phone calls she had instructed Alix to,

'Let us know when you're coming home. Niall will come and collect you from the station.' Well, now that Alix had her own transport Niall wouldn't need to play chauffeur for her ever again.

As for coming home . . . strangely enough, it did feel that way.

Calling in at the shop for a few essentials, Alix was cheered by a warm welcome from Maggie Gillivray: 'We've missed you! Are you well?' How friendly Lachanbrae felt, closing round her like comfortable cushions. Soon the hearth at the lodge was bright with flame, the water was heating, and Alix settled contentedly into familiar routine as daylight waned and evening came.

Hearing the Range Rover approach, she listened for it to go by as usual, but the engine slowed and stopped outside her gate. A glance through the window told Alix that Niall was on his way to see her. Well, fine, she thought, trying to ignore the panic that seethed inside her. Panic, stupid hope, helpless despair . . . She had been longing to see him, wanting to apologize, but after the way they had parted what would this meeting bring?

She opened the door, her face composed into a mask of polite disinterest though her palms were damp with nerves. He stood on the path, shoulders hunched, hands deep in the pockets of his thick belted jacket, eyes hard and accusing beneath a tangle of

167

windblown hair. The expression on his face made her heart sink.

'Am I interrupting something?' he demanded.

The blunt ferocity of the question made her blink. 'Sorry? What . . .'

'I thought you had a visitor. The car . . .' He gestured to where her Mazda sat by the hedge.

'It's mine. I bought it in Edinburgh. Drove back, all on my own.' She felt proud of this achievement and hoped he might applaud her nerve.

He only looked even more disgusted. 'Oh, I see. Decided to come out of the closet, have you? Started throwing your money around?'

Oh, Lord! Alix's heart drooped into her slippers. 'Dame Janet told you, I guess.'

'What did you expect, for God's sake? I do happen to be involved, you know. I'm the factor—the estate manager. How long did you think you could keep it secret?'

Opening her mouth to answer that attack, Alix paused to reconsider. 'Don't be so juvenile, Niall! Look, I don't intend to stand here with the door open letting all the heat out. Come in and let's discuss this like adults.'

'No, thanks. I have to get home and cook a meal.'

'Well, fine. Goodbye.' She started to close the door, but when he made as if to stop her she paused enquiringly. 'Well?"

He glowered at her in silence for a moment, then grudged, 'I suppose your intentions are good. Dame Janet's on cloud nine. You just don't understand . . .' The sentence trailed off as he shrugged deeper into his coat and looked down at his shoes. 'So how was Edinburgh? Did you see Sir Anthony?'

'I could hardly avoid it when I was staying at his house!'

That made him look at her from his eye corner. 'Did you find out what you wanted to know?'

'Yes.' She could be obstinate, too, more so because she was hurting. 'By the way, I gave Catriona your message.'

'And?'

'And she thought it was hilarious. Is that what it was—a joke?'

'In a way. I thought you might learn something from her reaction.'

Suddenly she was furious with his obliqueness. 'Well, thank *you*. I surely do appreciate being the butt of your private jokes! Wouldn't it have been simpler just to . . .' She stopped herself, though her temper was pulling at the leash. 'You're right, Niall—I don't understand. I don't understand you at all. And, you know what? I'm beginning to think you're not worth the effort, anyway. I'm sick of being constantly on pins. Why don't you just stay away from me?'

Dark lashes veiled eyes in which she fancied there might be a hint of pain. Or was she imagining it, reluctant to admit how stupid she had been? He said, 'That's what I came to tell you—that I think it will be best—for both of us—to forget . . . to not get any more involved than . . . What I'm trying to say is . . .'

Alix said it for him. 'Goodbye, Niall,' and closed the door before he could see how close she was to crying.

It was for the best, she assured herself, to write a final full stop. Obviously their relationship had no chance. No chance at all.

*   *   *

Despite Niall's resentment of Alix's offer of help, it appeared that he and Dame Janet had been busy discussing possible ways of using the new capital. The lady laird was delighted to have Alix back and to tell her all about the projected improvements—crofts to be modernized, barns erected, the village inn enlarged to accommodate more visitors, especially during the shooting season; the big house itself was to be rewired and the roof repaired—vital work—plus a hundred other minor refurbishments to fences, streams, forestry and game preserves. Future projects might include organized photography courses, fishing or painting weekends, a ski lift . . . Much to Alix's gratification, Dame Janet had lost her worried look and seemed to have shed ten years.

But whenever the subject came round to Niall Drummond, when Alix tried to discover what made him tick, she got exactly nowhere. She ought to have known from past experience that Dame Janet did not discuss other people's affairs.

'You'd better ask *him*,' she kept saying. 'I'm sorry, my dear, but he wouldn't thank me for gossiping.'

'Trying to get anything out of Niall is like trying to talk to an oyster,' Alix sighed. 'Why is he that way—all shut up inside himself?'

But Dame Janet only smiled. 'You don't need an old spinster like me to tell you how to handle a man, do you?'

*   *   *

By chance—and it was pure chance, Alix assured herself afterwards—she encountered Maura in the shop one day. Niall's sister looked pale and had a terrible chesty cough. So Alix, merely being neighbourly and caring, offered her a ride home, and when Maura asked her in for a cup of tea it would have been churlish to refuse, wouldn't it? Especially when Fergus was so pleased to see a different face.

'You're too much a stranger, lassie,' he beamed. 'Come away in and sit yourself down.

171

Maura, fetch some of those scones.'

Alix was *not* prying. Honestly, she had only the best of intentions. Was it her fault if Fergus liked talking about his family?

Thirty-odd years before, Fergus had been a widower, working as a gamekeeper out near Auchinveray with ten-year-old Maura to raise; then he had met and married pretty Amy McFee, who became Niall's mother. Photographs taken through the years showed how the children had grown and altered. Fergus was proud of them both.

'This was taken just before Niall went to Canada. Och, well, a lad has to try his wings, I suppose. I did mysel', as I recall.'

'But Niall only went because—' Maura began, and stopped when her father cleared his throat and said, as if she had not interrupted, 'It was over there that he met Barbara. Sadly, we never had the pleasure of meeting her in person. She had no family of her own, so they were married quietly, and then they had their home to get sorted. They were planning to come home to Lachanbrae the following spring, maybe, but . . . Well, there was an accident. They were out walking in the snow and one of those ski-sled things went out of control—some youngsters playing the fool, you know how it can be.'

Having heard some of this story before, Alix made appropriate comments.

'The lad was in a fair pickle for a while,'

Fergus continued sadly. 'We wanted him to come home, but he wouldn't hear of leaving Canada. Until his mother took sick. It was a terrible time for him. He lost his wife, then his mother, then I had my accident, and . . .'

'And then we all came to Lachanbrae,' Maura put in, laying a comforting hand on her father's arm, 'because Dame Janet—'

Again her father stopped her, his hand reaching up to cover hers as he turned his head and they exchanged a look that made Maura flush. 'Dame Janet,' said Fergus firmly, looking back at Alix, 'had need of a good man to help her manage the estate. So Niall became her factor and Maura and I moved into this cottage, where he can keep an eye on us.' The smile in his eyes reached his mouth as he added, 'And we on him, eh, Maura? Now that's enough about us. Tell us about yourself, lassie. Maura'd love to hear about America.'

So Alix told tales of the States, being vague about details of her own life—raised in Kansas with adoptive parents, studied English and History in New York, remained there to work . . . 'And then when the chance arose, when Sir Anthony suggested it, I decided to come and see Scotland, to work on my book in peace and quiet.'

The cliché had an ironic ring to it. Quiet, possibly. Peaceful? Not exactly. But she allowed Maura and Fergus to think she had found a true haven in their glen.

Later, she kept replaying that conversation in her mind, wondering what Maura might have said if her father hadn't stopped her from chattering. They had not been entirely frank, that was clear. But then, come to that, neither had she.

Maybe she was not the only one who had secrets to hide.

*   *   *

After that day it seemed only friendly and neighbourly to drop in on the Drummonds now and then, at first to check how Maura's cold was progressing, then to give her a ride to the shops when it was icy, or to bring Fergus a pack of his favourite pipe tobacco. Alix looked forward to those friendly cups of tea. She liked Niall's father and sister a lot. But she learned no more of his personal history. Every time his name cropped up, Maura looked at her father as if seeking permission even to speak.

Since Niall himself was a regular visitor to the cottage he must have known that she was seeing his family at frequent intervals, but he never called there when her car was outside. Back at Glenwhinnie, his Range Rover continued to pass her door every day. He was staying away, as he had said he would. Alix told herself she didn't care, but it was a lie.

Now and then, a few oblique hints did drop,

174

though they only added to the puzzle. One time in the shop Maggie Gillivray remarked that it was an odd coincidence that Niall had ended up working for Dame Janet.

'How do you mean?' Alix asked.

'Och, well, people will put two and two together and make five, or six. What I always say is, least said soonest mended.' This from an inveterate gossip! 'Anything else I can get you now?'

Obviously there was something the village knew, or suspected, but such private local secrets were not to be shared with an incomer. The saying went that you'd have to be resident in Lachanbrae for at least thirty years before you could begin to be accepted as a member of the community.

*　　　*　　　*

The silence between herself and Niall grew especially irksome when she realized she needed to talk to him. She had too much pride to make overtures he might misinterpret but, darn it!, she had good reason for wishing to speak with Dame Janet's factor on a matter of mutual concern. A business matter. Therefore, she would approach him in a businesslike way.

On a bright, clear day near the end of February, she walked up to the big house and into the side wing. The door to the reception office stood open and behind the desk Joan McNab was tapping away at a keyboard.

'Is the factor in?' Alix asked.

'Yes, he is.' Joan's tone made it a question.

'May I see him?'

The secretary used the phone, eyes filled with curiosity behind the old-fashioned glasses. 'It's Miss Grant to see you . . . Right.' She replaced the receiver, 'He says to go straight up.'

Alix climbed the stairs, her shoulders squared and her mind braced to be crisp and businesslike with Niall.

His, 'Come in,' answered her knock. She found him standing by the window, his back turned to her, thumbs hooked into the belt loops of the black jeans he wore with a scarlet sweater. As she closed the door, he glanced briefly over his shoulder before returning to his contemplation of the courtyard. 'Something I can do for you?'

'I've had an idea. A surprise for Dame Janet. But I shall need your help.'

'I'm listening.'

'Dame Janet will be seventy-five in June, won't she?'

'Yes.'

'It's quite a milestone. Three quarters of a century.'

'And?'

'And I've been thinking it might be fun to throw a special party for her. She talks about the fancy balls they used to have here. So I wondered . . . Why don't we go ahead and clean up the ballroom, make it look like it used to in the old days, invite all her friends . . . ? I know it will take some organizing, but if we work together we could—'

'Wait!' he broke in and slowly, wearily swung round to face her. 'Are you out of your tiny mind? That is probably the most ludicrous idea I have ever heard. Renovate the ballroom, when there are a million more important things need doing?'

'We could do it if we wanted,' Alix said stiffly. 'This won't be included under the loan arrangement. You can send all the bills straight to me. It will be my special gift to her, to thank her for everything she's done for me.'

He said nothing, but his expression was eloquent, pouring scorn and animosity.

'Just imagine how it would please her!' Alix insisted. 'And it wouldn't be wasted. Afterwards you could hire out the ballroom for special functions. Company dinners, wedding parties . . . People would come for miles to spend an evening in these surroundings. Maybe in time we could use part of the house as a hotel, and . . .'

Niall glowered at her across the office, more angry than she had ever seen him. 'Got it all planned, have you? What is this—a takeover bid? Perhaps, while you're about it, you'd like to come and manage the whole blasted estate!'

All at once Alix was sick of walking on eggshells, trying to reason with a man who took a jaundiced view of her every action. 'Grow up, Niall!' she snapped. 'What the hell's wrong with you? Can't you stand the thought of a woman having ideas, and energy and money enough to carry them through? I'm darned if I see why I need permission from you to do this. If you won't help me, I'll ... I'll go ahead and do it without you.'

Niall's hands flexed as if he wanted to fasten them round her throat. 'You'd do it, too, you blasted interfering female! What gives you the right to come in here and—' The sentence cut off as the phone rang and, swearing succinctly, he strode to answer it. 'Yes?! ... What? Oh ... Yes, Joan, put him through ... Good afternoon, Mr Cameron.'

While he dealt with the call, Alix took his place by the window. Outside, shadows lengthened across lawns where snow still lingered, while pale February sunlight angled across the façade of the main house. She imagined how it might look in June, with cars arriving and visitors flocking into the ballroom, away on the far side of the house. No, she would not let Niall deny her that dream. She sank onto the window board, frowning at his averted profile, idly noting that his red sweater was thinning at the elbow. No! Do not let yourself go soft, girl!

178

'I'll have the letter in the post this evening,' he said into the phone. 'Yes, thank you, Mr Cameron. Goodbye.' Dropping the receiver back into the cradle, he sat down at his desk to scribble a note. 'As you can see, I'm busy, so if you'll excuse me . . .'

'I'm not through yet.'

'But I am. Look . . .' Tiredly, he turned his head to look over his shoulder. 'You may think this loan gives you some rights here, but I'm afraid you're mistaken. We appreciate the financial support, but if you ever want to reap a dividend from it don't expect me to waste my valuable time on mad schemes you've dreamed up just to cause me grief. Now, kindly go away.'

'You think I'm doing this to annoy you?!' Choked with disbelief, she came off the windowsill and went to stand over him. 'Boy, your ego's even bigger than I thought! The only reason I came here was to enlist your help—because you're the factor and I can't possibly organize this without your co-operation. Believe me, if there was anyone else who could handle it, I'd go ask him. But it seems you're it, so I've no option. All it'll take is a little of your time and your co-operation, but if that's too much to ask for Dame Janet's sake, then . . . fine, I guess we'll have to call it off.'

The scathing tone of her voice made him look uncomfortable. 'Let me think about it.

179

Maybe we could arrange something.'

'You're too kind, Mr Drummond! Thank you so much. Please don't let me delay your vital work any longer.'

'Before you go . . .'

Halfway to the door she paused, waiting, her back turned to him, stiff as a flagpole.

'. . . I'd be grateful if you would stop hassling my family. I don't know what you think you'll gain from it—or from cross-examining Dame Janet about me. I'll say to you what you once said to me—stay out of my life, Alix.'

Unexpected tears pressed behind her eyes. Hassling his family? Is that what he thought? She bit her lip, keeping her back turned, but despite her efforts her voice came out hoarse. 'You mean that?'

'Yes!' he exploded, and must have shot out of his chair because she heard a crash as something hit the filing cabinet behind the desk. 'How many times do I have to say it? You're as bad as Cat McKenzie. Worse, even. At least she comes straight for me with her wiles, she doesn't go sneaking round my family trying to ingratiate herself.'

Alix spun round, wounded to the core. 'Don't you *dare* compare me with Cat McKenzie! And don't you dare cast doubts on my friendship with Maura and Fergus. I visit them because I like them. And they seem to like me, even if you find that hard to believe.

They're lovely people. How someone like *you* ever came to be kin to them—'

'That's enough!!' he roared.

'I'm not through yet!!' she yelled right back. 'Yes, I did want to know more about you. Of course I did. I must be naïve. I was starting to care about you. I wanted to understand you, so I could maybe . . . well, no matter. OK, I *will* stay clear from now on. I can't imagine any reason I should ever want to see you again!!'

She slammed the door violently behind her and clattered down the stairs in a rush. She caught one glimpse of Joan McNab's astonished face and then she was out in the cold air, running, running, almost blinded by tears.

*   *   *

More snow fell, choking the roads again. Alix wondered if the endless winter would ever turn to spring, but her calendar told her it was March. Soon, she decided, she must start to think about going home. Wherever that was.

She missed her chats with Maura and Fergus, but nothing would have induced her to call at their cottage without a specific reason, not after the insinuations Niall had made. Did Maura and Fergus believe she had been using them? Well, let Niall explain her absence to them, if he could. It had been his idea.

She tried not to think about Niall, but inevitably her thoughts turned to him whether she willed it or not. And still the Range Rover passed to and fro every day, reminding her of dreams that had died before they were even half-formed. He was not for her. Well, she had known that from the start, hadn't she? But next minute she would remember occasions that told a different story—the lovely pashmina he had given her; the way they had danced and kissed in the cold ballroom at Christmas; the Hogmanay dance, the snow, sleeping in his warm arms until morning, when they had so nearly made love, when he had been as happy as she was. But since then nothing. Nothing but silence, hostility, resentment . . . What had she done? What had she said?

That snow proved to be winter's last thrust. Cold rain came in, gradually washing away the remaining snow and eating into the piles of dirty slush. The trees dripped, but their tips were swelling with new buds and the woods came alive with birds in full mating song. In the lodge garden, as in many other sheltered spots, snowdrops nodded their beautiful, delicate heads.

*　　*　　*

Returning from a trip to Auchinveray, Alix in

her Mazda encountered Niall in the Range Rover, both of them arriving at the Glenwhinnie gates at the same moment. They both stopped, but since he had right of way she gestured him to go ahead, fully expecting him to drive on towards the big house. However, to her surprise he pulled in just beyond her gate and got out to wait for her.

'Something wrong?' she enquired, making for the trunk to unload her shopping.

'No, not exactly. Here, let me help, those look heavy.'

Deciding not to argue, she let him load himself up while she went to unlock the door and led the way through to the small kitchen, where Niall dumped the bulging bags on the table.

'Thanks.'

'Welcome.'

She waited. No, she would not ask his reasons for being here. Nor would she invite him to have a coffee. She wished he would go away.

'Looks like spring's on the way,' he commented.

'Sure does.' Turning her back on him, she filled the kettle.

'Maura's been saying how she hasn't seen you lately,' he remarked.

That was too much! She whirled on him with an angry exclamation, but he held up a hand to stop her, saying, 'I know. I know! And

I'm sorry. Maybe I was wrong. They miss your visits. So if you feel like calling . . .'

'You mean I have your permission?! Well, how frightfully kind of you, Mr Drummond, thanks so much, that makes me feel a heap better.'

His expression said he knew he deserved her sarcasm. 'Alix, please . . . I didn't come here to continue the quarrel. I wanted . . . I wondered if you would have dinner with me one evening.'

Astounded into speechlessness, she could only gape at him.

A dark flush spread up his neck to stain his face as he stuffed his hands into his pockets, regarding her from under lowered brows. 'If you still want to throw this party for Dame Janet, we have to get together to discuss how we're going to do it.'

'"We"? I thought you wanted nothing to do with such a stupid idea.'

'I didn't say it was stupid.'

'No, sorry, the word was "ludicrous", as I recall.'

'I only meant . . . I did also say I'd think about it, if you remember. Well, I've done that, and I feel we should discuss it in more detail. Over dinner. Somewhere discreet. I thought perhaps the Bridge Hotel in Auchinveray.'

Alix blinked. Was she hallucinating? 'You don't have to take me to dinner just so we can discuss arrangements for a party. Why can't we talk here? Or, better still, I'll come up to the office some time.'

'No, that's not . . .'

'Not discreet enough for you?'

He hesitated, blue eyes uncertain and anxious. 'Look, I'm trying to make amends for the things I said last time we met. I was in a foul mood and I let my temper get the better of me. I'm sorry. Please forgive me.'

Remorse twisted inside her like a fist as the anger drained out of her. He sounded utterly sincere. Strange how a few softly-spoken words had the power to change everything. Besides, she hated to see him look so unhappy. 'I lost my temper, too,' she admitted.

His mouth quirked though his eyes remained bleak. 'You said once that we should just enjoy knowing each other while we can. Can we do that? Just be friends?'

Alix doubted that was possible, but she said softly, 'We can try, I guess.'

'Then how about dinner? Saturday night? I'll book a table. Pick you up . . . around seven?'

'OK.'

Again he hesitated, his gaze locked with hers, then without another word he turned around and left the lodge. Alix switched off the boiling kettle, staring at her distorted reflection in the shiny metal. Friends, he had said. She only hoped she could find the strength to let it stay like that.

All week she lived for Saturday night, planning what she would wear and how to fix her hair. She found time for a visit to Dame Janet (though she didn't mentioned her date with Niall) and she also dropped by to see Fergus and Maura, who greeted her with delight and asked anxiously after her health. Apparently Niall had told them she was working very hard. Alix added that she had also been suffering from the blues, which was true enough. Funny how her depression had suddenly lifted.

Now she really noticed all the signs of spring, how the days were lengthening, the sun staying longer in the sky, even though clear skies at dawn and sunset still brought a touch of frost and the hills remained crowned with snow.

*   *   *

In the powder room at the Bridge Hotel, Saturday night, pink light flattered her reflection. She had had her hair high-lighted with blonde streaks and she wore a fitted jersey silk dress in a subtle shade of lavender that looked well with the soft pashmina she had donned for extra warmth. Would Niall approve? What a fool she was even to wonder! They were here to discuss business,

186

that was all. As friends. And conspirators in a delicious secret.

The Bridge was an old hotel, full of dark wood and a hushed, romantic ambience induced by soft lamps in niches. In the bar, deep armchairs and settees stood around small tables where couples and foursomes sipped aperitifs, laughing and talking softly. Alix paused a moment, looking round for Niall, and saw him rising from a chair near the big bay window, broad and tall in his smart dark suit, a white shirt and patterned blue tie setting off his dark good looks. The sight of him did strange things to her heartbeat and her breathing. She hardly noticed the admiring glances directed at her by a group of young businessmen by the bar as she passed. Niall noticed, though. As she came nearer his glance slipped past her and shot evil daggers at the other men. He looked, Alix thought with an odd lurch of her stomach, almost possessive. Then his eyes met hers across the last few feet of space and everything else melted into insignificance.

'You're stunning,' he said under his breath, adding, with another dark glance at the men by the bar, 'and I'm not the only one who thinks so.'

Finding herself with no answer that made sense, she replied with a smile, sinking down into a chair, reaching for the gin and tonic she had asked for. 'Well, cheers. Or . . . what was it . . . ? "*Slainte!*" '

His swift smile said he was pleased that she remembered the Gaelic toast he had taught her. He resumed his own seat and replied in kind.

For a while they occupied themselves studying enormous menus and ordering their meal. Waiting to be called, they made awkward small-talk, both of them ill-at-ease, with long silences punctuating inconsequential conversation. Eventually Niall took out a pen and notebook, saying, 'We might as well get down to business. About this Birthday Ball . . . I've had to include Murdo in the secret—he's as close-mouthed as they come so he won't blab. He's been checking what needs to be done and I've had a couple of estimates from builders. The stairs will have to be replaced, for a start. It won't come cheap.'

'It doesn't matter. Whatever it takes.'

'You're sure about this? This is only a beginning. When the building work is done the place will need decorating. And there'll be catering. And if we're going to do it properly we'll have to hire a band, and maybe a piper.'

'You *have* been busy,' Alix murmured. 'Maybe it wasn't such a ludicrous idea, after all. Yes, by all means let's do the thing properly. I can't wait to see Dame Janet's face. She's not to know what we're doing. If it's humanly possible she mustn't suspect until the very last minute. Oh—put down flowers.

We must have lots of flowers.'

Discussing details and planning ruses to keep the whole thing secret from Dame Janet took them from the bar to the dining room, where lighted candles graced tables laid with crystal and silver and blood-red table linen. Despite his initial antagonism, Niall's imagination had been caught by the project. Knowing that, Alix let her own imagination run free, though her ideas grew noticeably wilder as the bottle of wine emptied—more of it going into her glass than into his, as she realized belatedly.

'Hold on!' Niall objected eventually. 'You'll be wanting the hills floodlit next.'

'What a wonderful idea!'

'Alix . . .' He sighed, half amused and half exasperated. 'This is going to cost a small fortune as it is. Anyway, in June it hardly gets dark up here. No sooner are the stars out than dawn comes up. We shan't need to worry too much about lighting. Are you sure you know what you're doing? If you keep throwing money around like this you won't have any left.'

'Doesn't matter.' She leaned her chin on her hand, suddenly mournful. 'It's not really my money anyway. Doesn't feel real. I wish . . . I wish someone else had been burdened with it. Maybe I'll give it all away.'

'Now that *is* ludicrous.'

'Is it?' She sighed. 'OK, we won't go

overboard. We'll spend just enough to make it a marvellous evening for darling Jay—she asked me to call her that, you know, though it doesn't come easy. I'm very fond of her, Niall.'

'I know,' he said, his lips quirking ruefully. 'You're also just a wee bit squiffy. Black coffee for you, my girl, and then I'll take you home.'

My girl, she thought sadly, and heard herself say, 'I wish I was.'

He tilted a questioning eyebrow. 'Sorry?'

'Nothing. I'm babbling. You realize you gave me most of the wine?'

'Only because I'm driving,' he informed her with a smile that choked her up. To cover it, she made a dash for the ladies' room.

The night was clear and cold. Craggy hills formed a dark skyline and a sheen of frost showed on the road, but inside the big car Alix was warm and drowsy. When she turned her head she could see Niall's profile lit by an edge of light from the dashboard. She fancied she could have sat there for ever watching him, simply content to be with him.

Arriving at the lodge, he accompanied her to the door, where she fumbled with the key until he took it from her and opened the door before stepping back.

'Coffee?' she asked, and when he looked as though he might refuse she clutched at his jacket lapel. 'Oh, please, Niall!' She tried to pull him inside the house, but in her eagerness she tripped over the doorstep. She might have fallen on her face if he hadn't lunged to catch her, and somehow she was in his arms, inside the hallway. For a moment he held her painfully tight, telling her he was enduring his own kind of agony.

'Please stay,' she muttered into his shirt front. 'Just a little while. I'm not drunk, just a bit light-headed. I know what I'm doing.'

'I wish I did,' he muttered.

She peered up at him, wishing she could see his face clearly. 'Please stay. Have a coffee—just one coffee. You make up the fire while I put the kettle on. Please!'

Sighing heavily, he released her. 'All right. Just one coffee.'

As she moved around the kitchen she could hear him stirring up the fire and adding more peat. When eventually she went through with a tray Niall was standing on the hearthrug, looking at the photograph on the mantelpiece—the photograph she had brought from Edinburgh and displayed in a silver frame.

'Who's this?' he wanted to know.

'It's my father, Dr Duncan Grant. Sir Anthony gave it to me.'

'Ah.' The syllable held a note of relief. He studied her for a moment, then examined the photo again. 'I can see the resemblance, now you say.'

'Think so? Sir Anthony said the same. And whose picture did you suspect it might be? My secret lover?'

He sent her a sidelong look, a shrug. 'Just wondered.'

Liar, she thought happily. She knew jealousy when she saw it. 'Are you going to sit down?'

He did so, in one of the armchairs, where she couldn't sit close to him. Noting the fact, she sank into the settee, remembering how she had slept there in his arms, and how happy they had both been that New Year's morning, teasing each other over breakfast and working together to clear snow.

The wine had left her emotional. 'What happened to us, Niall? Where did it go wrong? What did I do? What did I say?'

When he looked at her she saw the veil back in his eyes, hiding his thoughts and his feelings. 'It's not *you*. Don't ever think that. You're a warm, beautiful, desirable girl. But I thought we agreed—'

'*You* agreed!' Her tears broke loose, dripping down her face, and she leapt to her feet. 'But you didn't give me any reasons for it. You never explain, Niall! Why don't you explain?!'

'Don't get upset. Please!' He came out of the chair and took her by the shoulders, blue eyes anxiously scanning her face before resting on her tremulous mouth. 'Don't, Alix.'

Feeling the magnetic pull between them, she lifted her lips invitingly.

192

He said, 'Oh, God, I can't—' and threw his arms around her, holding her tightly with her head pressed to his shoulder.

Alix clung to him, leaning pliant against him, her nerve ends drinking in the feel of him, the scent of him, thirsty as a flower left wilting for water. Closing her eyes she buried her face against him, her arms wrapped tightly around him. 'I love you, Niall,' she whispered brokenly. 'I love you. I love you. I love you.'

His arms tightened convulsively, making her gasp in pain as he dropped his head and found her mouth in an explosive kiss that made colours swirl behind her closed eyelids. His hands caressed her, pressing her ever closer as the kiss deepened into desperate passion.

Then suddenly she was free. She swayed unsteadily, breathless and bewildered as through misted eyes she saw Niall stride to the door. Without looking back, without a word of comfort or excuse, he walked out into the night and left her alone.

Alix's knees gave way and she sank to the floor, silent tears boiling down her face to drip unregarded onto the lavender dress. She had bared her soul to him, offered him her heart. And Niall had rejected her.

SEVEN

Somehow, she got through the night. She even slept, eventually, and when she woke she assumed her thick head was a result of too much wine and too many tears. She spent most of the day slumped on the settee, drenched in misery but slowly becoming aware of a virus brewing inside her—a cold, probably. The villagers had all been sneezing and snuffling.

But during Sunday night she felt worse, and on the following morning when she tried to get out of bed she almost fainted. She was really ill. Her throat felt like hot, dry sand, every muscle ached like crazy, and though her skin felt hot she couldn't stop shivering. She managed to drag herself downstairs to make a drink, then flopped on the settee wearing her warm wrap and the throw from the back of the sofa, gaining some warmth from the remains of the fire. Uneasy sleep claimed her, accompanied by weird, disturbing dreams. Once or twice she was shocked awake by the ringing of the phone, but she hadn't the strength to answer it.

The phone calls must have been made by Dame Janet; some time during the afternoon that redoubtable lady appeared and took charge. A doctor came, pronounced Alix stricken with 'flu, and supplied her with medication. Ailie Gordon appeared like the fairy godmother and between them she and Dame Janet put Alix to bed and provided more heaters to keep the small bedroom comfortably warm.

'And there you're to stay,' Dame Janet ordered. 'Don't worry about a thing.'

Word of her illness spread, as did all news in Lachanbrae, with the swiftness of a stag across the fells. Maggie Gillivray called bringing good wishes from half the village; Maura arrived with home-cooked goodies and messages from Fergus; even dour old Murdo Gordon had expressed his concern, or so his wife said—Ailie was in and out all the time, assisting Dame Janet with the nursing. As for Niall . . . 'He keeps asking after you,' Dame Janet told her. 'He's very concerned.'

At least he hadn't caught the 'flu from her, miraculous as that was. As for being concerned . . . maybe that was true. He had often expressed his damned *concern* for her. But he wasn't concerned enough to come see her, was he? Not that she expected him. Not after the way she had behaved. How she despised herself for letting the wine go to her head, for blurting that she loved him. He had made it very clear that that was not what he wanted. But the questions still plagued her. Why? Why? Why?

Finally she made her first unsteady trip

195

downstairs and from then on her weakness abated and her nurses came less often. The doctor called again, commented that she looked pale, and prescribed a tonic. However, the real cause of her pallor and *ennui* was not any medical problem. No tonic could ease what ailed her.

*　　　*　　　*

On a changeable mid-April day when daffodils and primroses were opening in the woods and the hillsides blazed with yellow broom, Catriona McKenzie appeared at Alix's door, dressed in layers of black like a messenger of doom. Removing her trendy woollen hat, she shook out her glorious hair, affording Alix a stare of pure green malice before shouldering past and sweeping to take centre stage in the sitting room.

Alix followed. As she closed the door Catriona swung round to face her, tragic and terrible as Lady Macbeth, declaiming theatrically, 'So! So! I suppose you thought I wouldn't find out. But I have a lot of friends in Scotland. You were seen.'

Leaning on the back of a dining chair, Alix said tiredly, 'Well, hi, Catriona. Come in, why don't you? How've you been?'

'And don't try to be funny! I'm in no mood for girly banter. You've been making a play for Drummond. Don't deny it!'

Oh, Lord, was that why she had come? 'His name,' Alix said heavily, 'is Niall. Look, Catriona, why don't we have a coffee, sit down, and talk about it like adults?'

'You had dinner with him at the Bridge!' Catriona cried. 'A very romantic dinner, making eyes at each other in the candlelight. I know you did because you were seen! Didn't I *warn* you to stay clear? I told you what would happen. Well, now I'm here to tell you it was no idle threat. You'll be sorry you ever laid eyes on Niall Drummond.'

She left as abruptly as she had come, leaving Alix wearily wondering at the other girl's immaturity. What a spoiled brat! Catriona McKenzie took the prize for stupidity. Would she actually carry out her threat? Would she bring a flurry of reporters and photographers to descend on Lachanbrae and ruin everything?

What was to ruin? Alix felt too depressed to care much. If they came, she would move on. She'd start packing right away, to be ready. Except that she didn't have the energy. It didn't seem to matter any more. Besides, where would she go?

One thing, however, seemed clear—one way or another, she would soon be moving on from Lachanbrae.

*   *   *

Dame Janet telephoned, inviting Alix to come up to the big house for tea. 'I'll have Ailie make one of those lemon cakes you like. It's been so long since you were here with us.' Clearly the lady laird had begun to wonder why Alix continued to avoid Glenwhinnie House now that she was recovered from her illness.

Since the day was fine, she walked up the drive, hoping to slip by the office without being seen—something she couldn't do if she were driving. She walked close to the side wing wall, not to be observed from the window of the factor's office, and even ducked her head as she passed the reception office window. Which was pretty foolish but she couldn't help herself.

She reached the porch and rang the bell, relieved when it was Ailie who answered and sent her in to see Dame Janet, who was— thank goodness—alone in the sitting room. But if Niall himself was nowhere to be seen he remained a vivid presence in Alix's mind. She dreaded their next encounter, their first after that night when she had made such a fool of herself. She blamed the wine—and the 'flu virus that had been brewing. She had not been herself.

'Has Niall been to see you lately?' Dame Janet's question came with a twist of grey brows and a shadow in her eyes.

With an effort, Alix maintained her

outward calm, setting her cup down on the saucer with great care. 'Not for a while. No reason why he should.'

'I'd have thought common courtesy demanded it, if nothing else. I thought the two of you were friends.' She paused, watching Alix and awaiting an answer.

'We are!' Had she put too much emphasis into that? 'But you've been watching over me like a guardian angel, and relaying the latest news, no doubt. He didn't need to visit me in person.'

'I suppose you know he's been seeing a great deal of Catriona recently? That red car of hers is forever appearing in the courtyard here. People in the village have noticed her passing by, too. Do you know what's going on? I thought all that was over.'

Alix gazed down into her tea. The liquid was trembling, like her hand. She too had seen the red Fiat come and go frequently over the last few days, ever since Catriona's melodramatic visit to the lodge. Presumably the on-off relationship was firmly on again. Would that stop Catriona from carrying out her threat to inform the press of the location of Alexis 'Lexie' Marisco's hideaway? Oh, she couldn't be bothered to fathom it. 'You'd have to ask Niall.'

'I've tried. But, as you once observed, Niall can clam up like the proverbial oyster when it suits him. Though lately he's been more like a bear with a sore head. Would you know anything about that?'

Saddened, Alix lifted her eyes. 'I'm the last person he'd talk to.'

'Indeed? I thought . . .' But whatever she thought, she decided against voicing it. 'Well, whatever's eating him it's making life very difficult for the rest of us. None of us can say a word to him without fear of getting our heads snapped off. The house is full of builders, too. Hammering and banging. Seems Murdo discovered some urgent renovations were needed. Part of the house is all sealed off—dangerous, so they tell me. But if they knock it about much more it will probably *fall* down.'

This was the one hopeful aspect in Alix's current dreary life—that plans for the party were going ahead. Recent traffic past the lodge had included a selection of builders' vehicles, so she knew that Niall was going ahead with the scheme.

Having ascertained the office electronic address from a notepad, she sent a carefully-worded e-mail enquiring about the work going on. As Catriona had observed, e-mail was quick and impersonal, ideal for concealing emotions. Niall replied from his personal e-mail, thus excluding Joan McNab from their exchanges, and from then on occasional messages flashed between them—brief, businesslike messages all concerning the planning for the party.

The Birthday Ball, as they had started to call it, was her only reason for staying. After it, she would leave Lachanbrae as swiftly as possible.

*   *   *

Knowing that she worked best to a deadline, Alix set herself the task of completing the first draft of her biographical novel by mid-June. Once that cathartic exercise was done, and with Dame Janet's surprise party accomplished, she would think about the future. She had to decide what to do with her life, and which place to use as a home base. In the meantime, if the press descended . . . like Scarlett O'Hara, she would think about that some other day.

Hard at work, with her mind back in Kansas, she heard the gate crash and a few moments later her doorbell began ringing. Alix got up, glancing out of the window, but saw no vehicle outside except her own white Mazda.

To her astonishment, the visitor was Maura Drummond, in a state of tearful distress.

'It's Niall!' she cried.

Alix's heart squeezed viciously with fright. 'What's happened?'

'You've got to talk to him, Alix! He'll listen to you. In the village they're saying . . . they're saying awful things. There's a girl—a girl with

201

red hair and a red car. They're saying she spends nights at Niall's cottage. They say he's going to marry her and go away from Lachanbrae, and if he does that I don't know what Dad and I will do.'

'Maura . . .' Relieved to know that Niall had not been hurt in some awful accident, Alix drew the frantic woman inside the hall and closed the door. 'Come on in where it's warm. Come and sit down. Let me take your coat. Now . . . take a few deep breaths. I'll make some tea and then you can tell me what this is all about.'

Alix escaped to the kitchen. As she prepared tea her hands shook uncontrollably. Had Niall asked Catriona to marry him? Oh, please, don't let it be true! Catriona herself had laughed at the very idea, hadn't she? Or had she changed her mind when the question was put into words? What woman could resist the thought of being Niall Drummond's wife?

When she returned with a tray of tea and biscuits, Maura lifted a tear-stained face, lips trembling as she tried an uneasy smile. 'I'm sorry. Got myself in a state, as Dad would say, but I didn't know what to do. When I heard them talking in the shop . . . I just ran out and before I could think about it I was on my way here. I didn't want to go home. Dad will be so upset. Oh, Alix, it's not true, is it? Niall wouldn't go away and leave Glenwhinnie, would he? Oh, why do people say these things?'

What she had heard, it transpired (much to Alix's relief), was a group of the villagers gossiping about the factor and his red-headed girlfriend from the city—most of what they said being pure speculation, based on the evidence of Catriona's frequent presence in and around the glen over the past days. No smoke without fire, so they agreed.

Alix had no idea how serious or otherwise the relationship might be. The pair seemed utterly ill-suited, but then opposite types were supposedly drawn to each other, weren't they? She never had known what really went on inside Niall Drummond's skull.

One thing became clear—he was as out-of-sorts with Maura and Fergus as he was with the folk at the big house.

'There's something badly wrong,' Maura sighed. 'I know him inside out and I can tell he's not happy. Oh, I wish that girl would go away and leave my brother alone!'

'Have you asked him about it?'

Maura's open, peach-furred face revealed her helplessness. 'I couldn't do that. Dad says he's a grown man and we shouldn't interfere, but . . . We *are* Niall's family, Alix! We *are!!* I can't suddenly stop caring about him.'

'Of course you can't.' Alix laid a hand over Maura's as she dissolved into more tears. 'No one wants you to.'

203

To her bewilderment, Maura suddenly leapt up, clapping a hand to her mouth, more distraught than ever. 'I shouldn't have said that. I shouldn't have! I swore I'd never . . . Dad will never forgive me! Oh, you won't say anything, will you? It's a sworn secret. Don't tell anybody, please!'

'Maura! . . . Maura, let me give you a ride home. Don't—'

Maura fended her off, grabbing her jacket as she passed, heading for the door. She would not be delayed, or helped in any way.

Alix confronted yet another mystery. For the life of her she couldn't remember what Maura had said that might possibly have been regarded as indiscreet.

However, after that day the little red Fiat was seen no more in Lachanbrae. When Alix ran into Maura in the village, Niall's sister was all apology for the fuss she had made. 'I got it all muddled,' she confessed. 'He's not leaving the glen. He doesn't even like that red-haired girl. He told me so.'

Thank heaven!

The gossips found other topics to amuse them. Life settled back into its usual pattern. And, for Alix, Niall Drummond remained a distant but maddeningly tantalizing presence.

*   *   *

Blossom by blossom, the glen put on its spring

mantle of flowers and fresh green leaves. Even Ben Lachan lost the last vestige of its snowcap. Soon, when the heather bloomed, the hills would change colour yet again, from green to purple.

The weather and the long, light evenings tempted Alix out for a walk after a long day at her laptop. Glad of the chance to stretch her legs and enjoy the air, she climbed up into the hills behind Glenwhinnie House, where a lookout spot afforded wonderful views. In clear evening light distant peaks looked blue, but the nearer mountains showed fresh green, patched with brighter lime where young bracken unfurled lacy fronds. Peewits called as they darted after insects and a flight of chaffinch came winging to arc away over the hilltops to where the loch stretched silver-blue between its rugged hills. The village looked like a toy town, half-hidden among trees painted in a dozen different shades of green.

Alix had promised herself to go home, come spring, and spring had come, but where was home? Kansas no longer held any meaning, except as the place where she had grown up. New York . . . she had acquaintances there, but not many who might be called close friends. Alix had never found it easy to make friends. Not before she came to Glen Lachan. That was odd, wasn't it? Home, she thought, was not necessarily a place: home existed among people who cared about you.

People for whom you cared in return. People like Dame Janet, Maura and Fergus, Ailie Gordon and her dour old husband Murdo, Maggie Gillivray, Sir Anthony . . . and one particular man with dark hair, blue eyes and a stubborn independence that maddened her, piqued her, attracted her helplessly . . .

She had, she realized, been naïve to believe that she could abstain from involvement in Lachanbrae. After almost eight months here, she was involved heart and soul.

Irritated by her thoughts, she began to walk again, knowing she couldn't get lost so long as she kept the loch in sight below. In damp places marsh marigolds clustered around the birthing of bubbling waters that fed a clear stream. Prickly gorse bushes shone with vivid yellow blossom.

Trying to think of nothing but the natural beauty around her, to store the memory away for the day when she needed it, Alix failed to note the changes taking place in the sky. All at once a rising wind took the warmth from the air and the sun went out as if someone had turned a switch. Shivering, she looked up and saw black clouds roiling in from the west. Rain stabbed down, soon soaking through her light sweater and jeans. Behind the rain came low cloud, swallowing the hills in a writhing mist. Within minutes it enveloped Alix in a world of chill grey, where all she could see was a few square yards of hillside. It will be all right, she told herself, shuddering in her wet clothes. Follow the downslope. Just keep your head and get down to the glen road.

After a while she knew she was headed the wrong way, or maybe going round in circles. One piece of rock-strewn hillside looked much like another. And then the light faded, minute by minute. She was cold to the bone, wet, near exhausted. But she forced her aching legs to go on. Some hint of her location must show before long, surely?

As the dusk deepened, pot-holes added their danger. Several times she stumbled and fell. But at last the ground began to slant downward and slowly the mist lifted to form a ceiling of cloud from which drenching rain fell. Far away below, to her relief, a light beckoned. Maybe it was a croft. Gathering her strength, she went on down the decline, stiff with weariness, keeping her eyes on that light.

The ground dropped away beneath her. She fell, and went rolling helplessly down a steep slope covered in soaking bracken. She fetched up against a low wall and, pulling herself up with numb hands, she peered over the dry stone barrier and saw the light still shining. It was fixed to a whitewashed wall, over a black door. So near. By an effort of will she scrambled over the wall and staggered down the path to lean on the door, pounding weakly with the flat of her hand, praying that someone was at home.

The latch clicked and before she could move the door opened, sending her lurching to her knees on a rough doormat, while above her a man's voice said, 'What the . . . Alix? Alix!'

It was Niall! Oh, how wonderful! Niall was here. She was safe. But what was he doing way up in the hills?

'I got lost,' she croaked. 'Sorry.'

'Oh, for Pete's sake!' he chafed worriedly, and lifted her as though she were a child, slamming the door with his foot. 'Haven't you been warned about wandering about on your own?'

He took her into a bathroom and propped her against the wall while he ran the bath. With water cascading into the tub and steam rising, he returned to where Alix was huddled helplessly. 'Let's get you out of these wet things.'

'No!' With numb hands she fended him off, horrified eyes wide in her pale face, hair plastered to her skull.

'Then you do it,' he said brusquely. 'Can you? No, you can't, see? You're too cold. Stop acting like a fool and let me help you.'

He stripped her roughly, as if she were a doll, and helped her into the bath. Shuddering uncontrollably, she slid down into the blessed heat, relieved that he had added foam which allowed her a semblance of modesty.

'All right?' he asked. 'Have a soak. Don't

you dare get out until you're warm all through. I'll be back.'

In his absence she relaxed. Her thunderous heart-beat returned to something like normal and slowly the hot water revived her numbed flesh, making it tingle painfully before marvellous warmth seeped all through her body. It also revived her mind, making her look curiously round the bathroom. Its décor was decidedly dated. The suite was avocado-coloured, for heaven's sake! What was this place? The factor's cottage?

She sat up, wondering whether to stretch for a towel, but Niall had left the door ajar and must have heard the water slop. He appeared suddenly, his mouth turning wry as she hastily leaned against the side of the bath, hiding her body from his gaze.

Taking a big towel from a cupboard, he tossed it towards her. 'Can you manage?'

'No problem.'

'When you're ready, you'll find a bedroom opposite. There's a dressing gown on the back of the door. Help yourself, then come through.'

After a while she was dry, wrapped in a bath sheet while a smaller towel turbanned her hair. Cautiously opening the door, she saw a narrow hallway with the main front door at one end and several rooms opening off. Music came from a room to her left but she slipped straight across the hall, as instructed, and found herself in what was obviously Niall's bedroom, white walls and no-nonsense navy-striped curtains, against oddments of wooden furniture. A plain white duvet was pulled roughly across the bed—a large double bed, she noted.

Niall's presence was everywhere—the scent of his after-shave, clothes thrown across a chair, books and magazines scattered, keys, cash, and a pair of navy pyjamas slung across the hastily-tidied bed. Rain still beat against the window and full night had come early under the pall of cloud.

A dressing gown made of some harsh, scratchy material hung on the back of the door. Alix took it down and pushed an arm into the sleeve, but her skin shuddered at the rough caress of the fabric. She couldn't wear that—it would make her itch like she'd rolled in poison ivy! Then she noticed the pile of freshly-ironed laundry folded on a chest. It supplied her with a grey flannel shirt which, though over-sized on her, felt soft against her flesh and covered her from throat to knee once she did up the buttons. Rolling up the sleeves, she gave her hair a final towelling, borrowed Niall's comb to straighten the tangle and, feeling as presentable as circumstances allowed, went through to the living room.

The music was an album by Sting—her taste, too, as it happened. Seascapes on the walls, and pictures of sailing ships, while the furniture matched that in the bedroom, bits and pieces collected from many sources. An electric fire glowed in the hearth, with Niall sprawled in front of it on a hand-pegged hearthrug, absorbed in a book.

He looked up, giving her a startled once-over, and got to his feet. 'I said the dressing gown.'

'I know. But it felt like sandpaper. I found this instead. Hope that's OK.'

'You look about sixteen,' he informed her with a glower. 'Have a seat.'

Gathering the shirt around her, she sat down on the brown cord-fabric settee, feet tucked under her. Niall brought her a glass containing some amber liquid, which she eyed with suspicion. 'What is it?'

'It's a whisky mac—whisky with ginger cordial. Medicinal. Get it down you.' He retreated to an armchair, lounging with one foot crossed on the opposite knee, but the deliberately casual pose only advertised his tension. 'How do you feel now?'

'Tired,' she admitted. 'But I'm OK.' The room was filled with undercurrents that sang along her nerves, rippling her skin. 'When I saw the light, I had no idea this was your place. I thought I was miles from here.'

'Maybe that will teach you to listen to good advice,' he said roughly, shifting in the chair. 'This hill country can be treacherous, at any time of year. And you've only just recovered from that flu. Only an idiot would have stayed out so late, with the weather closing in.'

Recognizing the cause of his irritation, she peered into her glass. 'You're right, of course. And I'm sorry. I won't stay any longer than is necessary.'

'I didn't mean—' He let out his breath in an explosive sigh and shot to his feet, pacing restlessly. 'I've got your clothes in the tumble dryer. It's not the most efficient machine, but it shouldn't take too long.'

'Thanks. Niall, I'm sorry to be a nuisance, but . . . I was planning to see you some time this week. I . . . I shall be leaving Glenwhinnie soon.' She couldn't bring herself to look at him but she sensed that he had gone quite still, staring at her bent head.

'When?' was all he said.

'Soon. I planned to stay six months or so. Until spring. Well, it's May already.'

But . . . what about Dame Janet's birthday bash? You can't go before that.'

'I'm not planning to go back to the States. Not quite yet. I thought I might spend some time in London. I've always wanted to see London. I could fly back for the party.'

Niall returned to his chair, leaning forward anxiously. 'The whole plan depends on it being your birthday, too—on your being here to help us fool Dame Janet into thinking—'

'Oh, you can think of some other ruse!'

He came out of his chair, towering over her,

212

saying passionately, 'You can't go!'

Her hands gripped the glass so tight she thought it might shatter. The whisky mac was almost slopping over the rim. 'Are you asking me to stay?'

The silence stretched out unbearably. The album had ended and still the rain lashed against the window, driven on a high wind, while inside the room tension hummed like the string of a bow ready to fire.

Another sound joined the wind and rain—a car engine, coming closer. The vehicle's lights swept across the drawn curtains and it stopped.

'Hell!' Niall made for the hallway. 'Some people seem to think the factor should be on call twenty-four seven.'

Alix remained where she was, unable to move, unable to think. What was it this time— a fallen tree, a flooded bridge, a car slid off the road . . . ?

The most unwelcome sound she could think of came floating to her ears—the sound of Catriona's light, breathy voice, saying, 'What a perfectly filthy night! Darling, no! Let me come in. Don't send me away in this weather, it would be too cruel. I only want to talk. We've got to talk, darling.'

'How many times do I have to tell you?' Niall said, his voice low but cold and hard as steel. 'I said all I had to say a year ago.'

'But I've changed my ways, darling! I swear,

I'm a new woman. Please let me in. It's cold out here, and tipping with rain. Please . . . !'

'No, you don't!'

There was a crash, a shout from Niall. Alix leapt to her feet as Catriona, her scarlet raincoat dripping as she threw back the hood, marched into the room. She stopped dead, paling visibly at the sight of Alix standing there wearing nothing but a flannel shirt. Niall's flannel shirt.

'*You!*' Being the person she was, she didn't fail to reach the obvious conclusion. 'No wonder he didn't want me to come in!'

Behind her, Niall appeared with a hand clapped over his eye. 'You vicious little bitch!' he said through his teeth.

'You should have let me in when I asked!' Catriona stormed. 'Or you should have moved before the door hit you. It's not my fault. So! Broken up a cosy evening, have I? What a damn shame! I am so, so sorry.'

'This is not—' Niall began, but Alix over-rode him, saying sweetly, 'It's all right, Niall. We're all grown-ups here. It was time Catriona found out the truth, anyway.'

'You two-faced harpy!' Catriona sneered. 'So cool with it. Butter wouldn't melt in her mouth. Well, fine, Miss Alix Grant. Or should I say Miss Lexie Marisco?' she spat the name with slow venom. 'You know what will happen now, don't you?' with which she turned and shoved Niall out of the way. 'And as for you,

214

Mister Drummond . . . This was your last chance. I won't be back again. You're not the only fish in *my* sea.'

A rush of cold air, a slam of the main door, and Catriona had gone. Through the beating of the rain they heard her car start up and drive away at speed. Alix stared at the plain green curtain, waiting for the question she was sure must come. But when eventually Niall broke the silence what he said was: 'Why did you do that?'

Only then did she see the red weal swelling across his eyebrow, where the door must have hit him. 'Niall! Your face!'

He grimaced, a brusque gesture telling her to stay where she was. 'I'll live. Now answer the question—why did you let her think . . .'

'Seemed like a good idea at the time?' No, humour didn't help. Spreading her hands helplessly, she added, 'What do we care what she thinks?'

'It doesn't bother me if it doesn't bother you,' he said grimly. 'Maybe she's finally got the message.'

'Then you and she . . . you're not . . .'

'Not any more, thank God!' Sighing, he ran a hand through his hair and perched on the arm of the chair nearest the door—furthest from where Alix sat, she noted. 'Yes, I did get involved with Catriona for a while. She has friends—the Pattesons—who live not far away. They're in the venison trade, so I

215

became acquainted with them. Christmas before last, they asked me to a dinner party—to make up the numbers, I suspect. Cat was there and . . . well, you must know what she's like. There was I, a lone widower, ripe for the taking, so . . .'

'Yes.' She held her breath, unwilling to break the mood. Was he actually *talking* to her at last, telling her something important about himself?

'I'd been alone a long time. But I knew almost at once that she wasn't my sort. It was a fling, for both of us. She'd have dropped me soon enough when she'd had her fun. Problem was . . . *I* was the one who ended it, and that annoyed her. Ever since, every time she gets bored with life, she weekends with the Pattesons and comes over to Glenwhinnie, calling in at the office, turning up here unannounced. It's been even worse since you came. She had the gall to talk Joan McNab into giving her the spare keys to this cottage. I came in and found her cooking dinner, wearing nothing but an apron and some flimsy black underwear.' His voice was thick with disgust. 'I threw her out. It's a stupid game she's playing. But every time I send her away it only makes her more determined. She seems bent on proving that no man can resist her.'

Even in flimsy black underwear, Alix thought. What a blow for Catriona's ego. But

216

then she herself had seen examples of Niall's strength of will, however sorely tempted. Look at him now, doggedly keeping his distance despite the tug of mutual desire that he must be as aware of as she. Or was the need for his nearness only in *her* mind? Was she fooling herself, as Catriona had done?

'Have you told this to Maura and Fergus?' she asked. 'You do know how worried they are?'

'Of course I do.' He sighed. 'As it happens, I saw Maura just after she'd been to visit you—haring down the road in floods of tears. Naturally I stopped and took her home, and set the record straight with her and Dad.' He slid her a sidelong, half-ashamed look. 'I hadn't realized what was being said. Sometimes I get so immersed in my work I forget what's going on in the rest of the world. But thanks.'

'For what?'

'For telling Maura she ought to ask me about it.' Another edgy glance, veiled and questing. 'She, um . . . she was really upset, wasn't she?'

'Beside herself.' Remembering Maura's visit, and the way it ended, she ventured, 'She didn't make a lot of sense, to be honest. She seemed to think she'd let out some secret, but . . .'

After a distinct pause, he said evenly, 'What sort of secret?'

'You tell *me*, Niall. What sort of secret might it be?'

He quirked his mouth into a rueful curve. 'Maura gets the wrong end of the stick, sometimes. You must know that. She misunderstands. Misinterprets. Anyway . . . We'd better see if your clothes are dry. It's late. I don't know about you, but I have to be at work early tomorrow.'

Some twenty minutes later, he drew the Range Rover up outside her gate, they said a casual, 'Good night,' and Alix climbed down. But just before she could close the door Niall spoke her name and she paused to look back at him in the faint light from the dashboard. 'Yes?'

'You're not really planning to go away before midsummer, are you? I mean, we shall need you here if we're going to spring the surprise the way we planned. It was all your idea, after all. Without you, it won't work.'

'I know,' Alix said quietly.

'Then you'll stay—until after the ball?'

'Until then.'

His smile broke her heart. 'I'm glad. Thank you. It will mean a lot to Dame Janet. Good night.'

She didn't cry. She felt too empty. Putting her aching body to bed, she lay awake for what seemed like hours, going over everything that had happened between herself and Niall. Had she totally misunderstood his feelings for

218

her?

*   *   *

She woke in the middle of the night, from a nightmare involving a witch-like Catriona and a flock of gulls that came swooping round with thrusting microphones and flashing cameras. Heart thudding, Alix lay listening to the steady patter of rain on her window, while her mind threw off the dream. Evidently she wasn't quite so sanguine about discovery as she had thought. The prospect of being invaded by the press was especially unpleasant when the privacy being disturbed belonged not only to her but to Dame Janet, and everyone else in Lachanbrae. Who knew what patterns of scandal some nosy reporter might weave from threads of idle gossip? Would Catriona be mean enough to carry out her threat? She had hurled Alix's real name at her last night—for 'real' read most well-known, most notorious, most . . . Wait!

Her scurrying thoughts snagged on a mystery that had got pushed to the bottom of the heap beneath the more compelling reality of Niall and her overwhelming need of him. Now, puzzlement wrote the question large across her mind: why hadn't Niall reacted to the strange name Catriona had flung at her? Why hadn't he asked what mischief Catriona might make to punish Alix?

219

Despite the hour, she went down and activated her lap-top to send an e-mail to Niall's personal electronic address: *I need to see you. It's important. You choose where and when.*

In the morning, she noted the Range Rover arriving, taking Niall to the office. She connected her laptop and waited. Twenty minutes later, the reply came: *Fairy Bridge. Ten o'clock. What's wrong?*

Alix decided it might be safer not to reply.

*   *   *

The so-called Fairy Bridge lay only half a mile or so from the lodge, where the footpath along the lochside crossed the burn—as Alix had learned to call the small river. Since the path would be muddy after the previous night's downpour, she pulled on wellington boots and a rainproof blue jacket with her jeans.

Morning had brought the sun up but the trees still dripped, light sparkling in the young leaves. The burn was running fast and high, but not quite covering the planks on the little bridge. Secluded as the spot was, especially with the trees in leaf, the larger bridge carrying the glen road was visible twenty yards away. Niall had chosen precisely the right location, ideal for a private chat, but public enough to prevent too much intimacy developing. Well, fine. Neutral ground was just right for some straight-talking.

She stood on the little plank bridge, leaning on the hand-rail to watch the water foaming beneath her, checking her watch every minute or so. He was late. Would he come by the road or along the path?

Even though she was watching for him, he took her by surprise, coming not from the direction of Glenwhinnie but from the east, further up the glen. His left eye was swollen, surrounded by a blackening bruise where Catriona had hit him with the door last night. The thought of it made Alix wince, but she was too bitterly angry to let sympathy deflect her from her purpose.

Niall stopped on the path six feet away. 'I'm late. Sorry. Problems up at Jock Moray's place. What's this all about, Alix?'

'How long have you known my real identity?'

'Ah.' It came very low, but his tone and his expression told her enough—her assumption had been correct.

'How long, Niall?'

'Three months, give or take.'

Her hands clenched on the wet wood of the rail as she stared down at the rushing burn, too numbed to say anything except, 'I see.'

'It's true, then? You're Claudia Cantrelle's daughter? The one who went missing after her funeral? The one the press have been looking for?'

'Catriona told you.'

'No. That is . . . yes, she did, a couple of weeks ago, but . . . I already knew. It was Murdo who recognized you. From a photograph in the paper.'

'*Murdo?!*' Incredulity half choked her.

'He and Ailie follow all the celebrity gossip. He sort of hinted at it on New Year's Day— when we were clearing snow. I didn't believe him. Laughed at him. But he seemed pretty convinced and then . . . when you came up with this loan . . .' He shrugged. 'It began to make sense. I tackled Murdo about it again and he produced the newspaper clipping with your picture in it. He'd kept it since November.'

'Who else knows?'

'Just the four of us at Glenwhinnie— Murdo, Ailie, Dame Jay and me. Since we knew you'd come here for privacy we all agreed not to intrude. We assumed you'd tell us the truth in your own good time, when you were ready.'

They had known. All this time. The four of them. Alix didn't know whether to scream in pain or laugh like a loon. Instead, she beat her fist on the hand-rail, said hoarsely, 'Damn it, Niall!' and turned to stride away from him. She might have run, but the path was slippery and with tears hot in her eyes she couldn't see too well.

After a while, she stopped to lean her back against a tree and recover her composure. How did she feel? Like an idiot, that was how. Foolish and lost and very much alone.

She heard Niall following her. He stopped a few feet away but she stayed as she was, staring down at her mud-caked boots.

'You want to talk about it?' he asked.

'No.'

'Are you angry with me?'

'Yes.'

'Why?'

Of all the fatuous questions! She looked up, blinded by tears. 'Because you let me go on thinking . . .' As he reached for her, she fended him off. 'No, don't! Don't touch me. Don't!' She beat ineffectually with her fists against his chest. 'I hate you, Niall. I hate you!'

Ignoring all her struggles and protests, he folded her into his arms and held her safe and warm against him, his head bent over hers while sobs wracked through her like waters from a broken dam. All she could do was cling to him helplessly, not thinking beyond the moment. She needed him and he was there. That was everything.

Niall didn't try to console her with words, nor did he tell her not to cry, he simply held her close against his heart until the wrenching sobs and tears turned to shuddering deep breaths. In the end it was Alix who, returning to her senses, eased a little away from him. She was reminded of another time he had held her, when mascara had smeared his white sweater. This time her tears had wet the front of a grey flannel shirt. A very familiar grey flannel shirt.

Aware that her face was a mess, her eyes swollen and red-rimmed, she looked up at him, slantwise. 'That's the shirt I had on last night.'

'I know.' That was all he said in words, but his eyes held a hundred tender messages and as he bent slowly to kiss her she lifted her lips in response.

This time, she was sure—he cared for her just as much as she cared for him.

EIGHT

They walked by the loch, making away from Glenwhinnie House, past the lay-by where Niall had parked his Range Rover and on to a spot where flat rocks provided adequate seating. An arbour of trees rustled above and behind. The loch rippled away into the distance, blue beneath the sky, bearing a mirror-image of Ben Lachan rearing highest among the surrounding hills. There, finally, Alix was able to talk truth.

She tried to tell it with humour, making

224

light of the heartaches—how she had grown up in Kansas, adopted daughter of a couple named Marisco, Bette turned thirty and Arturo in his forties, married for over ten years and childless until she came along. 'They always called me "Lexie"—short for Alexis. They said my birth mother had died having me, and nobody knew who my father was, nor was there any other family. So I was up for adoption and they went along and "chose" me. That was all they knew. At least ... that's what they told me.'

Ironically, when Alix was almost three Bette Marisco finally gave her husband a longed-for child of his own, a son, Tom. After that, it became ever more evident that Art Marisco considered Lexie a charity case, under his roof only so long as she worked for her place. When Bette fell ill with multiple sclerosis Lexie was the chosen housekeeper and main carer.

'I didn't mind,' she said. 'I loved Mom. She was always good to me and tried to make up for . . .' for all the times Pop was indifferent and young Tom unkind, she meant, though she didn't say it. 'Anyway, she died the year I turned eighteen and I decided it was time to leave. I went to New York to study. Worked in a bookshop part-time, and did some waitressing to make ends meet.'

She had not made many friends—lots of acquaintances, but none of them had got too close. Easier to keep people at arms' length rather than risk more hurt, though at the time she hadn't realized that was what she was doing.

Niall flung a stone across the lake, to skip and hop over the surface. 'That Marisco man ought to be horse-whipped! How could he do that to a child?'

'He did his best. He wasn't a bad man.'

'No, just totally self-centred. And all that time . . . How did Claudia Cantrelle fit into the picture?'

'I knew she was Mom's sister, but . . . well, at home she was kind of a taboo subject—I always thought that was because she'd broken away, done forbidden things. Mom and Dad were strict Presbyterians and to their mind Claudia had gone beyond the pale. All those husbands, the scandals, the lovers . . . She used to send me things, Christmas and birthdays, always from "Aunt" Claudia. I met her briefly, a few times, but Mom's ditzy younger sister, who blew in now and then bringing presents, seemed a separate person from Claudia Cantrelle the movie star.

'After I went to New York I hardly ever thought about her, let alone talked about her. It would have been like attention-seeking, and people would've asked too many questions I couldn't answer. Just after Mom—Bette Marisco—died, before I went to New York, I got hold of my real birth certificate. The space for the father's name was blank and under mother's name it said "Mary Jane Sanders". I knew Bette had been a Sanders before she married, and when I tackled Pop about it he told me Mary Jane had been the youngest of the sisters and that she died having me, her illegitimate child. They were all shamed by it, he said, and that's why they'd kept it a secret.' Fighting renewed bitterness, she took a deep breath before adding, 'That was when I knew I had to get away, to be on my own and . . . "find myself", I guess. Find out who the real me was, if I could. I never imagined I'd ever find out who my real parents were.'

'But you did.'

'Yes. I did. Last July. I learned it from Claudia's lawyers, after she died. They informed me she had made me her sole heir.'

The sudden death of movie star Claudia Cantrelle the previous summer had made headlines across the world, with stories of her most recent divorce, her wild excesses, her drinking, and of the final party when half of Hollywood had been present, when Claudia had vanished into the night, driving her new Mercedes. The car went off a road above the sea and next morning they had found Claudia's mangled body among the wreckage. Some said she had been drunk; some said she had been snorting cocaine; some said she was out of her mind with sadness. Some called it suicide. The inquest verdict was 'accidental

227

death'.

Alix had shared the shock and pity that accompanied news of the tragic end of a glamorous actress in her mid-forties (she had claimed to be 36, helped by plastic surgery). Alix had been sad for her little-known 'aunt'. But that was all, until the letter with its embossed heading and its incredible news had arrived.

Re-living that time more clearly than she had done for months, she watched the loch, hugging her knees and speaking in a low, husky voice. 'She had written a letter for me. How sorry she was for lying to me. How she'd suffered for it over the years. How deeply she had loved my natural father. How she wished it had all been different. It was all about *her*. Trying to ease her conscience.

'When the news broke—when the press came after me—I went back to Kansas and made Dad tell me the rest of it. What he didn't know, I learned from Sir Anthony last February.

'It seems Claudia had an affair when she was over here in Scotland shooting scenes for her first proper movie—'Hope Springs', if you ever saw it. She was only eighteen and already being hailed as the next screen goddess. In Edinburgh she met this good-looking young doctor, Duncan Alexander Grant. Fell for him big time. He wanted her to stay with him, but he had no money until he'd established himself. And she was ambitious, she wanted to be a movie star, not a doctor's wife. They quarrelled, and she went back to the States— apparently without realizing she was pregnant. She thought about an abortion but she'd been raised to believe that would be sinful, so she was torn. She went back to Kansas and then her childless sister Bette agreed to adopt the child. After I was born, apparently Claudia took a few weeks getting back in shape, and went right back to Hollywood, back to her interrupted career.'

'Oh, Lord, Alix . . .' Niall breathed, reaching to touch her.

She sprang up and moved away, unable to bear his sympathy, hunching into herself as she stared at the blurred sparkle of the loch. 'The lawyers assured me they'd keep the news of my existence quiet, but of course someone told the press. They found out where I was living and descended on me. I couldn't move without cameras flashing, microphones thrust in my face, reporters yelling . . . They disrupted my entire life. I fled back to Kansas, but Pop was furious with me when the press started clamouring at his door. I wasn't thinking straight. I hardly knew who I was any more. Everything I'd ever believed about myself had been a lie. I had to get right away for a while, to get my head together. But there was nowhere I could run to, except . . .

'In her letter, Claudia had told me to get in

touch with Sir Anthony McKenzie if I wanted to know more. He was the one person I could think of who the press couldn't possibly know about. So in desperation I phoned him and asked for help. When Sir Anthony suggested I might come here, to Lachanbrae, I went for it. The rest you know.'

'Is your father still alive?'

'No. He died nearly twenty years ago. In Africa. From malaria.' She leaned against a tree, her cheek against the rough bark. 'Claudia hurt him badly. Sir Anthony says he never got over her, just concentrated on his work and stopped caring about his own welfare.' She retold the story she had had from Sir Anthony, of his fortuitous meeting with Claudia two years before, and her shock on learning the circumstances of Duncan's blighted life and early death. 'He said she was distraught. Nearly fainted.'

'Don't you believe it?'

'I don't know what I believe any more. I never really knew her, did I? Maybe she *did* have regrets. Maybe she did feel bad over Duncan. Maybe she was worried abut her career—she couldn't go on being the beautiful ingénue much longer, could she? She'd already had so much plastic surgery she looked about as human as Barbie Doll. Oh . . . Who knows what she really thought or felt? She probably didn't know truth from fiction any more. She was the star of her own fairy story and Duncan was her "lost love".' Alix managed a hard laugh, shaking back her hair as she looked up into the shimmering leaves above. 'Excuse me if I sound cynical but . . . She never cared about me. What did she do for me, after all? She lied to me, she disowned me, and then she turned me into a media circus, a freak. I felt like a fugitive. Like a hunted animal. That's why I came here and tried to merge into the scenery. That's why I've been so uptight and crazy. I was terrified someone would find out who I was and start the whole thing up again.'

'Oh, hell,' Niall said sombrely from close behind her. 'If that happens now it will be down to me, won't it? Because of Catriona's stupid, spoiled-brat jealousy . . . I'm sorry, Alix. It's the last thing I'd have wanted to happen.'

Very slowly, she turned to look at him, seeing him more clearly as her tears dried. A wonderful calm certainty was stealing through her, like sunlight breaking through heavy cloud. 'No, you don't understand, Niall. If it happens now, I can face it. Let Catriona do her worst. I know who I am now. I'm not Lexie Marisco, the unwanted adopted child; I'm not the bastard-born Alexandra Mary Sanders, nor am I Claudia Cantrelle's guilty little secret. I'm me—Alix Grant. That's what Lachanbrae has done for me—it has given me my own self.'

231

'Then I'm glad you came.'

She reached for his hand, holding it between her own. Niall didn't pull away but neither did he respond. 'Whatever happens,' Alix said, 'you mustn't feel responsible. In some ways I hope Cat *does* break the story. It would be a relief. Except . . . I wouldn't wish it on my friends here. You, Dame Janet, the people in the village . . .' As a new thought occurred, she let a corner of her mouth curve in a cynical twist. 'Or would it put Glenwhinnie on the map? Bring more tourists in?'

Niall was frowning, looking inward onto his own thoughts and evidently what he found troubled him. He said slowly, 'No, not right now. We can do without a load of sensation-seekers raking up the muck.'

'I don't believe it will come to that, though. Whatever Catriona may have threatened to do, I don't believe she'll dare call the press. Her father would have something to say about it if she did. He promised me total privacy while I was here.'

'Time will tell, I suppose.' He still looked and sounded dubious.

'So it will.' She watched him through lowered lashes, wondering—as always—what was going on in his mind. 'Niall . . .'

But as she made a move towards him he shook free of her grasp and bent to scoop up a final stone, flinging it duck-and-drake across the loch's glassy surface. 'It won't be for much longer, anyway,' he said almost to himself, watching the spreading ripples where the stone had skipped and plopped. 'When we've got this midsummer fling over, the world's your oyster. You'll be free to go anywhere you like. London, New York, Rome, Paris . . .'

'Or Lachanbrae?' she ventured.

When he looked at her he had put on a smile that curved his mouth but left his eyes bleak. 'You wouldn't want to stay here, Alix. You don't belong in this backwater and you know it. And speaking of time . . .' with a glance at his watch, 'I'd better be getting on. Duty calls.' He clambered lithely up to the rocks and strode past her, leaping the last gap back to the path. 'See you, Alix.'

Alix stood for a moment staring after him in numb disbelief. Was that all he had to say? Did he really mean that there was no place for her in his life? She didn't believe it. She refused to believe it!

Or was it that she didn't *want* to believe it?

*   *   *

She went up to the big house to see Dame Janet, able at last to be honest with the old woman and to thank her for her protection these last months. Reckless of any possible risk of revelations in the red-top scandal-sheets, she also went to see Fergus and Maura

233

and told them the truth about herself. To them, her true identity didn't seem to make much difference: she was still their friend Alix, just as welcome in their home, and just as teased by Fergus. They certainly would not gossip about her private affairs.

It appeared that Niall had not talked about her intention to quit Lachanbrae in the near future, for no one mentioned her coming departure. They did, however, comment that Niall was sporting a 'beautiful black eye'.

'Walked into a door, so he says,' Dame Janet snorted.

'It's the truth,' Alix replied. 'I was there when it happened.'

She reassured Fergus and Maura on the same point, though that caused more problems because Niall had told them he was alone when the accident occurred. They drew their own conclusions—if she had been at Niall's cottage and he had deliberately omitted to mention the fact . . . well, well! But they seemed to approve rather than otherwise, which distressed Alix.

Although she knew that she ought to begin making plans for leaving Glen Lachan, instead she found herself inventing excuses to delay. First she was too tired after her ordeal in the hills, and then she couldn't decide how to go about packing, or where to go. London was still favourite as a beginning, but exactly where in London, and when? Somewhere in her mind she knew she was clutching at straws, but she couldn't help herself. She simply didn't want to think about life beyond Lachanbrae and she certainly couldn't put her mind to it until after the birthday ball, due to take place on the twenty-fourth of June. The ball, and pleasing Dame Janet, were the biggest excuses of all.

She personally supervised all the details for the coming party. Determined to have everything just perfect she found herself discussing buffet menus with caterers, flowers with florists, staircase construction with carpenters, flooring with carpet-layers, and subterfuge with, of all people, Murdo Gordon. She saw Niall frequently, usually at a distance though there were occasions when the two of them had to get together to discuss some aspect of arrangements for the ball. Every meeting served only to increase her heartache. She loved Niall Drummond, dreamed of him each night and woke with his name on her lips and his image in her mind. Remembering many tender moments they had shared she felt sure he cared for her too, to some extent, in his own strange Celtic way. So why, why, why did he keep her so firmly at arms' length? She might have begged him for explanations, but having been firmly rejected more than once her pride objected to inviting yet another rebuff.

On a day when the June heat grew unbearable, Alix donned a bikini under a sundress and, with a towel and some bottles of mineral water stuffed into a back-pack, followed the river up into the hills, paddling some of the way in the blessedly cool water. Far off any beaten track lay a spot Dame Janet had shown her during one of their walks, a shady place full of the scent of birch trees, where local people occasionally came to swim in a deep pool dappled by sunlight through green leaves. Trout lazed among fronds of weed in clear cold water that rushed down the hillside in a low rocky fall to fill the hollow before rippling over a stony brink and tumbling on towards the loch.

That day, Alix had the place to herself, a perfect location to relax and, perhaps, to decide what to do with the rest of her life. She waded carefully in, gasping as the cold water reached higher. When it covered her to the waist she ducked right under and, every nerve alive with the chill shock on her skin, began to swim. After the heat of the last few days, the water came as a blessed relief.

She let herself float, eyes closed, her mind roaming, testing possibilities. For a woman with ridiculous amounts of money (she couldn't put an exact figure on it but rounded out it ended in a string of noughts), almost any dream might come true. Houses, jewellery, clothes, business opportunities, charitable ventures . . . Problem was, whatever prospect opened in her imagination it all looked pretty empty and futile without Niall Drummond as part of the picture. Money can't buy me love? How right the Beatles had been!

Something small and hard hit her outflung arm. Thinking she had drifted towards the edge of the pool, Alex turned over and stretched a foot for the stones below, only to find the bottom was out of her depth. She went under and came up wiping water from her face.

Someone was standing on the bank, half-hidden in the dappled shade. As her eyes adjusted she saw that it was Niall, playing with a handful of stones. He wore blue jeans, his shirt hanging open outside them, and to judge from his tan he often went shirtless when his work took him out of doors. He was barefoot, too, shoes and socks thrown in a tangle with a small towel on the rocks not far away.

'I thought you were a salmon,' he said, skimming another pebble, aiming it some feet away from her this time. 'This happens to be my private swimming hole. How did you find it?'

'Dame Janet showed it to me.'

'I might have known. Nothing's sacred any more.'

Kicking lazily, Alix floated toward him. 'The water's great. Why don't you come in?'

'I was planning to. I just hadn't expected company.'

'You want me to go?'

Casting her an evil look, he tossed off his shirt, took a few strides to where a flat rock reached out over the deepest part of the pool, and dived in with hardly a splash.

Hauling herself up to sit mermaid-like on the flat rock, Alix watched him swim strongly under water the length of the pool, take a breath and dive to come back again, athletic as a seal. He surfaced in front of her, hair plastered to his head, water streaming from brown skin over rippling muscle. Sky blue eyes flung a challenge into hers in the moment before his lashes flickered and his gaze ran over her, making her aware of how much of her was on view. Her body responded helplessly, making Niall's mouth go grim. He vaulted from the water and took a few jerky strides to where her towel hung from a branch, flung it at her and turned away to snatch up his own towel and start to scrub it over his skin, his back turned to her.

Entirely aware of the strong sexual current running between them, Alix said lightly, 'Do you usually swim in your jeans?'

'I prefer skinny-dipping,' he growled. 'When there aren't any trespassing females around, that is. Are you decent yet?'

238

Alix was towelling her hair, the heat of the day warming her skin. 'I'd say so.'

He looked round, one glance taking in the sight of her slender curves barely concealed by the damp bikini. 'You call that decent?'

'Sure I do! On any beach in the world I'd be fully dressed. Overdressed, on some.'

'Yes, but this isn't a beach,' Niall pointed out. 'Put some clothes on, for Pete's sake! A man can only take so many cold showers.'

'You wouldn't need cold showers if you weren't such a puritan!' Irritated, she wrapped her towel round her sarong-wise. 'This will have to do. Sorry, I forgot my long black robe and yashmak. And maybe you'll be kind enough to put your shirt on—I'm not made of wood, either. And if you say it's different for a man, Niall, I swear I'll hit you!' She moved away, furious with him, and sat down on a grassy bank in full sunlight, arms clasped round her knees as she scowled across the shimmering pool.

Sighing audibly, Niall slung his shirt round his shoulders and came to sit beside her. 'What are you so grumpy about?'

'You know the answer to that. You're inhuman. You're not normal.'

'I'm all too normal. That's just the trouble.'

Alix looked round, meeting blue eyes that said things his lips seemed unable to form. And then, as if he couldn't hold back any longer, he reached for her, kissing her with

239

tender longing as he pressed her back onto the grass, stretching himself close beside her.

Alix slid her arms round him, glorying in the feel of cool damp skin that warmed under her touch. This was what she had hoped for, longed for, for so many weeks. She was ready to take the next step, to make this relationship complete. Once they had made love it would be different. She knew it.

When he lifted his head she gazed up at him through a mist, seeing his face as a dark blur against the sky. 'Niall . . .' the murmur sighed out of her.

He said, 'I love you.'

'What?' Alix felt lightningstruck, joy and disbelief surging through her.

She tilted her head, trying to see his face more clearly, but before she could read his expression he pulled abruptly away from her and sat up, picking up a small pebble that he tossed in his hand. Through gritted teeth, his voice deep with disgust, he added, 'You heard what I said. It's true, God help me, though it doesn't make the slightest difference to anything.'

Alix could find no answer. She lay watching him, her heart beating suffocatingly fast. How many times could he do this to her? How many times would she allow it? To give her hope and then slap her down . . .

After what seemed forever, he said, 'You've never asked me about Barbara, my wife.'

'No.' She lifted herself on one elbow, watching his profile, wondering what revelations waited. 'I figured you'd tell me when you were good and ready.'

The silence lengthened. Alix heard the water rushing softly, into the pool and out again, while a warm breeze flirted among the trees and birds chirped. High in the sky a large bird hung with outspread wings. An eagle? She couldn't see it clearly for the hurting brightness. Somewhere far off a sheep bleated plaintively and was answered by its lamb.

Niall said, 'I loved Barbara very much. I had never felt that way before and never expected to feel that way again. It doesn't happen twice. I believed that with all my heart and soul. When she died, so soon, so young . . . I thought I was destined to be alone. And so I have been, for nine long years. Apart from occasional physical flings. Like with Cat.' He hurled the pebble into the river, watched the ripples spread, and eventually added, low-voiced, 'And then *you* came along.'

Half-turning, he let his glance slide over her, along her bare legs and the drying towel draped round her, to her slender arms and shoulders, her tangle of fair hair, her face. 'You,' he said again, and the single word held memories of all the months they had known each other, when he had fought against his attraction to her only to have it grow ever stronger.

241

He turned away again, as if he couldn't bear to look at her. Hurting for him, Alix scrambled up to kneel behind him, her arms circling his shoulders and her cheek on the back of his neck. 'I'm glad you loved Barbara. But if she loved you the same way she wouldn't have wanted you to be alone. Nine years . . . it's an awful long time, Niall.'

'When she was lying in that hospital . . . We both knew she wasn't going to make it. I vowed there'd never be anyone else for me, but she . . . she said that she hoped I'd eventually find someone else, and be happy. That's what she wanted for me.'

Alix moved to where she could see his face, a hand on his cheek making him look at her. 'So what's stopping you?'

The pain in his eyes made her heart turn over, but he didn't answer her question. Instead he said, 'Shall I tell you something funny? For a while back there . . . I got it into my head you might be John McDonald's daughter.'

'John McDonald? Oh . . . you mean, Dame Janet's black sheep brother?'

'When you said you were hoping to find out more about your father . . . It seemed like the most obvious answer. Why else would you have picked Glenwhinnie?'

'But Duncan Grant was my father. I showed you his picture.'

'Not until weeks later. Stupid, wasn't it?'

'Absolutely crazy,' she agreed, perplexed. 'But what's that got to do with anything?' She waited, but he didn't answer. 'Niall, you're still not being honest with me!'

'There's nothing else I can say.' He got up without haste and stood shrugging into his shirt, running his fingers through his hair to tidy it. 'I'm sorry, Alix. This wasn't supposed to happen. I had no right to tell you how I feel. I shouldn't have said anything at all, but . . . No, I can't explain. You and I . . . it's not going to happen. It's not possible. The best thing you can do, for both our sakes, is to go away—as soon as this blessed party's over—and forget that we ever met.'

*   *   *

For the rest of that month Alix did her best not to think of the numb pain that existed where her heart used to be. She had been hurt before, but not quite like this. Lately she had allowed herself to believe that maybe some people did care about her—people like Dame Janet, and Fergus and Maura, Ailie Gordon and even dour old Murdo, and then Niall . . . petal by frozen petal she had allowed her feelings for him to unfurl until her most vulnerable self was open to him. She had let it happen in spite of all the warning signs. Like a fool. Hadn't she learned by now? Her whole life had been based on rejections, one after

243

another. Why had she let herself dream that this relationship might turn out different from the rest? What an idiot she was! A stupid, dreamy idiot. Prince Charming existed only in fairy tales.

In private, alone at the lodge, she began to pack her belongings. In public, among her friends in the village, she talked of leaving by the end of June, so that everyone should regard her departure as a long-planned occurrence, a natural if regrettable end to her sojourn among them.

'But what about Niall?' Fergus Drummond asked in consternation when she dropped by the cottage one day. 'I thought you two—'

'We've been friends,' Alix said, her voice seeming to echo in the emptiness inside her. 'We shall go on being friends. I'll keep in touch. Maybe you and Maura can come visit me some day, when I've decided where I'm going.'

'Ach, lass . . .' His hand came warmly on her arm. 'If ye've no one waiting for you, no place to call home . . .'

'Oh, there are lots of people!' Alix lied brightly. 'And lots of places. I haven't quite decided which one is right for me.'

Dame Janet, too, expressed her sadness at the prospect of losing Alix's company, though her over-riding concern appeared to be that Alix should not leave until after their joint birthday celebration.

'Our little dinner party wouldn't be the same without you,' the old woman said. 'I'm so looking forward to sharing the occasion with you. And, as a preliminary . . . why don't we go to Edinburgh for a couple of days? Just the two of us. I feel in need of a little break and I'm sure it would do you good, too.'

Alix feigned surprise but allowed the old lady to persuade her into agreeing. In fact, the Edinburgh trip was all part of the plan to surprise Dame Janet, getting her well out of the way while the final touches were added to the ballroom. Alix's aim while in the capital was to persuade the lady laird to buy an evening gown suitable for their 'small dinner party'. Meanwhile unsuspecting Dame Janet, prompted by Niall and Ailie, was under the impression that it was she who was to enveigle Alix into buying a glamorous outfit for the same occasion.

Staying at one of the best hotels in Edinburgh, Alix gained much secret pleasure and amusement from watching Dame Janet try to manipulate her, all innocent of what was really going on. Alix allowed herself to be manoeuvred into an exclusive fashion designer's salon, where she pretended reluctance to try on the lovely gowns.

'Aren't they a bit over-the-top for a dinner party?'

'Nonsense! This is my one and only time to turn seventy-five, so . . . well, I've persuaded

245

Niall and Ailie to turn it into a full dress occasion. We're doing the thing properly. Go the whole hog, as they say.' She slanted an arch look at Alix. 'Niall looks magnificent in a dinner jacket, you know.'

Alix was sure that he did, but she hid the momentary twinge of regret that assailed her. 'In that case, what are *you* going to wear?'

'Me? Oh . . . one of my old concert gowns will do. Nobody's going to be looking at me.'

'Oh, come on, Jay. Your old concert gowns must be way past their sell-by date. Let's get you something new. After all, you're the lady laird of Glenwhinnie. You have to look the part.'

It took most of the afternoon, but by the time they returned to their hotel it was a case of 'mission accomplished' for both of them.

Alix drove back to Lachanbrae on the afternoon of the twenty-third, time enough for Dame Janet to rest and revive her energy overnight before starting to get ready for the expected 'dinner party'. Having dropped the old woman off at the big house, Alix returned to the lodge and phoned the office to make sure all was going according to plan. Niall assured her that the ballroom looked magnificent; however, all doors leading to that area had been locked and the keys confiscated—Dame Janet had been told that the area was dangerous because of the renovations and recent toxic spraying for

246

woodworm, and in case she got curious dust sheets had been hung over the windows.

Dame Janet, however, remained sweetly unaware of the surprise being planned for her.

*   *   *

Next morning Alix was surprised and touched by the amount of mail that arrived for her, a score of cards and greetings from her new friends in Lachanbrae. They had accepted her for the person she was, and several of them expressed their sorrow at the news that she must soon go away from the glen. Niall had sent a card with a picture of trees overhanging a pool, a painful reminder of their last private encounter. The message saddened Alix anew: *With warmest wishes. May you find your heart's desire.* He had signed it simply 'N' though he had added a kiss as if to mitigate the starkness of it. The message was a clear goodbye: he had not changed his mind. That being so, his wish for her to find her heart's desire rang hollow—the only thing her heart really desired was for ever out of reach.

But however bad she felt inside she had to wear a happy face for one more day. For Dame Janet's sake. Alix determined that nothing should mar the surprise she and Niall had long planned for their favourite surrogate aunt.

To begin with she had persuaded the old

247

woman to join her and have a hairdo, which was actually a ruse to transport Dame Janet well out of the way so that the caterers and florists could move in. Accordingly she drove up to the big house early, picked up Dame Janet, and took her into Auchinveray, where she had made hair appointments for them both. First they must have coffee (to take up more time), and after the hairdresser had coiffured them both into glamour and elegance Alix delayed her old friend further by treating her to a protracted lunch at the Bridge Hotel, assuring her that Ailie would have everything under control back at the house.

Mid-afternoon, turning in at the main gates, she stopped outside the lodge and went in to collect her new dress, protected inside a plastic cover, along with the small overnight case she had packed in readiness. Dame Janet had insisted that Alix must come to Glenwhinnie House to prepare for the party and to spend the night afterwards: 'You don't want to be driving up here in your party frock, or trailing home on your own late at night,' had been her reasoning. Alix had not argued; being at Glenwhinnie suited her purpose fine.

While in the lodge, she made a quick call to the office, to make sure all was going to plan. It was Murdo who answered: 'Aye, it's all tickety-boo. Come ye on home now. Over and oot.' Come home . . . The steward never ceased to amaze her!

She paused a moment, surveying the packing cases and boxes which stood ready for tomorrow. She would not spend another night in this little house where she had felt so safe. Come morning she would be gone. It was all arranged. Edinburgh first, then on to London, and then . . .

Beyond that, the future hung shrouded by mist. So many possibilities lay open, everything she could ever imagine doing with her life . . . Except what her heart most longed for.

No, don't think about it. Worry about it tomorrow. For now, just concentrate on the next few hours. This was to be her farewell, and her sincere Thank You, to her dear friend Jay McDonald. Everything must go exactly to plan.

When at last they arrived in the front courtyard at Glenwhinnie House, Alix noted with relief that no telltale vehicle remained in sight. Apart from the yellow Range Rover, parked as usual near the side wing, the courtyard was empty, with no outward sign of any activity taking place behind the peaceful sun-washed façade. Climbing out of her Mazda, Alix glanced up at the office window, where Niall was waiting to give her a thumbs-up sign. She replied with a surreptitious wave before going round to help Dame Janet.

In the house, Ailie was doing her bit to add

to the deception by laying a dinner table for eight guests, with all the best silver and glassware polished to a high sheen. Dame Janet inspected the dining room, enquired after the progress of the food, and wanted to start helping.

'No, I'll help Ailie if she needs it,' Alix insisted. 'I'm sure she has it all under control.'

'All well in hand,' said Ailie. 'Don't you think Dame Janet ought to rest before dinner, Miss Grant? It will be a long evening, and she's still tired from your excitement in Edinburgh.'

Dame Janet argued that she wasn't in the least bit tired, but eventually they persuaded her to go to her room and put her feet up. When Alix checked a short while later, the old woman was asleep. Good. Satisfied that the lady laird remained unaware of the real celebration being planned, Alix summoned all her reserves of cool detachment and went along to the factor's office to liaise with Niall on the final details for the surprise.

'It's all going according to plan,' he assured her. 'Murdo and the lads will stand guard to direct cars round through the woods and bring people into the ballroom via the French doors, where Dame Janet won't see them. The guests are all primed to be here by eight o'clock sharp.'

'And she's not expecting the "dinner guests" until eight thirty,' Alix confirmed, checking her watch. 'Four hours to go. I've never been so nervous! Does it all look OK?'

'It looks amazing. Don't worry, it's all going like clockwork. Even the weather's co-operating.'

'Oh, don't!' Alix peered out of the window at the sunlit courtyard. 'It could pour with rain before eight o'clock. Your Scottish weather's unpredictable.' Much like some Scottish men, she nearly added but bit her tongue and shook the thought away. She would not get angry. She would not cry. Damn it, she would not!

When she looked round, Niall was behind his desk, opening a drawer and bringing out a big old key. 'This is the one you need. Keep it safe now. Don't lose it. We're all relying on you.'

'I only hope I can carry it off.' She reached across the desk, careful not to touch him as she took the key and folded her hand round it. 'I'll see you later, then.'

'Yes. Later. Good luck.'

'You, too.'

She left the office, closing the door quietly behind her. She hadn't looked him in the eye once.

NINE

Shortly before eight o'clock that evening, Alix was ready, waiting in the guest bedroom with palpitating heart and restless mind and body. Ten minutes ago she had helped Dame Janet put the finishing touches to her toilette and seen the old woman safely down the stairs, with promises to join her in the sitting room shortly. Now all that remained was for the drama to begin. Let it go well. Oh, please let the ruse work as she had dreamed!

She wore the strapless black gown she had bought in Edinburgh. The top fitted close to her body, leaving her arms and shoulders bare, and the skirt fell in softly draping silken folds, moulding to her thighs as she moved, both concealing and revealing. She had never considered herself a beauty—certainly she could never have competed with Claudia—but tonight, examining her reflection in an antique cheval glass, she had to concede that the dress suited her well, elegant and dramatic against lightly-tanned skin and fair hair touched to gold. She had kept her make-up minimal and wore simple gold ear-rings, necklet and bracelet. After all, tonight was Dame Janet's night.

Holding out the beautifully-cut skirt, she examined the effect of the deep split that would reveal a glimpse of thigh at certain moments. How would Niall react to the sight of her tonight? Could a dress, and a few hours at a party, make any difference? Probably not. Niall had made it quite clear that their relationship had no future. But he hadn't told her why. How could he expect her to stop hoping when he hadn't told her—?

'Alix?' Dame Janet's voice floated up the stairs, audible through the door which Alix had deliberately left ajar. 'Alix, are you ready? They'll be here soon. It's nearly eight.'

Without answering, Alix picked up the key Niall had given her, clasping it in a hand that was damp with nerves.

'Alix!' the call came again. 'Are you there?'

Still keeping silent, Alix slipped into the corridor, staying well away from the stairs and moving as quietly as she could towards the locked door which gave on to the gallery above the ballroom. The notice announcing, *'Do not enter. DANGER'*, had been taken down. Softly, Alix fitted the key into the lock.

Behind her, she could hear Dame Janet muttering to herself in annoyance as she struggled to climb the stairs. Her stick thumped on the treads and she huffed and puffed, swearing to herself in most unladylike fashion. One final thump must have brought her to the landing, where she rapped on the guest room door, snapping, 'Alix!'

'I'm here.' Alix hurried to where she could

253

see her friend, who looked grand in a blue satin skirt and matching blouse, grey hair groomed in soft waves. 'I'm sorry, Jay, were you looking for me?'

'Whatever are you doing?' the old woman demanded crossly. 'We said eight o'clock. It's not like you to be late. I thought something had happened to you. I'd have sent Ailie but she was busy basting the joint or something.'

'I didn't hear you calling,' Alix lied, high on excitement as she moved away back to the gallery door, luring Dame Janet to follow. 'I was being inquisitive, I'm afraid. I came nosing along here and noticed . . . Look, they've taken down the warning sign, and there's a key in the lock. It leads to the gallery, doesn't it? The gallery over the ballroom? Do you mind if I take a peek at what they've been doing?'

Dame Janet came closer, her own curiosity aroused. 'Might as well, since we're here. But do be careful! They may have removed those old stairs. Don't want you falling and breaking your neck at this late stage. Our guests will be arriving soon. I expected Niall by now, but . . .'

Closing her eyes in a last silent prayer that Niall had everything set, Alix turned the key. The door opened. Beyond it the newly-fitted gallery gleamed with polished wood. Complete silence reigned and long shafts of evening sunlight slanted through high-level windows.

'Good heavens!' Dame Janet breathed behind her. 'Whatever . . .'

Alex stepped out on to the gallery, one glance taking in the scene in the ballroom below. The place had been transformed. Banks of glorious flowers surrounded the polished dance floor, showing off the renewed panelling, the gleaming chandeliers, the sweep of the staircase as it curved down. As Alex moved aside to let Dame Janet come past, the skirl of bagpipes sounded in the ballroom below, where a mass of people in full evening dress—some of the men in kilts—swarmed by the foot of curving stairs, faces lifted in smiles and anticipation. When the lady laird appeared they all burst into applause, joining in as the piper played 'Happy Birthday to You'.

Waiting by the door, breathless with anxious hope and unshed tears, Alix saw Dame Janet lean on the gallery's new rail, her face working. A tear trickled down her lined cheek as she stood and let the birthday song run its course, followed by more applause, and then three cheers called for by a male voice Alix couldn't identify.

Under cover of the noise from below, Dame Janet looked round, her blue eyes awash. 'You wicked girl,' she chided, her voice hoarse with emotion. 'You wicked, lovely girl! *You*'ve done this.'

'Only with a lot of help,' Alix muttered. She

255

kissed the old woman's cheek, thrilled that it had all worked out, even better than she had dreamed it might. Then from her eye corner she glimpsed Niall coming up the stairs as planned, to escort his employer down to meet her guests. 'And here's your handsome . . .' She couldn't go on. For all her dreaming and scheming, this was something she had not anticipated—the sight of Niall Drummond in full highland dress.

The deep pleats of his kilt flared behind him as he climbed the last few stairs. The kilt was of Drummond tartan—mostly deep red, banded with pine green and cross-woven with white and yellow. Alix remembered Fergus showing her an example of his clan's tartan and explaining the highland dress, much as Niall was wearing it, shining black shoes and white socks, tasselled and complete with knife (a *'sgian dubh'* Fergus had called it) tucked into a sheath. At the front of the kilt hung a furred sporran adorned by a gleaming amber cairngorm jewel, the outfit completed by a short fitted jacket of black velvet worn over a shirt with snowy ruffles frothing at throat and wrists. He looked, she thought, half barbarian and wholly magnificent, robbing her of speech, breath, muscle-power . . .

Giving Alix a swift, speaking glance, he bowed gravely to his employer, offering her his arm.

'Hah!' Dame Janet scoffed under her

breath, her voice still cracked with tears. 'Young Lochinvar, I presume!' But she tucked her hand under his arm and leaned on him as she made her slow way down the stairs, stately as a queen.

Choked with emotion, Alix remained where she was, not wishing to intrude on the old lady's grand entrance. It was a role she had become accustomed to, to observe but never quite to be part of whatever was going on. Still, she was glad to have created this moment for dear old Jay. That was what mattered.

As the lady laird reached the ballroom, her guests crowded round to offer good wishes and to be recognised and greeted with delight and kisses. They had come from far and near, all old friends of Dame Janet, some from her personal life, local friends and neighbours; others from her days as a concert pianist. One or two were international celebrities, instantly identifiable from TV or newspapers. One famous conductor had flown in from Vienna. But all of them seemed delighted to have been part of the surprise; they had enjoyed the subterfuge in which they had connived, all to please their dear friend Dame Janet McDonald.

Reluctant to draw attention to herself by going down the stairs, Alix went back into the bedroom corridor and made her way down through the quiet house. Outside the kitchen she encountered Ailie, bearing a tray of sweet pastries crisp and hot from the oven, with helpless tears running down her face.

'Whatever's wrong?' Alix felt dismayed.

'Nothing's wrong!' Ailie wept. 'Oh, it was so beautiful. The look on her face . . . Thank you, Miss Grant! May God bless you for doing this. No one else in the world could have pulled it off.'

'Here, let me take those.' Embarrassed, Alix relieved her of the tray. 'No, it's fine. You go and dry your eyes and get back to the party. You're a guest tonight—that's why we hired the caterers, to do all of this. Ailie, go!'

Ailie went, back into the kitchen to restore her composure, while Alix carried the tray on through the house, making for the ante room to the ballroom. 'No one else in the world . . .' Ailie's kind words echoed in her head. It wasn't true, of course. Fact was, Alix had simply been in the right place at the right time, with resources enough to accomplish this gift for the woman who had become a dear friend. Why, then, was Alix doing what she had been programmed to do and letting herself feel like an outsider? She had told Niall she had conquered that lack of confidence, her true identity discovered, her confidence restored. Fine words. In reality it wasn't so easy to throw off years of adverse psychological brain-washing. But surely she could claim to have earned a small place

258

here? She felt more at home in Glenwhinnie and Lachanbrae than she had felt anywhere. The people liked her, and she liked them. Given a few more years she might even become one of them, an accepted part of the glen scene. Why, then, was she contemplating running away again? Because Niall Drummond said she must?

No.

She stopped, hearing the strains of distant music and chatter. No, it wasn't right or fair. Why should she throw away her chance to find a real home at last, for reasons that Niall refused to discuss? He could not be allowed the last word. She had some say, surely? Was she a twenty-first century woman or was she a meek little mouse?

*   *   *

In the ante room, the caterers had erected buffet tables laden with all manner of foods, including two whole salmon curved across huge plates and sprinkled with parsley and lemon. One of the waitresses seized the tray of warm pastries and took them away to be arranged on serving dishes and added to the desserts, while Alix admired the display of succulent dainties. Sliced meats, savoury nibbles, salads, fruits, trifles piled with cream, and yet more flowers . . .

'Where have you been?' Niall demanded

from behind her. 'I've been looking all over for you. We did it, didn't we? Is it OK?'

Alix turned with a smile, sharing his delight in the effect they had created between them and determined to think only of her pleasure in the moment. 'It's just wonderful!' she informed the lacy froth at his throat. 'Thank you, Niall. It's just the way I hoped. She was pleased, wasn't she?'

'She was absolutely knocked out. It was kind of you to plan it all. But then you are kind. Sweet, thoughtful, and . . .' he dropped his voice to a whisper only she could hear, 'you look absolutely stunning.'

Startled into it, she lifted her eyes to his and found herself captured by what she read there. Her mind resisted, crying for caution, reminding her of other occasions when she had let him enchant her only to be let down at the last, but her heart wasn't listening. This was the man she loved. This was the man she wanted. She was going to fight for him with all her feminine wiles.

'Dance with me,' she demanded.

'Now?' Wide-eyed, he glanced into the ballroom, where a band was playing 'Edelweiss' but the guests still mingled in merry, laughing groups, none of them taking to the floor. 'I can't waltz,' he objected.

'No? You could waltz well enough last Boxing Day.'

'We didn't have an audience on Boxing

260

Day!'

'Somebody's got to start and we can't expect Dame Janet to do it. I think it's up to us to set this birthday ball rolling, don't you? Come on, Niall.' She took his hand and half-dragged him out to the centre of the dance floor, turning to him with a challenge in her eyes. 'You're supposed to hold me. It's traditional.'

Having little option, he took her in his arms and began to lead her into the slow waltz dictated by the tune. A little scatter of applause rippled round the room, and with murmurs of approval other couples joined them, swirling about until Alix and Niall were just part of the dancing crowd.

After a while, feeling Niall begin to relax, Alix said past his shoulder, 'You might have warned me you were planning to wear the kilt.'

'Why, don't you approve?' His deep voice reverberated against her ear as he drew her closer and their feet moved in ever surer rhythm.

Oh, it wasn't fair! She considered half a dozen replies—joking, sarcastic, taunting, prosaic—but with his arms about her and his warm body so near she couldn't think straight. 'You know,' was all she could sigh as she closed her eyes and leaned her head on his shoulder, feeling his arms turn tender as he cradled her against him.

After that there were no words. There were only the two of them, sharing a few minutes out of time.

The party continued. Beyond the hills the sun sank in golden splendour and a warm evening breeze came questing in through French doors that shone like mirrors, polished and bright. Not filmed with greasy dirt as they had been six months before, at Christmas, when Alix had first danced here with Niall.

She danced with him several more times that midsummer evening, but she also had to do the social thing, talk with the guests and be introduced to all Dame Janet's friends—the world-renowned conductor, a lord, a marquis, a well-known soprano, along with several highland lairds, neighbours and business acquaintances. As the hours passed and the wine flowed, her confidence increased. Everyone accepted her without question. Many of them complimented her on the success of the evening. And no one mentioned Claudia Cantrelle.

Sir Anthony McKenzie secured her for a dance and rather stiffly expressed his pleasure in seeing Dame Janet so radiant and happy: 'You couldn't have pleased her more. I know how much the estate means to her and if you can restore at least some of its glory it will be a gift beyond price. I believe she has come to look on you as the daughter she might have had. But she tells me you're leaving soon. You think it's time?'

'I've already stayed longer than I intended,' Alix replied. 'I'm not too sure of my plans, to be honest. But, yes, I think I'm ready to face the ravening hordes of the press. Always assuming they're still waiting. Could be I'm yesterday's news by now.'

'I certainly hope so. If you want my advice, I'd say that the best way to handle these journalist johnnies is just to refuse to talk. Keep a low profile. Give them nothing to write about. They'll soon grow tired of it. Some very well-known people manage to keep their private lives private, you know.'

That was true, Alix thought. And it might work, unless . . . 'How's Catriona?'

'Oh, fine, as far as I know. Gone off touring Europe with a group of friends. Not sure when she'll be back. She'll be sorry to have missed you.'

'Give her my best,' Alix said, wondering how any man could know so little of his own daughter. One thing seemed fairly sure, though—Catriona had forgotten her plan for revenge. Maybe she had found other amusements, or some other unsuspecting man to pursue.

At eleven o'clock, when the long daylight was fading and lights in the ballroom grew brighter, Alex found herself in Niall's arms again, dancing in silence but still in communication. Between them, words had

263

never been necessary to express their deepest feelings. On the contrary, it was words that always caused the complications. But before the evening ended, she promised herself, there would be words in plenty. She intended to demand answers. For now, though, just being with him was sweet enough. She felt like Cinderella at the ball. Let midnight wait.

As the music ended and they reluctantly drew apart, they saw that Dame Janet was taking a stance part way up the stairs, where she could be seen by everyone in the ballroom. Below her, the kilted and bonneted piper, a dark McDonald plaid slung round his shoulder, played a few rousing notes that drew all eyes to the imperious figure of the mistress of Glenwhinnie. She beckoned Alix and Niall to join her, to stand close by the foot of the stairs.

'Just stay there,' she bade them. 'I want to say a few words and don't either of you dare move or interrupt me.'

Alix was amused. 'Bossy, isn't she?' she murmured to Niall, but when she looked at him she found him watching Dame Janet with furrowed brow and suspicious glower. 'Niall?' She slid her hand into his and felt him respond, his fingers clasping hers rather harder than was comfortable. What was he so tense about?

Lifting a hand to command a silence that spread throughout the company, the lady laird launched into an emotional impromptu speech, first chiding them all for conspiring to mislead her, and then thanking them for their presence on her seventy-fifth birthday, and for the gifts they had brought. 'But most of all I want to scold—and to thank—those of my dear friends who told me the most dreadful whoppers just to get me here tonight. Ailie and Murdo Gordon.' She sought them out among the crowd. 'I shall never trust either of you again,' she warned them. 'Well, not entirely.' Which caused a wave of laughter. Even Murdo managed to look a touch less grim than usual. 'And Niall Drummond, my factor, who as all of you know is my rock and my support . . . And Alix Grant—my darling Alix, who was mad enough to dream up this whole event, and generous enough to make it come true for me. There's only one thing she could do that would please me more, and that's stay here with us at Glenwhinnie.'

Murmurs of agreement arose, and applause broke out as Alix looked at the floor and wished Dame Janet would stop. She clutched Niall's hand for comfort, felt him stroke her knuckles with his thumb though he didn't look at her.

'Wait!' the lady laird's command gave pause to the rising noise. 'I haven't finished yet.' She waited until she had everyone's attention again, then said seriously, 'As you all know, I'm no longer a young woman. Oh, I trust I have a few more years yet, but at my age one never knows. I never married—you all know that, too. Well, no man was fool enough to ask me!' Laughter rippled among the guests, with cries of dissent and someone calling, 'No man would dare!' which caused more laughter.

'Whatever the reason,' Dame Janet went on, enjoying herself, 'it has meant that I've not had the pleasure of children of my own, to whom I might have passed on Glenwhinnie and all it means to me. But since you're all here, you might as well know that I do have an heir, a true McDonald in his own right.'

As the guests murmured with interest, intrigued, Alix felt Niall stiffen. His hand fastened so tightly round hers she felt her bones crunch together. 'Niall!' The whispered protest made him look down at her as if he had forgotten she was there. His look seared her in the moment before he abruptly unclasped his hand, withdrawing from her both physically and mentally. She couldn't read his face as he stared up at Dame Janet, but she saw the lady laird's tight, defiant smile of reply.

'And before he rushes up here to strangle me,' the old woman added, speaking to the crowd but trading electric blue glances with Niall, 'I want to assure him that I have permission to make this announcement.'

Curiosity buzzed audibly among the guests and Alix saw Niall's jaw work as he clenched

266

his teeth, looking bitterly angry, muttering, 'No . . .' Worried, Alix looked back to where Dame Janet was smiling down on the assembly of her friends and neighbours, blithely ignoring her factor's fury.

'When I'm gone,' she said clearly, 'I shall be entirely contented to leave the estate in the capable hands of . . . my nephew—my nephew Niall Drummond.'

She might have added more but her voice was drowned in a gasp of surprise followed by rising applause as everyone realized the import of her announcement. Alix had the feeling that many of the local people had guessed what was coming. Their faces told their pleasure in the revelation. But Alix herself felt numbed. Was it true? Niall was Dame Janet's nephew, rightful heir to Glenwhinnie?

As she glanced at him, Niall spun on his heel, the kilt flaring behind him as he shouldered roughly through the startled crowd and strode into the ante room, out of sight. Behind him he left a trail of exclamations and mutterings at his brusqueness. It was so unlike Niall that Alix felt disorientated. What was going on? She might have made after him, but an unsteady Dame Janet was coming down the stairs, reaching a hand for Alix's support.

The old woman seemed tired, but her blue eyes blazed with satisfaction. 'He's furious with me,' she observed, her grim smile including everyone within earshot. 'I expected no less. You'll have to excuse him, this is a battle that's been raging between us for quite some time.' Her gaze settled on Alix's face as she added more quietly, 'Let's go through to the sitting room, my dear. I need a breather.'

Fending off further offers of help, along with anxious queries as to her health, she leaned on Alix's arm as they made their way through the ante room and along the shadowy passageways to the sanctuary of the quiet sitting room. There, the old lady sank down into her favourite chair, while Alex switched on a few lamps and drew the curtains against the deepening twilight. On this shortest night of the year the sky remained a pale duck-egg blue against which the mountains loomed dark and craggy.

'Pour me a whisky, will you?' Dame Janet requested. 'I never did have much taste for champagne and after a speech like that I need some fortification. Maybe I was wrong to spring it on him like that, but I had planned to do it before long—and Fergus agreed with me. It was high time the truth came out. Now everyone can stop speculating and gossiping. They'll know the facts.' As Alix handed her the glass, the old woman took it in a slightly unsteady, thin and knobbly hand. But the look in her eyes was direct and penetrating. 'You, too,' she added. 'He hasn't even told *you* about this, has he?'

Alix's mind had been busy, recalling gossip about the lady laird's rake of a brother, and rumours about Niall's mother. Lachanbrae, it seemed, had long suspected the truth. All at once her memory focused on a day when Maura had come to visit her, upset about Catriona's chasing Niall, and had let slip something that made her cry in anguish, 'We are Niall's family! We *are!*' Poor Maura had thought she had given away a secret, though at the time Alix hadn't understood any of it.

'You mean . . .' she said slowly, 'Fergus Drummond isn't Niall's natural father?'

'No, he is not.' It came on a heavy sigh. 'Niall's natural father was my reprobate brother, John McDonald. Poor John . . . He had a miserable marriage. One of those dynastic things, you know, settled by both sets of parents. Oh, the girl—my sister-in-law, Liz—was willing enough, but John agreed only under protest, so before long the rot set in. John found consolation in the arms of a girl named Amy McFee, the daughter of one of our crofters. Pretty little thing, she was. Lively and spirited—though years younger than my brother. Of course she fell for a child. Well, John couldn't marry her—Liz and her family were Catholic, didn't believe in divorce—and my father wasn't about to allow any scandal here if he could help it. He found a post for John down in London, and he married the girl off to a widowed game keeper on a neighbouring estate—Fergus Drummond, of course.'

'It sounds like something out of history!' Alix commented, appalled.

'I agree. But here in the Highland's we're a wee bit old-fashioned still. Well, some of us are. It wasn't quite as straight-forward as I've made it sound, but . . . that was the gist of what happened. John and Liz went to London. Both of them lived their own lives. He started to drink. There were other women, scandals, upsets. He died, and she remarried. All gone.'

'Except for the child he left behind.'

'Quite so.'

They fell silent for a while, Dame Janet enjoying her whisky while Alix thought over the revelations and their import.

'Jay . . . when Fergus married Amy, I assume he did know she was already pregnant?'

'Of course he did. But he was content to help her out. Amy was an attractive girl and Fergus needed a wife—he'd a job to do and a daughter to raise. I believe my father added a financial consideration, too, and it worked out all right. Amy was happy enough. The marriage was a success, so I believe. It suited them all.'

'And Niall?' Niall was Alix's main concern in all of this. 'Did *he* know about it? Did they tell him the truth?'

The old woman took another sip of scotch, avoiding Alix's eyes. 'No, I'm sorry to say they didn't. I was the one who told him, eventually. Around the time he was born I was away a lot, busy with my career. I didn't know what had happened until much later. When I did come home for the occasional Christmas, or the Hunt Balls—and for my mother's funeral— well, we hardly ever mentioned my brother John. He was gone from our lives. My father preferred not to talk about it. It was only after he died that I found out I had a nephew. I became the main heir, but my father left some money for Niall. I sent for him—he'd be about nineteen then—and I told him he was my brother's son and that some day, when I was gone, he'd be laird of Glenwhinnie.'

Alix was horrified. 'You told him . . . straight out? Just like that?'

'Well, of course! No point beating about the bush.' But her voice was gruff and her face twisted, betraying her regret. 'In retrospect I don't think I handled it very well. But then I didn't realize how devilish proud he was. He was furious with the lot of us—me, his mother, Fergus, my father . . . He used his legacy to take himself off to Canada and vowed he'd stay there. He worked with the loggers, forestry and all that.'

So that was why he had gone away—for almost the same reason that Alix had come to

Scotland.

'He might have stayed away longer if his mother hadn't taken sick,' Dame Janet went on. 'That was what brought him back eventually. He loved her, of course. And he cared about Fergus and Maura too. Besides, by then . . . Canada had become a place of unhappy memories.'

'His wife. Yes, I know.'

'Ah—he told you about that, did he? Good.' She drank some more whisky, shaking her head. 'Poor Niall. I suspect his mother gave him a good talking to because eventually he came to see me. I can see him now, standing over there by the door, stiff as a ramrod, brow like thunder, glaring daggers. I told him then, whether he liked it or not, I had made him my heir. We argued bitterly—you can imagine. But in the end he said that if he was to inherit the estate then he'd do the job properly. He'd get some qualifications for estate management —his experience in Canada gave him a good start, of course, it was the kind of job that appealed to him—and then he'd come and work for me, and be the best damn factor this estate had ever had.' The memory made her eyes gleam. 'Hah! That boy's a real McDonald.'

'I still don't understand why it had to be a secret,' Alix said.

Dame Janet sat back in her chair, shaking her head ruefully. 'That was Niall's idea. You should know by now, he doesn't believe in taking the easy way out, always has to create difficulties for himself. He insisted we should keep our real relationship a secret for Fergus' sake. As far as he's concerned, Fergus is his real father. Fergus raised him and cared for him. Niall was afraid of making the old boy a laughing stock for being stuck with a cuckoo in his nest, and he didn't want to cast shame on his mother's name, either.'

'But everyone *knows!* ' Alix exclaimed. 'I've heard snippets of gossip and rumour but I never understood them.'

'Yes, well, there's been gossip, I know, but no one has been entirely sure. Until tonight. Now, the secret is well and truly out. Well, it was time. Past time, as I've been telling Niall for over a year now. After all, I am not going to live for ever and the people on the estate deserve to known that there'll be continuity.'

'Is that what you were arguing about at Christmas?'

The old woman shot her a rueful look. 'Probably so. It's the one subject we never could agree upon.'

So this was Niall's dark secret, Alix thought. Was it also his reason for believing they had no future together? It wasn't logical. They had so much in common—both of them deceived about their true origins, both devastated by discovering the truth, both learning to find their own identity, both reluctant

273

beneficiaries—he was heir to Glenwhinnie, and she had inherited a fortune. That was amazing! Wonderful! Between them they could bring Glenwhinnie back to life, create jobs, bring visitors flocking. His expertise allied with her capital . . .

Her flying thoughts stopped there.

Of course! Suddenly everything made sense. What a blind fool she had been not to realize . . .

Anger began to burn deep inside her. Oh, Niall Drummond! What a stubborn, mule-headed . . . It was almost as though he were afraid to let himself be happy. At first he had resisted her because of loyalty and a promise made to his late wife, Barbara—a reason Alix could understand and respect; but then at New Year's, just when those barriers were breaking down, Murdo Gordon had shared his suspicions about Alix's identity, and Niall had also entertained some confused idea that she might be another of John McDonald's illegitimate offspring, and therefore his half-sister, which would have made her taboo. And by the time that red herring had rotted in the sun he knew for sure that she was an extremely rich woman. Which, to the proud and puritan Niall Drummond, was probably worse than all the rest put together. Damn the man!

'He needs you, Alix,' Dame Janet said quietly. 'We both need you. We both love you.

Must you leave us?'

Alix found herself rigid with bitter thoughts. Aloud, she answered, 'You're right about his pride—his rotten, arrogant, stinking male pride. If I hadn't a bean to my name it might be different, but as it is . . . Where do you suppose he went?'

'I guess he's gone to see Fergus. To make sure he's not going to be hurt by all of this. But he'll be back before long. Proud and prickly as he may be, he's also aware of his duties and responsibilities. He won't stay away for long. Come, we'd better get back to our guests. I have a lot more explaining to do.'

*   *   *

Back in the ballroom, the old woman was immediately surrounded by a crowd of eager, inquisitive people, many of them made even more loud and inquisitive by alcohol. Alix drifted away, playing second-string hostess, making small talk and ensuring that all of the guests had everything they needed in the way of food or drink or comfort. But more and more she felt as if she were on auto-pilot. She seemed to be surrounded by an invisible cloud of unreality. Where was Niall? When would he come back? If he came at all. What was he doing? What was he thinking? What would he have to say when he did reappear?

Needing fresh air and, if possible, a few

minutes to herself, she went out via the French doors to the lawns behind the house, where some of the guests wandered beneath trees strung with lanterns. Far above, the midsummer sky had darkened to blue velvet, stars pricking out one by one.

Glancing back at the brightly-lit ballroom where dancers jigged and swirled beneath a glitter of chandeliers, Alix was reminded of the dream in which she had seen herself shut out and begging to be allowed in. Now the doors stood open and she was free to come or to go, as she herself chose. That was the reality.

Walking precariously in her high-heeled sandals, she made for the hillside behind the house, through a stretch of woods to a twilit slope where she could be completely alone. Behind her, down in the curve of the valley, the lights of Glenwhinnie House still gleamed, music and laughter floating softly on the night breeze. How lovely it was, come fall or spring, winter snow or summer heat. She loved the place, and its people. She could be happy here and do so much to help, if only Niall . . .

Despite the distance between them, she recognized the tall, kilted figure who appeared in the open doorway leading from the ballroom. He spoke to some people going by and they turned and pointed in the direction Alix had taken. Niall set out in pursuit.

276

Wanting no witnesses to their encounter, Alix climbed a little further up the hill, to where the land dipped into a shallow basin, taking her out of sight of the house and everyone in it. It wasn't quite dark—at that time of year the light of one day had hardly faded before the dawn began to spread the first hint of the next—and the air remained balmy, under a velvet blue sky sprinkled with stars. Alix stared up at the arcing heavens, praying that she would find the right words.

'Alix?' Niall's voice came faintly.

'I'm here,' she replied, turning in the direction the call came from.

A few moments later, Niall appeared on the edge of the hollow. He had taken off his close-fitting jacket and in the starlight the white ruffles on his shirt gleamed. She couldn't read his expression. His presence made her feel weak with love and longing, but mingled with it was anxiety, and not a little irritation. Oh, he was a proud, stubborn Scot. She would have to play it cool and canny.

'So there you are!' he said on a note of relief, coming down to join her. 'You keep disappearing on me.'

That was too much. '*I* do?! You're the one who stormed out!'

'I know. I know!' He swept a hand through his hair. 'I'm sorry I deserted you, but I had to see Dad. I *told* Aunt Jay she was not to worry him with all of this—not until I'd talked it all

277

out with him and made sure he was entirely comfortable with the possible consequences. But *she* thought differently, so as per usual she decided to take a unilateral decision. That's typical of her—she always knows best.'

'Must run in the family,' Alix breathed to herself.

'What?'

'Nothing. So what did Fergus have to say? Is he going to be mortified now the truth's out?'

'No. No, he's not like that. But that's not the point, is it? He's still going to be in for some stick. What are people going to say?'

'I imagine they'll throw their bonnets in the air and give three hearty cheers. From what I've heard, the villagers have suspected the truth for a long time. No one thinks any the less of Fergus, or your mother—or you, for any of it. They blame John McDonald. Which seems reasonable to me. If he'd behaved himself Amy would never have got pregnant. On the other hand, if she hadn't got pregnant *you* wouldn't be here, and that would be a disaster for Glenwhinnie, wouldn't it?'

'Would it?'

Alix's temper snapped. 'Of course it would!' She swung away, arms wrapped round herself and fists clenched. How she longed to slap some sense into that obstinate head of his.

After a while, Niall said, 'I gather you've been talking to Aunt Jay.'

'Bright of you. And since when has she been "Aunt Jay"?'

'For quite a while. In private. She told you the lot, did she?'

'Most of it.' Taking a deep breath to calm herself, she turned back to face him. 'I must have been blind not to guess it before. Why the heck didn't you tell me yourself?' She threw out her hands in exasperation. '*Why*, Niall? You surely knew that I'd understand? Good grief . . . suddenly being told you're not who you thought you were . . . You've been through the same mill I have.'

A rueful smile tugged at a corner of his mouth. 'I hadn't thought of it that way. Anyway, I couldn't have told you. The secret wasn't really mine to give away. It was mother's, and Fergus . . . I was trying to save Fergus from being hurt by thoughtless gossip. You know that.'

Slowly, deliberately, she shook her head at him. 'That was only one of your excuses. What about the rest of it, Niall?'

'How do you mean?'

'You know very well what I mean! There's the money, too—the fact that Claudia Cantrelle left her fortune to me. So I'm impossibly rich. A millionaire several times over—dollars or pounds hardly matters, it's still a ridiculous amount. While *you* . . . You're heir to a crumbling mansion and an estate that's almost bankrupt. You desperately need

279

an injection of capital. And when you do eventually inherit there'll be—what do you call it, death duties?—to pay, won't there?'

'Inheritance tax,' he amended in a low voice. 'Yes.'

'But sooner than share these problems with me—because you knew what I'd say—instead of that, you invented reasons for saying nothing. Even though you know I'd be happy to be useful here—not just to you but to Dame Janet, the people on the estate, the people in the village—you're just too damned stiff-necked to accept help, especially from a woman. Isn't that the bottom line?'

Niall watched her levelly, saying nothing either to confirm or deny her charges. He didn't need to. Alix knew she was right.

'You'd rather send me away,' she went on, 'even though I'd be miserable without you. You'd rather risk losing Glenwhinnie, going bankrupt and drowning in debt. You'd throw away the chance for us to build something good, for ourselves and the people here, for our children, and their children after them. The Drummonds of Glenwhinnie. Will you let your stupid male pride prevent them from ever being born?'

'That's female thinking,' Niall said. 'I can't look that far ahead. All I know is, if you stay here . . . if we were together . . . everyone would say I'd married you for your money.'

Irritation prickled across her skin like ants

280

on the march. 'And would they be right?'

'No, they would not!'

Alix moved away from him, looking up at the bright stars in a midnight sky. 'Ever since Dame Janet told me the truth, I've been wondering what I should say to change your mind. Maybe I should lose my temper. Maybe I should cajole and beg—use tears to get through to you. Maybe I should point out that a mere century and a half ago you'd have been legally entitled to marry me and claim all my money as your own, and nobody would have blinked an eye. Or possibly I should remind you that I have nowhere else to go. Nowhere to go and no-one who cares about me. And wherever I went my life would be empty without you in it, because I love you incredibly much even though you drive me mad at times. Or maybe . . . maybe I should just simply stick around, anyway, whatever you might say. Stick around, get involved as a business partner. After all, I'm entitled to decide my own future, aren't I?'

'Of course,' he said gruffly, and cleared his throat. 'Of course you are.'

Staking everything on a gamble, she turned to face him, hands spread. 'I'm not going to do any of those things. You see, Niall, I have some pride, too. Too much to stay where I'm not wanted. I won't interfere in your life. So, just the way you wanted, I'm leaving Lachanbrae.'

281

'What?!'

'You heard me.'

'Alix . . .' he muttered.

Softly, sadly, she stepped close to him, laid a hand on his arm and reached up to kiss the corner of his mouth, murmuring, 'Goodbye, darling.'

She felt the shock that ran through him as he stared down at her, a hand circling her wrist to detain her. 'You're not . . . not going right this minute, surely?'

'It seems best.' Gentle easing free of his grasp, she began to walk away. 'I've already done my packing. The carriers are coming at ten in the morning to collect my boxes—I've left a note for Murdo, asking him to be there to supervise things, and I'll leave the key in the lock. My flight leaves Edinburgh around mid-day.'

'But . . . I thought you'd be staying at least a few more days. The end of the month, isn't that what you said?'

'It *is* the end of the month, more or less.'

'But surely . . . You haven't said goodbye to everyone. Does Dame Janet know?'

'No. I can't bear goodbyes. I'm going to slip away to my room while the party's still going on, get changed, drive through the dawn to Edinburgh. You tell Jay for me. Give her my love and tell her I'll call her very soon. Maura and Fergus, too.'

Heather rustled as he came striding after

her to whirl her round to face him, his hands clasped round her upper arms. 'You're not serious. You can't just walk out like this. I won't let you drive to Edinburgh without getting some sleep first.'

Alix's hard-held calm shredded on the edges of raw pain inside her. 'So what do you want me to do?' she cried. 'Another night. A few more days. A while ago it was "stay until after the ball". Well, the ball is over, Niall. If I've got to go, let me go now. That *is* what you want, isn't it?'

She saw his inner struggle, felt his hands painfully tight on her arms as his brow furrowed and his mouth twisted and hardened. 'No,' he got out. 'No, it's not what I want. You know it's not.' He took a deep breath, adding fiercely, 'Just understand this—I fell in love with you long before I knew anything about that bloody money. Other people can think what they like, but you have got to believe this—it's you I want, rich or poor. You, Alix. Not capital for Glenwhinnie.'

'My darling love . . .' she managed. 'I never doubted it.'

He threw his arms round her, holding her tight as he buried his face in her hair. 'I love you. I love you so much I hurt. I thought I could let you go, but I can't. I need you too much.'

'Then marry me!' she whispered forcefully, her arms clasping round him. 'Will you, Niall?

Will you?'

'Alix . . .' he muttered, bending to find her mouth. 'Alix . . .'

*　　　*　　　*

A day or two later, when Lachanbrae was still buzzing with the news that the heir to Glenwhinnie had chosen himself a bride, Alix and Niall sat in the garden of the Drummonds' cottage enjoying tea with Maura and Fergus. Bees hummed in the roses and gulls cried as they wheeled over the loch.

Ingenuous as ever, Maura wanted to know details of how it had all happened, especially when and where Niall had asked Alix to marry him.

Laughing, Alix confided, 'He didn't. Not in so many words.'

'Actually,' said Niall with a grin, '*she* proposed to *me*.'

Maura's eyes popped. 'Did she, though? Jings! And what did you say?'

He looked at Alix, blue eyes alight with love and laughter as he reached to take her hand and rub his thumb across the amethyst ring he had given her—a McDonald heirloom that just happened to fit her perfectly. 'Oh, I let her persuade me—eventually,' he said.